Mystic's Touch

Dena Garson

DEDICATION

To my mom, who has always been my biggest fan. She's told me,
"You can do anything you put your mind to," since I was learning
to walk. And by golly, she was right! Love ya, Mom!

ACKNOWLEDGMENTS

I need to send a big thank you to Jennifer Schmidlin for her critiques, suggestions and calming words. Whenever I feel like I'm going off the tracks and taking my manuscript with me, she's able to show me that no, I just need to take a little step to the left.
hugz

CHAPTER ONE

Massive yellow paws pounded into the hot desert sand as he ran. His heart beat a rhythm in his ears and kept him moving toward his destination. Behind him, sand as far as the eye could see was marked with his passage, allowing the man on horseback to follow without being seen.

Neither the reflection of the sun on the white sand nor the heat radiating around him stopped the creature.

The goal was too important.

A hazy spot appeared on the horizon. The creature altered his course slightly and doubled his efforts. The spot grew with each ridge he crossed until it shifted and took shape. A tree emerged from one side of the creature's vision.

He crossed another dune and detected color in the distance. Greens and blues.

As more dunes were conquered, the almost indistinguishable tree became a cluster of palms. Nearby were a few other plants and a pool of water.

Yet another ridge was crossed.

The creature slowed not far from his goal, but within easy sight. When he crested the largest mound he stopped at its pinnacle. As he stood atop his chosen platform, blue eyes scanned the horizon for prey or enemy. His breath seemed to be taken more for scent than as a result of his race across the sand. When seemingly satisfied with what lay before him, the creature descended.

Cresting the next sandy mound in place of the creature was a

1

man. His face and body were darkened from the sun. His golden
hair glistened, much the way the creature's had. The linen
wrappings he wore did little to hide his masculine form. The only
testaments to his station were the golden bands bearing the king's
seal wrapped around his upper arms and the royal-purple sash
around his waist.

Muscles rippled gracefully as he marched over the final ridge
then into the shadiest area of the oasis. His sandals were silent as
he strode toward the glistening pool. The steeds belonging to the
small party waiting there danced nervously as he approached.

"My prince."

A man dressed in robes the color of wine dropped to his knees,
his head bowed deeply. Behind him, four others, dressed similarly,
dropped to their knees and mumbled a greeting. Only one man
remained standing.

"Cousin. At last you made it." The standing man crossed the
span between them to clasp forearms with the prince.

"Aleric. Good to see you," Prince Ceros greeted his cousin
coolly.

"Don't tell me you ran all the way from Shirghada." Aleric
frowned. "And alone, no less."

"No," Ceros said with a slight grin. "I am not so foolish,
Cousin. My escort is just beyond the third dune."

Aleric looked in the direction the prince had come as if to judge
whether or not he spoke the truth.

"You doubt me?"

"Of course not," Aleric said smoothly. "I simply wanted to
determine how far they had to travel so we could leave as soon as
they arrive." He quickly added, "Assuming they will be traveling on
to Licosia, that is."

Ceros simply nodded. "Who have you brought with you,
cousin? I assume by their robes they are members of the council."

Aleric made the introductions to the three council members. As
he finished, a solitary man appeared at the edge of the oasis. He
was similar in age and build to the prince but with dark hair on his
head and chest. The sword strapped to his back marked him as a
soldier. The beads that hung from the single braid in his hair
indicated he was a high-ranking, decorated warrior.

Everyone went silent when they noticed him.

"Ah, Gehiji." The prince walked away from the group to greet the newcomer. He said a few things to the warrior before returning with him. "Gehiji Talasona has been a close friend for many years. He is to be paid all respect and courtesy due an honored guest."

"Of course," Aleric once again spoke for all of them.

The men tipped their heads and murmured greetings.

Once the courtesies were completed, the prince turned to Aleric. "Have my sisters arrived?"

"They have. When we left, they were enclosed with the queen."

"Good. And what of Mother? How is she handling the news?"

"As to be expected of a queen. She grieves, but she may be counted on to maintain a strong front for the people of Licosia."

Ceros nodded. "What preparations have been made so far?"

"Your mother insisted we wait until you arrived to light the funeral pyre. She believes it should be your right and honor to send your father on his journey to the afterworld."

Ceros nodded again. "Are there others to escort us to the palace?"

"No, my prince. Just the council elders."

Ceros grunted. "Let us be off then."

"You do not require refreshment before we go?"

"No. I am anxious to see Mother." He glanced at the four council members who had made use of the limited shade nearby. "If they require rest, we will continue on unescorted."

"Oh." Aleric glanced to where the other council members stood. "I believe we can be ready to return as you do."

"Fine."

"We brought extra mounts in case yours were weary."

"Thank you. I believe I will take you up on that offer." He looked to Gehiji, who shook his head. "Gehiji will continue to ride his own."

"As you wish." Aleric bowed his head respectfully. "Oh, one other thing."

Ceros paused expectantly.

"We brought the ceremonial headdress for you to wear as you enter Licosia. The council felt it would be good for people to be able to recognize you and know that you have returned." He shrugged. "After all, you've been away for many rotations of the sun."

"I know, but I don't want to create a scene with my return." He grimaced. "Are you certain the headdress is necessary?"

3

"I'm afraid so."

Ceros nodded.

Aleric gestured for one of the servants to step forward. The servant carried a wood box covered with elaborate carvings.

Ceros groaned as soon as he saw it.

With great ceremony, Aleric removed the polished metal. Sunlight reflected off the rounded side and point. Other than its exaggerated height, the crown had a simple design. Ceros often wondered if his predecessors had been short men who wanted additional stature to feel more important.

Someone had replaced the silky fabric that lined the edge. Probably in an effort to ensure his royal head didn't become stressed under the weight of the gold, Ceros thought sarcastically.

Thank the Gods it wasn't covered in gemstones.

"If I may," Aleric gestured to Ceros' head with the crown.

"Very well," he said with a sigh. He went down on one knee in the sand to allow Aleric to reach him. The headpiece fit snugly and pinched when Aleric put it in place.

"There," Aleric said with a smile. "Your mother will be pleased."

Ceros stood and returned his smile. At least he hoped he'd managed a smile instead of a grimace. "Shall we?" Ceros gestured to their mounts, anxious to reach home.

"After you," Aleric said.

When they reached their mounts, Ceros took his reins and greeted his eligari with softly spoken words. As he stroked and soothed the animal, he checked the fastenings. Aleric stood nearby, looking at him as if he had lost all good sense. Ceros wondered when Aleric had become so stuffy and formal. Perhaps he had just been gone too long.

Before he could climb onto the back of his eligari, Aleric stopped him.

"I haven't had a chance to tell you that I am sorry about your father. He was a beloved leader and he will be missed greatly."

Ceros nodded. "Thank you. I just hope Mother is doing as well as she says."

"It's hard to say. Your mother is a strong woman and doesn't always let on when things are bothering her. Even when she should be asking for help."

"True," Ceros said with a slight grin, then grimaced. "I hate that

I couldn't get here any faster."

"I'm sure she understands."

"She does."

Aleric clasped Ceros on the shoulder. "I just hope everything is as you expect."

Ceros held Aleric's gaze for a moment. "As do I."

Aleric patted Ceros once more then headed to his eligari to mount up. Ceros watched him for a moment, wondering what to make of Aleric's comment. He felt a trickle of unease and wondered what he would find when he reached the palace. There would be many things to catch up on. Many people he would have to familiarize himself with. Old friends with whom he would have to become reacquainted.

There would probably be enemies waiting as well. Unfortunately those would take longer to uncover.

Ceros climbed onto the back of his eligari. As he settled himself into the saddle, he felt as if the ground began to dip and sway. He shook his head, trying to clear the feeling. He looked around the oasis to get his bearings, but everything had become fuzzy and out of focus.

"My prince, if you will lead the way?" the voice echoed.

Ceros' eligari danced nervously beneath him.

"Ceros?" Gehiji's voice registered from somewhere to his left. "Are you okay?"

"Something is not quite right, Gehiji." Ceros turned in the direction of Gehiji's voice, but he couldn't focus on his face. "My eligari seems to disapprove of carrying me."

"I'm not sure it's your eligari."

Ceros felt someone grab one of his arms and pull.

"Ceros? What's wrong?"

The edges of Ceros' vision became fuzzier and dark gray. "I think I need to dismount, Gehiji." He tried to lift his leg to remove himself from the saddle, but only felt the rush of air as he slid to the ground.

"Your highness!"

"Ceros!"

The voices faded further and further to the back of his mind and darkness swamped him into oblivion.

CHAPTER TWO

By the Gods, why can no one hear me!

Ceros continued to yell until even the voice in his head began to sound hoarse. Still no one responded. There were people in the room. He could hear them moving about and whispering. Since he couldn't turn his head, he couldn't see anything except the same ceiling view he'd had since he'd awakened.

Could be worse. My eyes could have been closed.

He tried to move an arm, a leg, a finger. He tried to turn his head again, but nothing worked that he could tell. One of the physicians had told his mother earlier they were bewildered by what ailed him. They only know half of the puzzle. His body may not be responding to any of the pokes and prods when they tested his reactions, but he could feel everything, hear everything and see the few things that passed through his line of sight.

He simply had no control over his own limbs.

Not being able to communicate had pushed him near the brink of madness. There had to be a way for him to tell them he was alive and functional inside his shell of a body.

Thank the Gods his mother insisted they feed him what they could. So far it had been water and broth mixed with some kind of herbs. All spooned in small quantities as someone encouraged his throat muscles to work. His body would soon wither away if they didn't find a cure for whatever had put him in this state.

With nothing else to do, Ceros replayed his memories of the morning and tried to discern what happened. He'd had no unknown food or drink since he and Gehiji left Shirghada. They'd packed their own rations before leaving and traveled alone.

Gehiji posed no threat. He'd protected Ceros' back more times than he cared to think about. And Ceros had done the same for Gehiji.

He remembered meeting Aleric and the council members at the oasis on the outskirts of Licosia. After that, his memory became clouded.

When he woke, his father's old physician, Darius, had been speaking with his mother. He couldn't see her, but he felt certain it had been his mother who clung to his hand. Darius admitted he didn't know what ailed him but promised to consult some colleagues and dig through his tomes to find an answer.

His mother came and went several times through out the day, but her own physician had cautioned her against staying and exhausting herself when there was nothing she could do to help. Ceros hated being the cause of more grief for her. She had just lost her husband, the father of her children, her king. She probably feared she would lose him too.

What if the throne were in jeopardy?

If it hadn't already been chilled, his blood would have run cold at the thought.

His father's death had been labeled a hunting accident but the absence of witnesses only created more questions in his mind.

Ceros had been away from the royal court and the related politics for years. There would be no reason for anyone to hold a grudge against him personally. If his present condition was the result of someone's attempt to kill him, it would most likely be someone who felt he or she had a chance to gain power, or perhaps even rule over Licosia.

He ran through the list of people who would step up in power if he died or was deemed unfit to rule by the council. While he'd been away, he allowed himself to get caught up in the politics of Shirghada instead of Licosia. He didn't readily remember all of the highest-ranking council members.

In his present condition, he couldn't ask anyone. He couldn't even make a list of the names he did know.

Damnation! If he got out of this predicament, he would remedy that problem as quickly as possible. He allowed himself a string of curses to relieve some of the tension he felt building up inside.

That's a very creative use of more than a dozen curses. And all of them used in a single thought too.

Ceros startled at the sound of a female voice inside his head. *Oh Gods, I've finally gone mad. Now I'm hearing voices.*

You haven't gone any more mad than I, the voice attempted to reassure him.

That isn't a comforting thought.

The voice laughed, the light sound dancing through his mind, soothing some of his frustrations.

Who are you? Ceros asked.

There was a pause before the voice answered.

I don't think I will reveal that just yet.

Do you know who I am? Ceros asked, allowing his royal breeding to show in his voice.

I believe so.

You don't know for sure?

I didn't at first, no.

How long have you been listening to my thoughts?

I first heard them this morning, but mistook them for echoes from somewhere within the palace. When I realized no one else could hear you and sensed how frustrated you were, I began looking for the source.

How is it that you can speak to me? Inside my thoughts, that is.

The voice paused again. *I cannot say.*

Cannot? Or will not?

A little of both I suppose. If it makes you feel better, I don't think I can hear all of your thoughts all the time.

What do you mean?

This is the first time I've heard anything. Today was, I mean.

That makes me feel somewhat better.

I suspect that your thoughts were projected due to your intense emotional outburst.

Ceros considered her theory. It made sense. *Do you think that anyone else can hear my thoughts?*

Again the voice paused. *It's doubtful.*

Why you then?

The voice sighed, or so it seemed. *Will you allow me to find the answer to that question before I tell you?*

Do I have a choice?

The voice chuckled. *Not really.*

Then by all means, take your time. I'll be here. Waiting patiently.

Now, now. No need to be petulant.

Me? Petulant?

Yes, you.

The voice laughed again, easing some of the tension that built up again. He was so relieved to have someone to talk to he couldn't bear the thought of breaking the connection, no matter who it belonged to.

How do I know you're real, not a drug-induced illusion?

He felt the bed dip as someone sat next to him. That same someone grasped his foot over the linen sheet that covered him.

Can you feel that? she asked.

Feel what? He didn't want to assume anything.

Me, touching your foot.

Yes.

Do your drug-induced illusions usually touch you? Physically, I mean.

It was Ceros' turn to chuckle. *No, not usually.*

Well, then, I must really be here.

I guess so. Thank the Gods. Ceros knew he wasn't really holding his breath, but it felt like it.

I heard that, you know.

You mean I have to censor all my thoughts now?

No. But if I'm somewhere nearby and you're upset, you might want to.

You have to be near me to hear my thoughts?

I think so. It's only a theory. One I'll test here in a moment, since I need to leave before anyone returns.

Do you really have to go? He hated the panic that rose with the thought of her leaving and never returning.

People will wonder why I linger if I'm seen in your room.

When will you be back?

It's almost time for the evening meal. I need to find someone who may be able to answer the question of why we can hear each other's thoughts. I doubt I'll be able to return until tomorrow. Perhaps while everyone is busy with the midday meal.

Can you do something for me?

If I can.

Will you get a message to my friend, Gehiji? Him and only him. Tell him that I am alive, inside this body and I will need his skills to find out who did this to me.

What reason would he have for believing me?

Ceros pondered that thought. She was right. Even if she could get a message to Gehiji, he would likely dismiss it as the fanciful wishing of a woman. Or worse, he could become suspicious of her intentions and try to keep her away.

Tell him that I will return the telos he gambled away if he is able to find out what and who was behind this.

A telos? Do I even want to know what that is?

If you deliver my message and I recover from this, whatever this is, I will tell you the story.

Very well. I will seek your friend out. But I won't promise to tell him how I know.

Fair enough.

A sound from somewhere nearby sent the owner of the voice scurrying to her feet. *I must go.*

You will return. Ceros knew it was more an order than a question, but he didn't care. He needed her to return. As much as he hated it, he needed her to keep him sane.

Yes. I will return as soon as I can. You should sleep. It's the best thing you can do to heal the body.

Ceros snorted. *Like I have anything else to do.*

He heard a door open and close but didn't hear anyone moving about the room. Something twisted in his chest knowing she had gone.

I will return. The voice whispered in his mind, easing the knot forming in his chest.

A moment later, he heard her asking, *Do you still hear me?*

Her voice had faded making him wonder if proximity or barriers between them impacted his ability to hear her.

Yes, somewhat.

Interesting.

What is?

I'll tell you tomorrow.

He chuckled and wondered what just happened.

CHAPTER THREE

The midmorning sun cast shadows along the covered walkway between the main entrance and the palace. Danet scurried past the main dining hall, but craned her neck to see who might still be taking their breakfast. One of the prince's sisters and her husband were just settling in but the queen was not present.

She made her way to the servants' area to find the one woman who would know what had been going on around the palace the last few weeks. Hesina, the most senior of the household staff, had served since she was a young girl. Her loyalty ran deep and she made it her business to know everything that affected the royal family.

"Hesina. There you are." Danet found the short, pudgy woman in the kitchen, inspecting the day's produce with one of the cooks.

Hesina waved for her to enter. The palace kitchens were off-limits to anyone not assigned to work there. That rule was strictly enforced by Hesina and her staff. Rumor had it the cooks had chased more than one person out with large knives.

A couple of the kitchen staff murmured greetings as Danet passed, which she returned in kind.

"I've been wondering when you'd make you way around here," Hesina said as Danet approached.

"I tried to find you last night, but your girls said you were busy and I needed to see one more patient before going home."

"You and that father of yours. Always running here and there, taking care of others when you should be taking care of yourselves." She clucked her tongue.

"You're one to talk." Danet smiled warmly at Hesina. "So tell me. How bad is it around here, really?"

The woman shook her head. "It's a sad state of affairs, child. Come." She motioned for Danet to follow. "Let's step out into the gardens."

The area Hesina spoke of was not the royal family's lush, cultured grounds but the functional space that grew herbs and a few fruit trees. Despite its utilitarian purpose, it was a lovely space. Danet and Hesina often sought refuge and quiet there.

"Has your father been summoned?" Hesina asked.

"Not that I know of."

Hesina grunted as she sat on the edge of a raised flowerbed. She had chosen a shaded spot far enough away from the doorway to allow privacy. "Probably won't be long before he is. Darius is frantic with worry that he won't be able to save the prince." She paused. "So is the queen."

"Understandable."

"And so soon after the king's death." Hesina shook her head. "I do not like the things that are happening here. Too much death. It should not be so."

"What do you mean?"

Hesina lowered her voice. "I mean something is not right about all of this." She tapped her chest with her fist. "Something tells me the king's death should not have happened."

"It was an accident, wasn't it?"

"That is what they say."

"Who declared it to be so?"

"The council." Hesina grunted. "Those weak-kneed old men who wouldn't raise a hand if the Zarenthia were beating down the palace doors."

"Didn't Darius have a say in it?"

"He did, but he had been to the southern border to check into reports of some kind of outbreak. It took almost two days to reach him and for him to return to the palace." Hesina looked Danet in the eye. "A lot can be hidden in two days."

"Strange that they summoned Darius when Father was already there. He'd even sent word to his colleagues to let them know the outbreak had been grossly exaggerated. There was one isolated case."

"Strange indeed," Hesina agreed.

"Do you believe the prince is in danger?"

Hesina glanced around the area. "I will say this. A council meeting has been called in three days' time. That meeting is to appoint an interim ruler until it is determined if the prince will be capable of assuming his rightful place."

"Is the queen not the interim ruler?"

"She is, but only upon the prince's authority. If he is no longer capable of assuming his place, thus granting his authority, then it falls to the council to appoint someone."

"Oh Gods."

"If my queen were of childbearing age, I would worry for her. A posthumous heir might have put her life in danger as well. The council has already asked her maids about her woman's cycle."

"Someone could be after the throne," Danet whispered.

"I may be seeing things that are not there, but it worries me greatly."

Danet grasped Hesina's hand. "Your worry may be well-founded. I will talk with Father."

Hesina nodded. "He will know where to look for answers."

"In the meantime, how may I get in to the prince's chambers so I can examine him myself? I assume he is under guard."

"Most definitely. The queen chose the men herself." Hesina stood. "But I believe we can get you in. Let's find the girl I assigned to his room for today. I believe she may be feeling ill and should go home and rest. That means someone else will need to take care of the prince's linens."

Danet smiled. "I seem to have a free moment to spare and could help with that problem."

"I thought you might." Hesina winked at Danet.

In no time, Danet found herself on the way to the prince's chambers with a basket of fresh linens and a pitcher of water. As she drew closer, she relaxed her mind to allow herself to pick up his thoughts. They came through with alarming clarity.

Damn all the hydotcha in the kingdom. When I am on my feet again, I'm having every one of those blasted flowers cut down. My nose itches and I can't scratch it! I don't know who keeps bringing them in but I may have them tossed out of the palace along with the flowers.

Are you always this cranky of an invalid or did you not get enough sleep? It's about time. Where have you been?

If she hadn't heard the relief in his tone, she would have taken offense at his high- handedness. *Good morning to you, too.*

The sun has been up for hours. What took you so long?

I warned you yesterday I wouldn't come until the midday meal, so actually I'm early. Even after checking on a few things.

Like what? he demanded.

Like possible reasons for your condition and why we are able to speak with just our minds.

And what did you learn?

Not much, I am afraid. She sighed. *There are several toxins that could cause this sort of thing, but nothing that matched exactly. I was advised by someone close to me, who has knowledge of healing, that I needed more information.*

Such as?

Visual clues. Knowledge of anything you were exposed to or consumed.

Did you tell this person you had spoken to me?

Of course not.

Didn't think they would believe you?

Didn't want to worry them. She corrected him. *Oh wait, I need to get past the guards.*

I guess telling them I said to do it won't help.

Not a bit. She smiled at the thought.

It didn't take much convincing to gain access to the prince's rooms even though there were orders to not admit visitors. Being well-known at the castle, particularly as one of the queen's own, helped.

Yesterday there had only been one guard on duty. While the maids cleaning the guest suite at the end of the hallway distracted him, she had been able to slip in, unannounced.

I'm here.

That was alarmingly easy. Either my security needs better training or you know something I don't.

Perhaps a bit of both. She took a moment to look around the room. She had never been in the prince's chambers before yesterday and even then she had been so focused on why she could hear his thoughts she didn't take in her surroundings. The furnishings were surprisingly sparse.

It's a functional space, he said, obviously picking up on her thoughts. *I haven't lived here for several years and my visits were often short when I did return home.*

But it is home.

Yes. He paused. *Yes, it is.*

Danet set the basket of linens on the floor not far from the bed. The bed itself was oversized, obviously made to accommodate the prince's large frame. However it was a simple structure. A mattress set upon a platform, neither far from the ground. The linens were plain but of the finest quality.

The prince had been placed in the center with a sheet covering his lower half.

Before she looked at his face, she reminded herself she had company in her head and shouldn't comment on anything she saw. The last time she had a glimpse of the prince she remembered thinking he was handsome enough that he would never have to worry about finding his princess.

So, how are you today? she asked, struggling for neutral conversation.

He growled. How he managed to project the sound in her head puzzled her, yet made her smile. *I am alive.*

Have the physicians checked on you yet?

Yes. I have endured poking and prodding again this morning.

Did they say anything?

I heard two people whispering that, other than an increased heartbeat, they didn't detect any changes. They worried that Darius would not be pleased.

I'm sure he isn't.

I worry more about Mother and how she is handling this so soon after Father.

Your mother is a very strong, capable woman. She will do what she has to do to see you well and to cope with whatever comes her way.

The prince paused. *You are right.* Another pause. *Thank you.*

I speak only the truth.

She allowed him a moment to let the thought sink in. As she waited, it occurred to Danet the connection had become stronger and she could hear him much better. It sounded as if he were speaking from across the room instead of down an empty hall.

I am going to change your bed linens to make myself busy lest it appear I came in here just to admire your princely beauty.

You may admire my princely beauty as well. His appreciation of her sarcasm came through their connection.

She snorted. *I am sure you have an ample supply of ladies to do that. I'll stick with trying to heal you.*

15

She pulled the sheets loose from the bed corners then wondered how she would get them out from underneath the prince. She had no trouble moving a child or small- framed woman on a narrow cot with no help. The prince was considerably larger and so was his bed.

The maids rolled me onto my side, pushed the linens around then rolled me onto the other side and onto the fresh one.

Ah. That makes sense. She set to work then said, *Tell me how you're feeling today. Everything you have an awareness of, no matter how small.*

Are you in a habit of telling your superiors what to do? His tone held a hint of amusement.

There are very few who I would consider superior. I have met many who, due to their birthright or good fortune, hold power in our part of the world. However, in either case, when they expect assistance with an issue they have brought to me, yes, I do tell them what to do. Like everyone else, it is their choice to follow or not.

Well said. He paused. *I heard one of the guards call you Mistress, but I couldn't hear your given name. What is it?*

Danet stopped what she was doing. She originally thought she could hide her identity, but that seemed a foolish notion now. If the prince or any of the royal family were in danger, she had no choice but to help however she could. Even if it meant risking her freedom and possibly her life. If—when—he recovered, he could easily learn her name anyway. It would be best if she didn't lie to the next king.

My name is Danet.

You are mated, Danet?

No. I was, but he passed several years ago.

Another pause. *Is Mistress a title then?* He sounded somewhat disappointed.

Yes, but not in the way you may be thinking. Because of the station I hold within your mother's staff, my degree of training and, perhaps partially due to my family's history, I am regarded as an elder.

How do I not know you then?

I serve your mother and on occasion your sisters. Before you left the palace, I was unmated. I would never have been called upon to serve you. We have passed a time or two, but nothing ever warranted a need for an introduction. I'm sure there are many in the palace you do not know.

He grunted but didn't deny it.

Starting at the top of your head, describe everything you're feeling. If it aches, tell me how or how much and, if possible, where.

All right. He managed to grumble even without vocal cords. *My head aches.*

Where?

At the temples and the back of the top part.

Now that she had both sheets loose and pushed next to the prince's body, she knelt on the edge and considered how to proceed.

I won't bite. Or, at least, not right now, he teased.

I know. Just give me a moment to figure out the best way to do this without moving you any more than necessary. She studied his still form from head to toe. He was a large man. And what wasn't covered by the sheet was very nice to look at.

Hopefully she'd managed to keep that thought to herself.

If it doesn't offend your royal person, she said with a lift of her lips, *I shall attempt to accomplish two things at once. I need to roll you over to remove the linens but I think I will also take the opportunity to do a visual inspection.*

Go right ahead. I couldn't stop you even if it did offend my royal person.

She decided to start her exam with something easy. Something that wasn't so, well…manly. She lifted his hand that lay closest to her and examined every part. Each finger, between the fingers, under the nails as well as the palm and top. Her hands were dwarfed next to his. The breadth of each of his fingers nearly doubled hers. While they didn't look like a laborer's hands, his had seen rough conditions. *Huh.*

What? he asked.

Sorry. I am surprised.

By what? Did you find something?

No. Nothing to explain your condition. There are no fresh wounds or puncture marks to indicate an infection or poison entry point.

Then what surprised you?

Your hands. They're, um… They're not what I expected to find on a prince.

What did you expect to find? Well-manicured and jeweled?

A little, yes. Yours have obviously seen a harder life than most princes would be expected to live.

That's probably true.

How so?

He sighed. *I assume you know that I went to school in Shirghada.*

Yes.

What you probably do not know is that I served in their regiments after finishing my learnings.

Danet's mouth fell open. *But their regiments produce some of the most elite forces in the world. How did you get in? And why did the king allow such a thing?*

The king didn't know at first.

But…

Some of the people I met at school planned to join, so I figured I might as well give it a shot. I didn't want to go home. There was nothing for me here as long as Father ruled.

But you could have been killed.

Possibly. I could have been killed getting thrown from the back of an eligari too. It's not as if I asked for suicide missions. However, the training was invaluable. I wouldn't trade the experience or the friendships I made for anything.

Pride and conviction rang in his tone. She didn't know what kind of training they did, but it had to be extensive and physically demanding for Shirghada to have the reputation it did. For any leader, the training would be an enormous asset. As a man, he probably saw it as a worthy challenge. There were obviously many benefits to what he did. Despite the risk.

It took initiative and drive for him to choose that instead of becoming a spoiled and pampered prince.

Impressive.

Not that I object to your holding my hand, but I'm going to be very disappointed in your abilities as a physician if that is the only thing you examine.

Danet dropped his hand as if it had bitten her. Her foolish woolgathering would get her caught if she didn't focus. *My apologies. I let myself be distracted.*

He chuckled in her head. The sound was like a warm caress. That kind of distraction she couldn't afford.

Your head hurts, you said. What else?

My hands are fine. One of them feels rather nice now.

If he could have, Danet felt sure he would have grinned at her. She chanced a look at his face. He was a handsome devil. Every woman in the city would be throwing herself at him as soon as he became mobile again.

She made a harrumph sound then moved to the foot of the bed so she could check his feet. Like the rest of him, they were large and masculine. She ran her thumb across the sole of his foot, checking for any protrusions that she might miss with her eye.

Believe it or not, my feet are somewhat ticklish.

You can feel that? She deliberately ran the nail of one finger from his heel to his big toe.

Yes!

You can feel it, but you have no physical response. Interesting. I had wondered if your ability to feel touch had diminished. That answers that question.

Taking pity on him, she checked his other foot and tried to not tickle him. Like his hand, she didn't notice any scratches or puncture marks.

She moved to the other side of the bed so she could check his other hand. His four extremities were the most likely place to have accidently come in contact with something poisonous. Unfortunately that theory expired when she found nothing.

Other than being a little sensitive to touch, can you sense or feel any difference in your feet or hands? she asked as she moved her inspection up his arm.

Nothing out of the ordinary, no.

And I don't see anything on this hand and forearm. She knew it had been a distant hope to find something so easily. *Do you feel discomfort or pain or heat or maybe even numbness anyplace unusual?*

Like a hot, prickling feeling maybe?

Possibly. Where do you feel that?

On the back of my neck.

She sat on the edge of the bed and ran her fingers along the side of his neck. It felt hot to the touch.

Where exactly? Can you feel my finger? she asked.

A little higher.

She pushed her fingers into the edge of his hairline. As she moved around the corner toward his ear she felt something. She jerked her hand away instinctively.

What?

I felt something. Let me get a linen and then I want a closer look.

Danet grabbed one of the thin linens Hesina had included in her basket and dampened one corner with water. She sat close enough to the prince so she could maneuver her head without impeding the light.

I'm going to turn your head just a bit. Tell me if it's uncomfortable.

Before you do, can you let me see your face so I know what you look like?
Does it matter what I look like?

It would be nice to have a picture in my mind at least. Besides, you know what I look like. Seems only fair that I at least get a glimpse of you.

She hesitated.

I could command you to do it.

She snorted. *And I could poke you with something sharp and leave.*

You wouldn't.

You don't know that. Thankfully he couldn't see her smirk.

Please?

Danet was so startled by his polite request she didn't know what to do. While the royal family had always treated her kindly and with a certain level of respect, she was still basically a servant. They didn't have to ask nicely.

She was humbled that it meant enough to him to do so. She couldn't refuse him such a small thing.

All right.

She pulled her hair to one side and twisted it around so it wouldn't hang directly in the prince's face when she leaned over. She wished for a mirror to double-check her appearance but that was foolish. He wouldn't care what she really looked like. He just wanted to be able to recognize her again.

She leaned across the prince so she could put one hand on the bed just above his shoulder then shifted until she hovered above his face. *Can you see me?*

Danet watched his eyes as if expecting them to move, but they didn't. The vacant expression made her heart ache.

There you are.

She started to back away.

Wait. Let me see your eyes. I want to know what color they are.

She looked him directly in the eye. *They're an odd green color.*

Why do you think they're odd?

I've never seen anyone else with this color.

There's nothing wrong with being unique.

Danet blinked and retreated so he couldn't see her blush. *I suppose not, unless you're trying to blend in.*

Why would you want—

Let's take a look at your neck and see what's going on there. It wasn't something she wanted to discuss. Especially not with the prince. *Tell me if this gets uncomfortable.*

She turned his head away from her so she could see more of the back of his neck. Using the dampened linen as a covering, she ran her finger around the place she had felt something. When she found the spot again she moved in closer to get a better look.

"I think there's something there," she mumbled as she tried to scrape at whatever clung to his neck.

Finally it fell off.

On the bed below where she had been working she found a tiny thorn. She picked it up with the linen so she could better examine it. It was dark, reddish-brown and had a curved point. It looked somewhat familiar, but since she didn't know plants as well as she should, her father would be a more reliable source.

Well? the prince asked.

The prickling you felt came from a thorn. More specifically, from your reaction to the thorn. It was stuck just inside your hairline so I'm not surprised it had been overlooked during your earlier exams. I probably wouldn't have noticed it if I hadn't been looking where you indicated.

Surely that isn't the reason for my condition.

I won't know until I find out what plant the thorn is from. It is possible that you could have an extreme sensitivity to whatever this is. And being so close to your head and spine might cause this kind of reaction.

I don't remember brushing up against anything with thorns.

Danet folded the linen around the thorn so she wouldn't lose it then tucked the linen into her bag inside the basket. She grabbed some salve she had in her bag then returned to his side and patted his arm in a consoling manner. *Don't worry yourself over it. Let me find out what kind of plant it came from then you might remember.*

As she dabbed on the salve, she added, *The thorn might or might not have been the problem. So don't get your hopes up too high.*

He grunted. *Well, you've done more than those fools who keep coming in here, poking and prodding me.*

They're doing their best. Is there any place else that aches or has discomfort?

My back is a little uncomfortable. That feels similar to when I've slept in a bad position for too long.

I wouldn't be surprised since you aren't able to arrange yourself comfortably. After I change your linens, I'll have you help me find a better position for you. Anything else?

Other than the itch on the back of my leg, no.

She smiled. *Which leg?*

My right one. Just below the knee.

She pushed the sheet aside then pulled his knee up so she could reach the spot he mentioned. Like the rest of him, his leg was firmly muscled and tanned.

When she scratched her fingernails over the area, he groaned with relief. *Right there. You just don't realize how a tiny itch can become so bothersome until you can't do anything about it.*

She chuckled. *I'm sure.* She patted his leg. *Okay. I need to finish these linens before the guards think I'm just in here napping.*

Thank you for taking care of my itch. And the thorn.

Once again, the sincerity in his voice touched her. *You are welcome, my prince.*

CHAPTER FOUR

Danet had just tucked the last corner of the bed linens under when the queen came in, followed by her usual entourage.

Danet turned away from the bed to make the proper curtsey. "My queen."

"Danet. What are you doing here?"

"Hesina was in a bind and I offered to help."

The queen regarded her for a moment before saying, "I see." She approached the bed and looked down at the prince. Her gaze turned tender, as one would expect of a mother watching a sleeping babe. "I suppose it would be too much to hope that he woke while I had luncheon."

"I have noticed no change in his condition since I arrived, my queen."

Well said. Not a lie, but not entirely the truth either. I'm impressed, the prince teased.

The queen nodded then sighed. She turned to her escorts. "Maya, would you please have tea brought in for us? And Theosa, I believe I could use my shawl. The pale-blue one, if you please."

The girls departed, leaving Danet alone with the queen.

"I am glad you're here. I had planned to send a message this evening if I didn't see you."

"How may I assist you, my queen?"

"I assume you did more than change the linens."

Danet tipped her head.

"Do you know why he is like this?" The queen indicated the

prince with a wave of her hand.

"I'm afraid not, my queen." The queen's shoulders wilted.

"Not yet," Danet quickly added. When the queen met her gaze, the pain and fear Danet saw made her heart ache. "I did a brief exam because I didn't know how much time I would have. Father and I both have questions. He is already looking into a few things."

The queen took Danet's hands. "Thank you."

"You should know we would not allow the prince to remain this way if there were something we could do."

"I know. But in this, I am a mother first and a queen second. I want my son well and whole and happy. Darius may be the king's physician, but I trust you and Sebak far more. Please help him."

Danet was honored the queen trusted them so much. But she feared how much faith she put in their abilities.

You're Master Sebak's daughter?

I am.

You could have mentioned that.

Would it have made a difference?

He hesitated. *No. But still.*

"Please, Danet. I will give you anything you desire if you make him well again," the queen added.

Danet couldn't believe her offer. "My queen, I am honored, but I fear your faith in our abilities exceeds reality."

"I do not believe that to be so."

"As much as I would aid you in anything that you asked, it would be an insult to Master Darius if either I, or perhaps worse, if Father were to take over the care of the prince. He would never let that happen without an uproar."

"I worry only for my son." The queen began to pace. "You are right though, and I know it, but I do not trust Ceros' care to Darius. I simply don't."

I don't either, to be honest with you, the prince added.

"If I might suggest an alternative?" Danet waited until the queen looked at her again. "What if I were appointed to oversee the prince's daily needs? To ensure his linens are changed regularly, that he is properly bathed and he receives some kind of nourishment throughout the day. That way I would have access to him. No one would question if I were examining him. Yet I could still carry information back and forth to Father and keep you updated as well."

"That is an excellent idea. And Darius would have no reason to get his nose out of joint."

"Exactly."

Nicely done.

Thank you. I do try.

"That would much relieve my mind, Danet." The queen grasped her hands once more. "I will have Theosa spread the word as soon as she returns." She hesitated, "You will begin immediately, yes?"

It really wasn't a question. "As you wish, my queen."

The queen's relief showed through her smile. She squeezed Danet's fingers then returned to Ceros' bedside. As she reached out to brush her hand across his brow she asked, "Do you think he will recover?" She looked up at Danet. "Tell me honestly."

"He appears to be a very strong, healthy man, which dramatically increases his chances for the better." She stepped closer to the foot of the bed. "But until we can determine the reason for his condition, I am afraid I cannot give you a better answer."

The queen nodded.

Tell her. Tell her that I'm in here. That I'm fine. Inside.

That would not be prudent.

Prudent? I do not give a damn about prudent. This is my mother. She is worried for no reason.

I'm afraid she is worried for a very good reason.

But—

I must insist, my prince. It would not be wise to tell her right now. Even if I were able to convince her, there are too many ears. We do not know who may be listening nor do we know if your condition is as a result of someone wishing you harm or a mere accident.

He went quiet.

Danet let what she said sink in as she bundled up the linens she had removed from the prince's bed.

The queen seemed content to simply sit beside Ceros and hold his hand. Probably remembering the last time she had seen him.

Your points are valid, the prince said. *I will concede. For now.*

Will it make you feel better if I promise to tell her as soon as we know more? And when I believe it is safe to do so? she added quickly.

Very well.

Danet took a cleansing breath. Gods and Goddesses above. Dealing with tender royal feelings could be exhausting.

I heard that.

She froze, despite the note of amusement he'd heard in his tone. Thankfully Theosa and Maya returned, saving Danet from having to respond.

"Your tea, my queen." Maya sat the tray on the table in the sitting area across the room from the bed. Theosa laid a shawl across the back of one of the chairs.

The cushioned chairs and table seemed out of place in the room, making Danet wonder if they had been brought in specifically for the queen's use.

She moved furniture into my room? the prince asked.

Danet grimaced. It was hard getting used to having someone else in her head. *I couldn't say for sure, my prince. I was merely speculating on the differences between the furnishings.*

Aren't you the diplomat all of a sudden.

Yes, well, that happens when I'm surrounded by royalty.

He chuckled. *I'm afraid that happens all too frequently. And here I had hoped you would be one of those genuinely refreshing people who would tell me what they really thought instead of what you thought I wanted to hear.*

You will probably hear more of my honest opinion than you should. Especially since I'm not used to having someone else in my head, hearing every stray thought I have.

It is a little unsettling isn't it?

To say the least. But I can't have you beheaded if I don't like something you think or say.

True. He sounded far too pleased with the notion. *But don't let that stop you from speaking freely.*

Danet settled for a grunt instead of a reply.

"My queen," Danet said as she stepped to the bed. When the queen looked up from her quiet reflection, Danet continued. "If I may, there are a few things I would like to retrieve from home. I should also let Father know my duties will be changing until the prince has recovered. I shall return as quickly as I can."

"Yes, of course. Give Sebak my regards and tell him we are sorry to pull you away from your duties at the clinic." She turned to Theosa. "Please have an escort readied for Mistress Danet." Before Danet could protest, the queen cut her off. "It will be faster and will save your energy for Ceros."

Danet knew it pointless to try to argue. She bowed her head. "Thank you, my queen."

"I'll have Maya speak with the guards while you are gone. And Hesina as well. We'll make sure everyone knows what I have asked of you. I'm sure it goes without saying that if anyone questions you or refuses any orders you give, you are to let me know immediately."

Danet tipped her head. "Yes, my queen."

"Oh, and one more thing, Danet. While I have the utmost faith that you will care for my son to the best of your ability, please remember to have a care for yourself too."

The look she gave Danet told her two things. One—the queen was not unaware of the threat leveled at Ceros, and by association, now her too. Two—the queen was genuinely concerned about her welfare.

Mother never was a fool, the prince said.

"I will," Danet said softly.

"Good. You may go."

"Thank you, my queen." She made her bow, gathered her basket and linens and headed to the servants' area once again.

How long will you be?

Not long. Especially with an escort to and from home. I want to get this thorn to Father as soon as possible so we can find out what it is.

Agreed. Mother is right however. You do need to take care.

I will. Word that I have been asked to help will not have gotten far yet, so I believe I will be safe for now.

Don't assume anything.

Yes, my prince.

I mean it. I need you.

Danet's foolish heart gave a little leap, but she quickly reminded herself he was concerned because she was the only one he could communicate with and because she and her father were skilled healers. *I will return,* she assured him.

You'd better.

CHAPTER FIVE

Danet's father and the housekeeper, Ryana, met her at the front door when she reached their home.

"What's happened?" Sebak asked.

"Nothing, really."

"Then why have you been escorted home? Are you ill?" Ryana asked.

"No, no. I am well, I assure you." Danet unwrapped her shawl from around her hair and draped it over a hook just inside the foyer. "The queen wanted me to return quickly and offered an escort, that is all."

"So you are to return to the palace then?" Sebak asked.

"Yes and soon. I just needed a couple of things." Danet reached for Ryana's hand. "No need for worry, Ryana."

"So we should not plan on you for dinner, then?"

Danet smiled. "No. But I will take some of your sweetbread for the morning if Father hasn't eaten it all yet."

"Even if he did, I would have another ready for you by the morning."

"You are too good to us."

Ryana took her cue and returned to the kitchens, allowing Danet a chance to speak to her father. Without a word, they went to his study.

"The queen sends her regards," Danet began.

Sebak nodded his acknowledgement.

"She has asked me to attend the prince during his illness.

Knowing Darius would likely frown upon interference from any outside parties, she has agreed that my role should be daily monitoring to ensure the prince's medicines are administered as ordered by the royal physician and the prince's every comfort is ensured.

"However, if I were to convey any observations I made to you and you were to suggest alternative care methods, the queen would be open to them."

"I see." Sebak fingered the edge of his robe. "It is a fine line that you walk, daughter."

"Yes, it is."

"Are you sure it is one you should travel?"

"You know I cannot turn away. Even if the queen had not asked it of me, I could not allow the prince to linger in that state when you or I may be able to help."

"I know. I just wanted to be sure you did. What have you learned of his condition?"

"All outward appearances indicate he is a healthy man. He seems to be in excellent physical shape. No infections or disease marks that I could see. When I inspected his hands and feet, I found nothing to indicate he had grabbed or stepped on anything."

"Very strange."

"Indeed. Until I found this." She pulled out the linen she had stashed in her bag and carefully unfolded it, revealing the thorn.

Sebak moved so the light from the window fell upon the cloth. "Where did you find it?"

"Buried in the skin, just inside the hairline behind his ear. Do you know what kind of plant it came from?"

"There is something familiar about this. Where have I seen this recently…" Sebak stood and crossed the room to one of his bookshelves.

"There is more, Father."

He turned to look at her, his hand poised in the air to retrieve a book.

Danet moved closer so she could speak softer. "I can hear him speaking." She paused. "In my head."

If he was surprised, he managed to hide it. Sebak lowered his hand and his eyes met hers. He took a deep breath and released it. "Are you sure it is him?"

"I am afraid so."

"And does he know who you are?"

"He does now. The queen came in while I changed the linens and spoke to me. She called me by name."

He nodded then turned away to stroll to the window. "Does he know why the two of you were able to speak to each other this way?" he asked as he looked out.

She chuckled. "No. I'm not certain, myself."

Sebak looked back at her, his eyes sad. "I think you do, child."

Danet tried to swallow the lump that had formed in her throat. "But how can that be, Father?"

He shrugged one shoulder. "It is something that is beyond our control. If he is truly your destined mate, it is for a reason. One that you may or may not be able to see in your lifetime."

"Is there no other explanation for it?"

"None that I know of."

"I had hoped that perhaps it was another of my gifts that had been triggered by the prince's outburst of emotion."

Sebak's eyes sparked back to life and he moved away from the window. "So he is conscious inside his unmoving body, then?"

"Yes."

He continued toward her. "Is he alert or groggy? Fade in and out?"

"When I have spoken with him, he's been alert and lucid. The only thing that seems to make the conversation fade out is distance." At his questioning glance, she added, "I cannot speak to him if we are far apart."

"That will get stronger over time." He held her gaze. "Assuming you want it and if the two of you are together."

"Oh Gods, Father. What am I to do about this?" Danet sat on a nearby chair and rubbed her hands over her face. "He is the prince. Actually, now he is the heir to Licosia. Even if I am able to hide my abilities from him, he's going to want an explanation. I'm sure once he's recovered, he'll try to learn anything he can about it. If I were him, and slated to be the next ruler, I wouldn't want a stranger having access to my thoughts."

Sebak came and stood next to her, his hand resting on her head. "It is a strange thing to become accustomed to."

When she looked up at him, she saw the sadness had returned to his eyes. "But when it is a connection between two people who love and respect each other it is a comforting and beautiful thing.

You're never alone. You know when the other is in need and you are certain of their feelings for you." He paused. "I miss it terribly. Almost as much as I miss your mother."

Danet reached for his hand and laid her cheek against it. "I'm sorry, Father."

"For what?"

"That Mother was not meant to stay with us."

"It wasn't for us to decide." He pulled her face up by her chin until she looked at him. "And I know that I will see her again when my time comes."

She smiled though her eyes were watery.

"You had best get your things and return to the palace."

Danet stood. "You are right."

"I will find out which plant this," he pointed to the thorn on the linen, "came from and I will send word as soon as I do."

"I plan to come home as often as I can."

"Do what you need to, my dear." He pulled her into a hug. "But take care."

"I will." She smiled as she pulled out of his embrace. She grabbed her bag then darted up the stairs to her room.

A change of clothes and a hairbrush went into a bag along with her journal. At the last minute, she grabbed a few hairpins and a length of ribbon. In case she needed to tie her hair out of the way, she told herself. Not because she wanted to look nice once the prince healed and became fully awake.

When she returned to her father's study she found he had piled three books on his side table to use as references. The scholar was already hard at work on the puzzle. Occasionally he would stop to take a glance at the thorn still displayed on the linen.

"Is there anything else I should be looking for or doing to help the prince, Father?"

Danet could tell he had to make an effort to drag himself away from his books. "If you treated the site where you removed the thorn, there is nothing more I can think of for now. Watch for fever and shallow breathing."

"I will."

He started to turn back to his books then added, "You might also try manipulating the muscles. It won't help with his condition, but it does seem to help patients confined to a bed once they are recovered."

"Good idea. I can start that this evening." She shifted the weight of her bag to a better position. "I will send word of any changes if I cannot make it home myself."

He mumbled some response but was already engrossed in his work so Danet slipped out the door to rejoin her escort. She had to admit to it being easier to get back and forth to the palace with a guard. The crowds in the streets made room to allow them passage and she didn't work up a sweat skirting around street vendors and boisterous children.

As she passed through the palace gates, she attempted to connect with the prince. *Are you awake?*

His voice came through, but it was faint and had a hollow ring. *Unfortunately for me, I am.*

Why is it unfortunate?

Darius has some poor soul cornered and has been telling him all about the days he spent studying with the great physician, Masiurus.

Oh dear.

I bet you didn't know that Darius almost single-handedly cured a town of some pox.

Actually, I have heard that story before.

Would you please hurry back so you can stuff something into my ears? Or perhaps just smother me. I don't care which at this point.

Danet giggled then tried to stifle the sound when one of her escorts looked at her oddly. *He's not that bad.*

He's been here for what feels like hours.

I haven't been gone that long.

So you say.

She rolled her eyes. *I'm coming in the front entrance, I'll be there momentarily.*

Despite her amusement at the prince's annoyance, she did not look forward to the confrontation with Darius. She knew it wouldn't be long before he made an appearance, but she had hoped to avoid him a bit longer.

The guards at the door of the prince's quarters didn't balk at her admission so obviously she still had authorization for his care. She glided into the prince's room and found Darius seated on the chair the queen had occupied earlier. A young man wearing apprentice robes listed to him attentively.

Darius must have taken on a new student to train.

She made her bows and greeted Darius. "Good afternoon,

Master Darius. How are you?"

"Good afternoon, Danet." He stood. "I am well, thank you." He swept a hand toward the young man, who also stood. "This is Ishaq. He has recently come to Licosia and will be studying with me as an apprentice."

Poor bastard, the prince mumbled.

Danet tried to ignore his comment, even though it amused her.

Ishaq tipped his head, not quite in a bow, but nor did he give her a formal greeting. "I'm pleased to make your acquaintance, Danet."

Inwardly she sighed. She couldn't tell if Darius failed to give her proper credit for rank on purpose or not. You never knew with him.

"Mistress Danet," she gently corrected Ishaq. "Welcome to Licosia. I hope your tenure is educational. Even though my tenure was served with another, I have frequently benefited from Master Darius' experiences here at the palace."

Well done. In one breath you let the new kid know where he stood in rank and left it open as to whether or not Darius' experiences were positive or negative.

Don't distract me while I'm verbally sparring.

She tried to maintain a neutral expression and not react to the prince's comments or Darius' borderline insults.

"Yes, Danet is the daughter of an old colleague of mine. I've known her since she was a babe. She has served the queen and her daughters for many turns of the sun."

"Ah." Ishaq glanced back and forth between them, obviously uncomfortable with the undercurrents in the room.

"Speaking of the queen." Darius made a poor segue to the subject he had really come to discuss. "I understand you will be handling the prince's daily care."

"That is correct."

"May I assume that any changes in the prince's condition you notice will be reported to me immediately?"

"Naturally."

Unless I tell you otherwise, the prince added.

"And will you be administering his medicines?" Darius asked.

"I will ensure they are given at the correct intervals and oversee the doses."

Darius held her gaze. "I assume you will monitor any food and drink also?"

"Of course."

"Very well." Darius straightened his robes. "I will make it a point to check with you each day to get a report."

Danet nodded once to show her concurrence. "Before you go, would you mind making a note of everything you have ordered so far?" She pointed to the desk across the room from them. "Any foods or drinks as well as any herbs or medicines would be good to know. I assume you have ordered bland fluids and water for now."

"Yes, for now."

"Then I will continue your suggested course."

The prince grumbled something about lack of nourishment.

"I expected no less. I've only ordered a few herbs until we can determine the reason for his condition with certainty." He scribbled a few things on the paper lying on the desk. "Ishaq and I must go. Aleric expects us shortly."

"Enjoy the rest of your afternoon." Danet pasted a smile on her face.

Ishaq mumbled some farewell as he followed Darius out.

As soon as they were gone, Danet rolled her eyes and mumbled, "Thank the Gods."

Is he always that condescending to you?

Yes. When he does bother to speak. Most of the time he ignores me.

I've often wondered how he acted with other people. I remember him as being very self- important and meddlesome yet highly submissive, all at the same time. It's rather annoying.

Unfortunately I've seen it in action so I know what you mean.

Danet retrieved the list Darius had written. Nothing unexpected there. However, she would verify with Hesina's staff that nothing had been left off.

Enough about him. Now that Mother has made it allowable for you to be in here, what's your plan?

My plan? It's simple really. Figure out what's wrong and stop it or make it go away.

Good plan. Any more information than that?

Not as much as I'd like, but we're working on it.

We?

Father is researching the thorn I removed from your neck to determine what kind of plant it came from. Once we know that we'll have a better idea of whether it is related to your condition or not. Speaking of which, how is your neck? Has there been any change in what you've been feeling there?

It is better. The burning has stopped and the tingling is fading.

Good. Danet was relieved to hear it but didn't want to get either of their hopes up. *Any other changes?*

Not that I've noticed.

Well, it hasn't been long since I removed it.

How much did you tell your father?

Danet stopped sorting through the basket of supplies she found near the bed. *Pretty much everything.*

Including the fact that we could talk?

Yes.

Did he think you were crazy?

No.

There was a pause. *He believed you then?*

Of course. I have no reason to lie to my father.

Another pause. *Did he have an explanation for why we could speak this way?*

Danet took a deep breath and debated how much to tell the prince.

Everything is what you should tell me.

It's very startling having someone in your head.

Yes, I know. Now, tell me what you know.

You won't like it.

Let me be the judge of that.

She set the basket aside and walked to the sitting area. It was silly, but she felt better putting a piece of furniture between them. *I come from a long line of mystics.*

Go on.

I have gifts, if you will.

Like?

I can grow almost any kind of plant and know many of them on sight or by taste as well as their healing properties.

That's not so strange. It could just mean you have a talent and can memorize things easily.

I see colors around most people and know they say something about the person, but not what they mean. My mother died before I learned most of the things I needed to know to fully realize my gifts.

So it is passed through your mother's line then?

Yes.

What else?

When I was young, I dreamed of things that would come to be.

You don't any longer?

No. Not since my mother's accident. Father thinks I blocked the gift since I wasn't able to see her death and warn her.

How old were you? he asked softly.

Ten. She took a few steps toward the bed.

Were there no other mystics you could have turned to for help or training?

Of course not. They're banned.

I know, but that was long ago. And only in the city. Surely you have relatives you could have gone to.

No. Mother was an only child. Her mother had a sister but they lost contact when she went into the queen's service. We've never been able to find where that branch of the family moved.

Your mother served as a handmaiden, didn't she?

Yes, she did. Just like her mother and her grandmother.

Your great-grandmother served my great-grandmother?

Yes.

During the Great Wars?

That's right. Why all the questions? Her nervous energy forced her into action as they talked. She fluttered about the room, checking for supplies and to see what she had access to. She also took a good look at the layout of the suite.

Two reasons. First, if you are a mystic from your mother's line, then there is a very good chance that your great-grandmother saved my great-grandmother's life.

I have heard the story.

You have? Was it your great-grandmother then?

I'm afraid so. Danet chewed her lip and worried what his reaction might be to know she was related to the woman who turned the tide of the Great Wars.

But… That's incredible! What is there to be afraid of? Your great-grandmother made a huge sacrifice and it was unfair that her bravery had to be covered up.

It was war and there were plots against the royal family that would have unraveled the balance of power. They had to cover it up.

Even today credit for finding the people behind the plot to kill my great-grandmother and grandfather has never been disclosed.

Obviously you've been told so they didn't hide it completely, she pointed out.

I'm part of the royal family, though, so it doesn't count.

If you say so.

Danet turned to look at the prince. He was a handsome man. She hated seeing him trapped in his body this way.

Don't try to distract me, the prince said.

How am I distracting you?

You were thinking of touching my hair.

I was not.

Yes, you were.

Danet harrumphed. *What was your second reason?*

My second reason?

You said you had two reasons for asking about my family but only mentioned one.

Ah, yes. I was trying to figure out how your family could be so intertwined with mine, but I don't remember meeting you before now.

We were introduced once, long ago. As I have already explained, it would have been improper for me to have served you or spent any time in your company. Besides, you have been away from home for many turns of the sun.

Why is it acceptable for you to be in my service now?

I am no longer an innocent maid. I was married for a short time. Besides, completing my apprenticeship allows me a great deal of freedom even though I am not mated. I believe your mother is more concerned with your well-being than any sense of impropriety. Besides, there is little danger of your ravishing me while in this state.

How does she know that you won't ravish me while overseeing my care?

She shot him a look that would have spoken volumes had he been able to see it. *Because your mother knows me better than that.*

Does she?

Yes. With one word, she made sure there could be nothing to argue.

How unfortunate.

An image flashed through her mind of her straddling his very naked body, both of them sweaty and flushed. Danet tripped over her own feet. She quickly stamped the image down, not knowing if she had conjured it or if he had.

Either way, no good could come of dwelling on it so she forced her thoughts in a more productive direction and began making a list of things she may need for the next couple of days.

Why are you not mated again? he asked, making her forget what she had just put on her list.

Danet shrugged. *I had just finished my apprenticeship when Okpara*

37

and I were mated. He died about six moons later in an accident. I busied myself with a demanding schedule at the clinic as well as here at the palace. Between the two, I haven't had the time or the inclination.

Interesting.

Why? Because something must be wrong with me if I didn't rush out to find the first available man to fill my bed?

That's not what—

Are you one of those men who think every woman needs a man to watch over her?

No. I—

Just because society has dictated they expect girls to marry by their twentieth year and have little ones a year or two later doesn't mean I have to comply.

That's true but—

I'm not a simpleton. If I had met a man I wanted as a mate, one who was capable of capturing my interest both physically and mentally, I would be joined with him.

I'm sure you—

As it stands, I have yet to meet such a man. And until I do, I won't just throw myself in the path of every available man just so I could say I am mated. Danet folded her arms across her chest and harrumphed to herself. Actually it wasn't really to herself since Ceros could hear pretty much everything that passed through her thoughts.

Are you finished?

She took a deep breath. *Yes.*

Good. What I was trying to say was that you seem to be a talented, intelligent and caring woman. I'm surprised that a dozen or more men haven't come along and turned themselves inside out to impress and please you just so they could have the privilege of being with you.

Oh.

I respect your decision to help your father at his clinic. It is probably rewarding work that you do. But I also know what it's like to lie awake at night and wonder how much more rewarding life would be if there were someone it could be shared with.

Danet swallowed the lump that formed in her throat. His admission mirrored her deepest longing. One that she kept locked down and rarely examined so she wouldn't be reminded of what she might be missing. It was too risky to allow anyone to get close enough to discover her "gifts". Especially when she didn't know the extent of them herself. The idea of passing unknown abilities on to a child made her gut clench.

She clamped down on her thoughts and her feelings before Ceros picked up on them.

You know you'll only tempt my curiosity by trying to hide things from me, he told her.

No. Just forget about any temptation. I sense you are an honorable man and you should be able to understand that we both need boundaries. I won't go dancing through your private thoughts if you'll leave mine alone.

If they impact Licosia, how can I just look the other way?

There is nothing in my head that truly impacts Licosia. She frowned. *At least, not that I can think of.*

And if there is?

You will just need to trust that I would tell you if there was. We just need to agree to stay out of each other's closed-off thoughts.

He fell silent for a moment. Long enough to make Danet squirm.

Very well.

She let out the breath she didn't realize she'd held.

I will trust you, he said. *But don't be surprised if I bring it up after all of this is over.*

She groaned.

I heard that, he reminded her.

CHAPTER SIX

Ceros' sisters came to check on him and provided a welcome relief from his relentless questioning. Danet enjoyed catching up with them and found it hard to keep the information about Ceros' true condition to herself. Harder even than it had been with the queen.

As she held one of the girls' newborn son, she realized she was missing a piece of her life she hadn't previously noticed.

It took a lot of focus to bury her thoughts about mates and what her connection to the prince might mean, but Danet felt as if she accomplished it. She hoped the prince's lack of questions on the subject was proof she had succeeded.

The next distraction came by way of Hesina and a few members of her staff.

As Hesina's girls busied themselves cleaning and straightening the room, Hesina pulled Danet aside. "It relieved my mind to hear the queen assigned you to the prince's care."

"He is still under Darius' care. I will simply oversee his daily needs."

"However you wish to look at it, I know he'll be in good hands now. And I'm sure your being here eases some of the queen's stress."

"I just hope we are able to figure out what is wrong with him quickly."

Hesina patted her arm. "I have faith that you will."

"Thank you."

"Now, what can we bring you? Knowing you, there are probably a couple of lists started."

Danet smiled. "Naturally." She gave Hesina a note with the things she needed.

"What about you? There's a rather comfortable lounge in one of the guest rooms that I can have brought in if you're planning to stay through the night."

"I hadn't decided whether I would stay or not. I told Father I would return home whenever possible, but I would wait to see if the prince's condition changed."

Have them bring in the lounge. If nothing else, you can use it for extra seating when my sisters return.

"How about if I bring it in just in case," Hesina suggested. "If it's not needed, it's no trouble to take it out again."

"Very well." The idea of walking home late at night didn't appeal to her anyway.

That is very much out of the question. Even if you do decide to return home after nightfall, you ask for an escort home.

Danet could sense his concern. Despite her deep-seated need for independence, she doubted she would win this argument. Besides, her father would tell her the same thing. *Yes, my prince.*

"I'll have the lounge brought in after dinner has been served, but the other things should be within the hour," Hesina said.

"Thank you."

"Remember what I told you." She leveled a look at Danet and dropped her voice. "If you feel as if you're in danger for trying to help the prince or if you need any help with anything, anything at all, you come find me."

Danet hugged Hesina. "I will."

Hesina cleared her throat. "Now get to work and get our young prince back on his feet before someone snatches his palace out from underneath him."

Danet groaned inwardly, knowing Ceros heard what she said. Thankfully he remained silent.

"Come along, girls. You did a fine job getting this place in tiptop shape." With one last look in Danet's direction, Hesina added, "I'll send a dinner tray for you in a bit."

"That would be lovely, thank you."

Finally the room fell quiet once more.

What did she mean by my palace getting snatched away?

Danet took a deep breath. *I haven't been able to confirm the significance yet, but Hesina learned there was to be a council meeting in three days' time.*

When were you planning to tell me?

As soon as I knew more about it.

He paused. *Is that why you were asking my sisters about plans for the next few days?*

Yes. I didn't want to mention the meeting to anyone but I need to find out who knows about it and who doesn't. From what Hesina tells me, the meeting is not common knowledge.

How did she find out?

Danet sat on the edge of the bed and took his hand in hers. As she spoke, she rubbed and flexed each finger and massaged his palm. *Hesina makes it a point to keep an eye on everything that goes on in the palace. Not for malicious purposes. She is completely loyal to your family and has served since she was a child. Like her mother before her. And probably her mother's mother too.*

And like my mother, she must trust you if she confided that information.

She is a good friend to have.

When I am recovered, I think I will have you take me on a tour of my own home so you can introduce me to the people I need to know.

She smiled. *I would be honored to do so.*

They fell silent as she worked the muscles in his arm. He had far more muscle than the little old men and women she typically treated in her father's clinic. She found herself having to dig in harder and longer.

That feels really good, he murmured.

It should keep your muscles from stiffening after lying for so long without movement, and speed your recovery once you're back on your feet.

Whatever the reason, keep doing it.

Danet chuckled. *Yes, my prince.*

She moved around to the other side of the bed so she could work his other hand and arm. Shortly before she finished, one of Hesina's girls arrived with a basket and a small bowl of broth. The basket contained most of the things she'd requested and the broth had been sent for the prince.

To give her own muscles a chance to relax after working Ceros', Danet spooned a few drops of broth between his lips and did what she could to get him to swallow it.

I hate not being able to feed myself, Ceros grumbled.

I'm sure you do.

And that soup is not something I would ever request again.

Probably not, but with everything your body is trying to deal with right now, bland is best.

If you say so.

Once she had worked a few spoonfuls into him, she set the bowl aside and went to inspect the things in the basket. She found the oil she requested and returned to Ceros' side.

I am picking up some kind of focused intent from you. Are you going to torture me like the vultures who were here this morning? he asked irritably when she sat on the edge of the bed.

I hope it's not torture. I had planned to continue to work your muscles if that meets with my prince's approval.

Oh, well, in that case, proceed.

She chuckled. *I thought as much.*

Despite her budding curiosity, she took care to not expose more of him than necessary as she uncovered his feet and legs. In case more visitors arrived. She poured a liberal amount of the oil into her palm then rubbed her hands together to warm it. When she rubbed it into the lower part of his leg, Ceros groaned in her head.

She finished coating his leg with oil then kneaded each of the muscles. The thick and well-defined muscles piqued more of her interest than they should have. It had been a long time since she was close to a virile, healthy man. But she didn't remember wanting to touch Okpara as she did Ceros.

Have you never done this to a man before?

Danet cringed, realizing he had picked up on her thoughts. *No.*

Not even with your mate?

I... Uh, no. Her cheeks burned with embarrassment.

He paused. *Please tell me he didn't leave you untouched.*

No, but our schedules left us very little time together. And if you're going to keep picking through my thoughts I'm going to put a lock on them.

I can't help it. They're just there.

Well, stop it. Some things are my own business. I'm making an effort to not trespass in your head.

My apologies. I don't mean to pry but I have to admit it's fascinating getting a glimpse into the mind of a woman. You are creatures who have confounded men for hundreds of generations.

Be that as it may, some things should be allowed to stay private.

You are right, he admitted. *I will try harder to not intrude on your privacy.*

They fell silent as Danet worked to compartmentalize her thoughts and push the ones she didn't want exposed into a dark corner of her mind.

Can you go back to doing that thing you were doing with my leg? That felt nice.

She made a harrumphing sound but did as he asked. When she finished working the second leg, she switched positions so she could manipulate the foot and knee in order to stretch and pull the muscles farther.

The queen swept into the room just as Danet used her weight to push against his bent leg. "While I trust that you know what you're about, what are you doing to his leg?"

For once, Danet didn't hop up to make her curtsey. She knew if she let go of his foot, she'd lose the progress she'd made stretching the upper thigh. "Father calls it manipulation of the muscles. He recommends it for those who are bedridden to keep the limbs flexible and alleviate any knots that may be forming due to a lack of use."

"So it's not something that will cure him?"

Danet allowed Ceros' leg to relax as she turned to face the queen. "I'm afraid not. He felt it would speed the prince's recovery once he was healed again though. Given the amount of muscle tissue I've encountered I believe it is a good suggestion."

I have to stay in shape to keep up with my sparring partners.

She dabbed her sleeve on her forehead to absorb the beads of sweat that had formed and smiled at the queen. "My patients at the clinic are usually women and children and not nearly as difficult to manipulate."

"I suppose I could see where that would be so."

Danet adjusted Ceros' leg to a more comfortable-looking position then covered it with the sheet. When she turned around she found the queen staring at his feet.

"Danet, I may be seeing what I want to see but I thought his foot just twitched."

Did it? he asked.

Did you move? she asked him at the same time.

I don't know, he replied. *I wasn't thinking about it. I was more focused on the relief I felt in my lower back now that you have worked some of the tension out.*

Danet uncovered both of his feet and stood beside the queen at the foot of the bed and watched.

Try to wiggle your toes or your foot.

His big toe twitched.

"There! Did you see it, Danet?" the queen exclaimed, excitedly.

"I did."

Did it really? That's a good thing, right?

Yes, that's a very good thing.

"Let me check his reaction to stimulus." Danet went to her bag and pulled out her case of tools and instruments. She selected a metal one with a pointed end. It was not sharp enough to cut, but would definitely poke.

She tested several points on his foot. Those closer to the toe elicited a response, but the others did not.

You can feel when I do that though, right?

Yes.

To the queen she said, "I will continue to check to see if it spreads to more areas."

"And keep doing whatever you were doing." The queen waved to Ceros' legs. "It might have helped."

I agree.

Danet forced herself to ignore Ceros' comment. "Of course, my queen."

With watery eyes, the queen grasped Danet's hands. "I'm so glad you agreed to take care of Ceros." She pulled Danet to the seating area then waved her to a chair. "I know these aren't your usual duties and it's a little unorthodox for an unmated woman to care for a man, much less an unmated one, but there is no one else I would trust his care to."

"Thank you."

"If you feel uncomfortable or that we are pushing the limits of propriety, I can send one of the senior maids to stay any time you are here. You only need ask."

"I am not worried about what people may think or say. I am past the age of participating in any courtship rituals where a question of my morals might matter. I trust that I will find my mate when it is time and whether or not I adhered to every rule society has lain down will not matter." She smiled. "I essentially thumbed my nose at society's rules when I completed my apprenticeship. If that didn't make me a social pariah, what can they say about this?"

The queen studied her. "Your mother would have been very

proud of you."

"I'd like to think so," Danet said with a fond smile.

They chatted about Ceros' sisters and the queen's new grandbaby. These were the moments Danet valued most about her position within the palace. When she and the queen were alone and they were able to relax while courtly manners were set aside along with rank.

Oddly enough, Ceros hadn't offered any comments while she and the queen had been talking. Perhaps he dozed off, bored by the girl talk.

No, I'm not asleep or bored. Just letting you have some space.

That's very considerate.

Would you mind asking Mother how she is doing after Father's death? It sounds as if she trusts you enough that she may open up a little at least.

I can try. I wondered the same anyway.

"While we have a moment, my queen." Danet hesitated, trying to find the right words. "I wondered how you were faring after King Rashidi's passing."

The queen took a deep breath. "It's hard. During the day I must put on a brave face and carry on for my servants, my children and for Licosia." She tugged at a spot on her robes. "But at night when I am finally alone in my chambers, I remember him and our time together. And I grieve."

Danet reached across and clasped the queen's hand to show her support.

"He was a good man," the queen continued. "Very few knew that he was a loving husband and father as well as a wise, caring ruler. I miss him terribly. I keep waiting for him to stroll through the doors as if he had been on another diplomatic visit." She lifted tear-filled eyes. "But I know he won't."

The queen's gaze roamed to the bed where Ceros lay. "And now Ceros. I don't know what to make of it." She looked back at Danet. "As far as I know, he was perfectly healthy. Gehiji, Ceros' friend who traveled with him, assures me Ceros had not been ill or injured before they left. He is equally as confused by Ceros' condition as the rest of us."

"Do you think someone would want Ceros out of the way?"

The queen patted Danet's hand then stood and walked toward the prince's bed. "As long as there have been kings there have been others who, for one reason or another, wished to step into their shoes. If you are asking, do I think someone is trying to kill my son so soon after my husband's somewhat questionable death, then I will tell you, yes, it has crossed my mind."

Danet let go of the last remnants of hope that Ceros' condition was a coincidence.

"Ceros has been away from Licosia long enough that he shouldn't have any personal enemies here," the queen said. "If anyone wishes him ill, I believe it would have something to do with his ascension to the throne."

"Who would be next in line?"

"Since Ceros was the only male descendant, the decision would fall to the council."

Danet said a prayer of thanks for her years of training that kept her face schooled in a neutral expression. Her impulse had been to roll her eyes and declare most of the council weak-minded fools.

Well said.

Unfortunately her years of training hadn't taught her how to keep her thoughts hidden. *Yes, well…*

I assume you have reasons for your opinion. Perhaps we will discuss those reasons at a later date.

"Is that why the high council meeting has been called?" Danet asked.

"Has it?" The queen sat up tall in her chair.

"So I was told." She quickly added, "However, I have not been able to confirm that with anyone on the council."

The queen stood and took a couple of steps before stopping and turning back to Danet. "Excuse me, my dear. I believe that is something I need to look into posthaste."

Danet stood as the queen hurried to the door. "I hope I didn't just create more problems for you, my queen."

The queen stopped and looked back at Danet. "You never create problems for me. I suspect that, as usual, you've just prevented me from being blindsided. And I intend to find out by whom."

I just stirred up a nest of snakes, didn't I? she asked Ceros.

If you did, the snakes had better be worried, the prince said.

Yes, but who else might get bitten?

CHAPTER SEVEN

As promised, Hesina had a dinner tray delivered with the prince's bowl of broth. She sat on the bed and fed them both.

What else did they bring you to eat?

After all your grumbling, I'm not sure you need to know.

But I'm hungry and your food smells better than what you're dripping into me.

Danet sympathized. *If I had any way of getting something more substantial into you I would. I'm thankful we're getting this much in.*

The first thing I'm going to do when I am recovered is have a feast prepared.

I wouldn't recommend that, she said as she chewed a piece of soft bread.

Why not?

After being ill like this, your body will need to adjust to its norm. Stuffing a bunch of food, especially rich or heavy food, will only send your stomach into spasms. You'd most likely throw up whatever you ate. Give it a week, then order your feast.

You physicians are just a bunch of naysayers.

She shrugged then ladled another few drops of broth into his mouth. *Maybe so, but some of us are right more often than we're wrong.*

A commotion at the door made Danet grab the knife off her dinner tray as she turned to see what was happening.

What's going on? he demanded.

I don't know.

She scooted to the end of the bed to look into the hallway.

Damnation! Not being able to move is extremely frustrating, Ceros groused. *I should be up protecting you. Not lying here helpless.*

Shush so I can hear. Oh Gods. I just shushed the prince.

Yes, you did. We'll discuss that later. What the devil is going on?

I still don't know. No one has come in and I'm reluctant to get very far from you even though I know there are very few people the guards will allow to pass.

The doors burst open and a flood of people swept in.

Oh this should be fun, Danet mumbled.

What? Who is it?

It's two of the high council members, Aleric, your mother, her usual attendants, two of your mother's personal guards and a man I do not know.

Danet put the knife back on the tray and stood to greet the visitors. "Good evening, my queen." She let her gaze sweep over the group. "Is there a problem?"

"There seems to be some confusion about who may and may not be permitted to enter the prince's chambers," the queen said. She wore an expression meant to convey royal boredom, but Danet recognized it as one the queen wore when she was truly worried about something but refusing show it.

"It is a ridiculous notion that council members are not be permitted entry," the older councilman grumbled.

"We were merely checking on the health of the prince," Aleric added.

"You could have come and asked," the queen pointed out.

"We wanted to see for ourselves," the other councilman said.

"No one is to be permitted entry unless I say so. And right now only Danet and family are allowed. Per his physician's orders," the queen added.

"Until we know what caused the prince's collapse, it is for the best," Danet interjected smoothly.

"And why is she here instead of Master Darius?" the younger councilman sneered.

"The prince is still under Master Darius' care," Danet clarified for the group. "I have been asked to monitor the prince's healing and ensure the best care is provided in order to hasten his recovery."

Well said. Politically correct yet interpretable in more than one way.

"I understand you have been able to get a response from the prince?" Aleric asked.

Danet looked to the queen. She gave a slight nod but otherwise, no facial expression.

"There were a couple of twitches in his toe but nothing more," Danet said.

"What did you do to get this reaction?" Aleric asked.

"The first time, nothing. The second time, I tapped his foot."

"You haven't given him any medicines or herbs or anything like that?" Aleric asked.

"The only herbs or medicines the prince is receiving are the few Master Darius ordered be given with the prince's broth," Danet said.

"The queen indicated you were trying something new with the prince," Aleric hinted.

"It is common practice to manipulate the muscles of bedridden patients. We do this by moving the limbs to stretch and extend the tissue to increase blood flow and prevent the muscles from forming knots or becoming lax due to lack of use." She shrugged. "There are no herbs or medicines involved."

"Is that what made the prince respond?" Aleric asked.

"It is doubtful unless the motions improved his circulation momentarily."

"Does this mean he is getting better?" the older councilman asked.

Everyone in the group looked to Danet for an answer.

"That would be for Master Darius to determine," Danet said smoothly. "I should hope it would be a positive sign, however."

"When will Master Darius return?" the younger councilman asked. Danet was taken aback by the thinly veiled hostility in his tone.

"I couldn't say. As he left, he mentioned he was late for a meeting with Aleric and would expect a report each day of the prince's condition. It was unclear if he would return this evening or wait until morning."

"I say we wait until Master Darius has a chance to examine him again," the younger councilman whispered not-so-quietly to Aleric.

"As you wish," Aleric agreed. He turned to the queen and bowed his head. "My queen. Our apologies for the disturbance. We will check with you when we require updates on the prince's heath." His gaze traveled the remainder of the group. "Good evening."

Danet and the queen's attendants bowed their heads in return and murmured their farewell. The queen tipped her head slightly in acknowledgement but otherwise remained rigid. The gentleman she didn't know hovered in the shadows near the wall.

After Aleric and the two councilmen departed, the queen mumbled, "Pompous asses," then crossed the room to the prince's side. She picked up Ceros' hand and clung to it.

"Gehiji, what did you think?" the queen finally asked.

Finally. The elusive Gehiji. Now she knew whom to look for.

The man stepped into the light. He seemed to be of a similar age to Ceros, but he had darker features. While he was handsome and moved with a warrior's natural grace, Danet found her attention still drawn to Ceros.

"I believe your description to be keenly accurate, your Majesty."

This elicited a chuckle from the queen. "I meant about the people we're dealing with."

"I think you have a couple of toothless snakes. Unfortunately, that doesn't make them any less venomous."

Gehiji always cuts to the heart of the matter.

"Quite true," the queen said thoughtfully. "Danet, any change?"

"No, my queen." She glanced about the room to ensure her attendants were out of hearing range. "But I haven't worked on his upper body yet. I was trying to get a little broth into him when you came in."

"It seems we have interrupted your dinner as well," Gehiji said.

"'Tis no matter. I can finish later," Danet said as she pushed her tray aside.

"I don't believe we have been properly introduced. I am Gehiji Talasona." He made a slight bow but didn't lower his eyes from hers. "Your name is Danet?"

"Oh, I am sorry," the queen interjected. "I forget you two have not been properly introduced. Gehiji, this is Danet. Actually, it is Mistress Danet, to be completely correct. Danet was one of my most trusted handmaidens until she completed her apprenticeship. Now she splits her time between her father's healing clinic in the heart of the city and here." She smiled at Danet. "She's agreed to take charge of Ceros' care." The queen swept a hand to Gehiji. "Danet, this is Gehiji, one of Ceros' closest friends. He traveled with Ceros from Shirghada."

Don't let his pretty face fool you. Gehiji is one of the most deadly and most decorated warriors in our unit. There's no one I would trust more at my back.

Danet dropped her head into a slight bow, hoping to hide any reaction Ceros' words caused. "Welcome to Licosia." She looked up once she felt certain her expression would remain neutral. "I am sorry your stay has been under such a cloud."

Gehiji looked at the prince, his face grim. "Me too. I hate seeing him like this." He glanced back to Danet. "And you have no idea what caused it?"

"We're looking into several possibilities. But no, we know nothing definite yet," Danet said.

Find a way to get Gehiji alone. You need to tell him everything.

I will try.

"Danet's father is a well-known healer and scholar. She has already enlisted his help. As soon as she knows something, she will tell me and then I'll be sure to find you," the queen reassured Gehiji.

"Please do." He nodded to the queen. To Danet he added, "And if there is anything you need assistance with or if I can answer any questions, please seek me out."

The queen patted Ceros' hand then called out to her attendants. "Let's return to dinner."

While the queen was distracted, Danet whispered to Gehiji, "I need to speak with you." She glanced in the queen's direction. "Alone."

He seemed startled but nodded once before following the queen and her entourage.

"Danet, should I have Hesina send you a warm tray of food so you can finish your dinner?"

"No, thank you, my queen. What remains does not require warming."

"I'll check on his condition again before retiring for the night." The queen paused again. "I assume you'll be staying?"

"Hesina has offered to have a lounge brought in for my use so I do not have to travel back and forth, so yes. I will stay."

The queen looked as if she wanted to say something, but thought better of it and simply nodded.

Finally the room fell quiet again and Danet breathed a sigh of relief.

I know I said I'd try to leave your private thoughts alone, but I can't help picking up on your worry for Mother. While I appreciate your care for her and your concern, is there some threat I don't know about?

Danet climbed up onto the bed to rearrange what was left of

her dinner. *No. It isn't a threat that worries me. It's the burden that your mother carries.*

How so?

I've always known she had a lot of responsibilities. I've helped with some of them through the years. But this is a load she has never faced before. One of her children is facing an unknown illness, something she has absolutely no control over. It has been my experience that no matter how old someone's child becomes, parents never quit worrying. Most would gladly take their child's place instead of watching them suffer. In many ways, an illness or injury is as hard on the parent as it is on the patient. Add to it that her husband has died, so the one person she could always turn to for comfort and strength is gone. With the daily stress of running a royal household, I don't know how much more she can take.

Ceros fell silent. Finally he said, *You are right.*

I don't mean to worry you but I can't help but be concerned.

You are a genuinely caring person. I find that refreshing.

Thank you, but I fear it will get me into trouble one day.

Not if you have someone watching your back.

Danet chuckled. *That would have to be a very energetic someone to keep up with my schedule.*

Perhaps.

Danet picked up the bowl from the tray. *Do you want any more of the broth?*

Not if I have any say about it.

I'd like to get a little more of something in. How about some water?

Since wine is obviously not an option, then I suppose it would be better than that foul- tasting liquid Darius ordered.

As she spooned in the drops of water, she noticed the sheet flutter over his feet. Did you move your toes?

Not intentionally, no, but things are not working the way I'd like them to right now.

Probably not. I think they twitched some more.

I'm taking it as a good thing since nothing hurts when they do.

I agree.

She set the bowl on the tray then scooted off the bed.

Where are you going? Ceros asked.

I'm getting the tray off the bed so I have room to work.

What are you planning to work on? he asked with reservation.

In a word, you. She set the tray on a table near the hallway but kept the bowl of fruit for later. *I need to finish working the muscles in your upper body. Most particularly your back.*

If you mean to do what you were doing to my legs, then I have no objections. I'm not sure how I'm going to accomplish it though.

She set the fruit on the desk then rummaged around in her basket of supplies for the oil and a linen cloth.

What do you mean? Don't you just need to run your magic fingers over all the places you think need it?

She snorted. *Magic fingers?* She poured some oil into a small bowl.

They feel like it when you're doing whatever it is that you do.

Have you never had someone rub you down after your training sessions?

Er… Not in this manner, no.

She stopped at the edge of the bed and looked down at the prince. *What other manner is there then?*

As part of the, er…recreational activities provided by specially trained ladies.

You mean prostitutes?

No. They were never paid.

They used slaves in that manner? Danet became incensed.

No, you mistake me.

Perhaps you should clarify before I jump to any more conclusions and spill all of this oil on your head then leave.

Sit and I will explain.

She hesitated.

Please, sit. You don't know how frustrating it is to not be able to reach for you to make you stay and listen, so I'm asking nicely.

Very well. She sat on the edge of the bed and set the oil and the cloths aside.

Thank you. You know Shirghada's strength is its elite class of warriors. The reason they produce the world's best soldiers is because their society is built around them. Men come from around the world to train. And with that many young, healthy men, women naturally follow.

And men, being men, indulge in that which is made available to them?

In most cases, yes.

As much as it made her uncomfortable to know, she asked, *And did you?*

In the beginning, yes. I won't lie to you. I sampled what was freely offered. But I soon grew tired of the games being played and the cold, impersonal episodes.

Not to mention the medicines you had to take to get rid of the aftereffects, she said cynically.

I was more selective than that.

Danet harrumphed. *How is what I am doing different than what those women did?*

Perhaps it is only my perception, but when you do it I feel you are doing it entirely for my benefit. To help me in some way or to make me feel better. There is no other agenda.

And when they did it, they wanted something?

Warriors are prized by these women because of the lifestyle they can provide. Some want a sponsor who will set them up with a place to live or pay for their expenses. Others hope to ensnare a warrior into a bonding.

How often do they succeed?

More often than you'd think.

But not you.

No.

The knot inside her chest eased. *I still don't understand how what I'm doing is any different than what anyone else who had a little bit of training would do.*

A skilled courtesan is able to make a man believe he is the most important, most virile man in the world, no matter what she really thinks of him. It didn't take me long to learn that you can lie with words and even looks, but not so much with touch. Your touch tells me you genuinely care. It isn't cold and impersonal.

I thought you meant there was something sexual that I wasn't doing that you felt I should be.

That isn't what I meant to imply.

Good. It's hard being trained as a physician but not having the same respect as men who do the same work. Danet pulled the sheet down to the prince's waist. Thankfully someone had dressed him in a loincloth. Despite the number of patients she had seen in varying states of undress, both men and women, it made her uncomfortable to be exposed to someone she was attracted to.

There were dozens of reasons she needed to ignore any feelings she had for the prince. He being a prince and her essentially a servant in his household topped the list. He was a gorgeous specimen of manhood and she had always been a girl boys ignored. He didn't know the extent of her gifts and if he did he'd toss her out of the city. But if nothing else, a physician should never become involved with a patient under their care.

But he was lovely to look at. His shoulders were easily twice the size of hers and looked as if they could hold the weight of the world. His broad chest made her want to curl up next to him and lay her head down. Despite her inexperience, her curiosity had been piqued about what might lie beneath the loincloth. In her darkest fantasies, it had always been someone like him who expanded her knowledge of the ways of men and women.

Danet. You're killing me.

Why? What did I do? Am I sitting on you?

No, but you are transmitting your thoughts loud and clear and I can't ignore all of them.

Oh Gods. Her cheeks burned hot in mortification. *This is a very bad idea. Perhaps I should take your mother up on her suggestion to have one of the others help me.*

No.

No? What do you mean no?

I mean I don't want anyone else. I want you to take care of me. Mother trusts you. My sisters like and respect you and a great many of the servants do as well. I think that speaks volumes about your respectability.

But I am obviously having some difficulty maintaining a professional attitude. And even worse, you know it. She got up and paced at the foot of the bed.

Let's just say that were the roles reversed, it would not be unexpected if I were to have the same thoughts or feelings.

But—

And how about if we agree to set the issue aside to be addressed later. I won't bring it up if you don't.

This is not appropriate.

I need you. You're the only one I can talk to. I need you to help me get well. He added, *Mother needs you too.*

Don't bring your mother into this.

I will if it helps my case.

A laugh bubbled up. *I really need to work on my mental self-control.*

I don't know. I kind of like it.

She sobered. *There are things you are better off not knowing about me.*

Danet, did it not occur to you that there are things in my head that you do not need to know about also? Things that I have been working to keep hidden.

Yes. That is why I have been trying to stay out of there.

Do you not realize that some of those things might get me killed if they were to become known? There are the things that I have seen and done that would make an innocent like yourself run for the hills. I don't want to do that to you. I don't want you to be afraid of me.

That makes two of us.

Well, aren't we a pair?

I guess so. She looked at his unmoving body. Once again she was struck by an overwhelming need to cure what was wrong with him. It was more powerful than anything she had ever experienced with any of her patients.

Come. Work your magic with your fingers. You may not be able to fix everything right now, but you can take your mind off your worries and make me feel a lot better.

She sighed. *Yes. I can at least do that.*

CHAPTER EIGHT

On a lounge across the room from the prince, Danet lay wrapped in what had to be the softest blankets ever made. She tried to remember what it felt like to sleep beside a man and wake in his arms. Okpara had not been much for cuddling, but she imagined it would be a wonderful experience with the right man.

Moonlight spilled onto the foot of the prince's bed, allowing Danet see the occasional twitch as he dreamed.

A rustle from somewhere behind the lounge alerted her that she was not alone. Her heart began to pound, making it hard to listen for other sounds.

Wha… What's wrong? the prince asked.

I'm not sure. I thought I heard something. Did it wake you?

No, your fright startled me.

You can sense that too?

Yes. What do you see?

Nothing from here, I was afraid to sit up and alert whoever might be in here.

Do you have a weapon?

I have a couple of instruments that could be used as such and the knife I kept from the dinner tray.

He grumbled something unpleasant. *Where is the knife?*

In the fruit bowl on the desk.

He mumbled another expletive. *If you are attacked, you yell loud and long for the guards no matter what they tell you. Understand?*

Yes.

A face appeared above her, startling her. She took a deep breath to scream, but a hand clamped down over her mouth.

"Danet. It's Gehiji," the man whispered.

She blinked and tried to make sense of what was happening.

Ceros released a couple more expletives.

"Don't yell. I'm not going to hurt you," Gehiji said quietly. "Do you understand?"

She nodded.

"I'm going to uncover your mouth. Nod if you understand and won't scream."

She nodded again.

As soon as he released her, she sat up on the lounge and whispered, "What are you doing here in the middle of the night? And how did you get in?"

"You said you needed to speak to me. I figured now would be the only time I'd be able to get you alone." He shrugged. "As for how I got in, let's just say I have a talent for it."

He does, actually.

Gehiji sat at the other end of the lounge. Danet scrambled to pull her blanket out from underneath him and wrapped it firmly around her body. She had left her clothes on in case something happened with Ceros during the night. Now she was grateful for that foresight.

"What did you want to talk to me about?" he asked casually.

Despite his relaxed posture, she could sense he was poised for most anything.

Go ahead. Tell him, Ceros encouraged.

"Ceros wanted me to tell you something," she blurted.

Gehiji blinked a couple of times. "What did you say?"

"Ceros insisted I tell you he was awake, alert actually, inside his body and that I can talk to him."

Gehiji looked to where the prince lay prone on the bed, then back at Danet. "Really?"

Don't forget what I said about the telos.

She took a deep breath. "I know it sounds crazy, but we are able to talk to each other." She pointed to her head. "In here."

"I see," Gehiji said slowly.

"He said to tell you that he needs your help and that he'll return the telos you gambled away if you are able to find out who is behind whatever is wrong with him."

Gehiji sat up straight, looked at Ceros then back at Danet. "When did he tell you this?"

The look in his eye made her lean back. "Yesterday, when I first discovered who I was hearing in my head. But I didn't know who you were or where to find you until you came in with the queen."

"This is the first time you've been able to talk with him this way?"

She nodded.

He stood and looked at the prince across the room then motioned for Danet to follow.

She pulled the blanket around her and followed him to Ceros' bedside.

What is he doing?

I'm not sure. He's standing over you. You trust him, right?

Yes, why?

Because if he pulled out a knife right now, there wouldn't be much I could do to stop him.

He chuckled. *No, actually, there wouldn't be.*

It's not funny. I don't know him and that isn't reassuring me.

Gehiji will not harm me. Of this I am certain.

"Is he awake?" Gehiji asked her quietly.

"Yes. You startled me when you came in, which in turn woke him."

Gehiji squatted next to the bed and whispered loud enough for both of them to hear, "Ceros, tell her what nickname you were given during our first year of training and tell her to tell me."

Ceros' laughter echoed in her head. *They called me Silent Night.*

"Silent Night?" Danet said. "That doesn't sound terribly insulting."

Gehiji's eyes widened in surprise. Obviously he hadn't expected her to be able to answer, but he recovered quickly. "It's the story behind the nickname that's funny."

Don't ask because no, I'm not telling you.

She looked at Gehiji. "He said I shouldn't bother asking because he won't tell me the story."

Gehiji laughed. "I wouldn't either." He wiped his hand across his face. "Okay, I have to be sure this is for real." A flash of pain crossed his face. "Ceros, what did we lose on that mission to Ismailia?"

A tightening in her chest made her breath catch. *Ceros?*

I'm sorry. I didn't clamp down on that memory fast enough.

Are you okay?

Yes. It's a very painful memory.

Obviously. She rubbed at a spot on her chest. Her movement caught Gehiji's attention.

"What did he say?"

Tell him I said too damn much.

"He said, 'Too damn much.'"

Gehiji nodded and looked to Ceros. "That we did, my friend." He patted Ceros on the arm then stood.

He towered over Danet, but he looked down at her with a new expression. Something gentler with a sliver of respect.

"So why you are able to speak to my friend this way?"

"I'm not entirely sure."

Gehiji stepped closer. "I sense a partial lie in that, but not enough for me to disbelieve you. Is it because you are not certain of why?"

"Yes, that would be accurate."

"But you have ideas."

"Yes."

"Ideas that you don't want to share."

"Not right now, no."

"Have you shared your ideas with him?" Gehiji jerked his thumb in Ceros' direction.

No. But you will soon, won't you?

"Not yet. I told him I need to do some reading on it first so no one jumps to any conclusions." She gave Gehiji a half-smile. "I figure it's the least of our problems right now anyway."

"You're probably right." He stepped around her and grabbed a chair from the sitting area. He placed the chair next to the bed then indicated Danet should sit on the bed next to Ceros.

Gehiji looked at Ceros then at Danet. "This is a little weird, knowing he's there and functioning but his body isn't moving."

"You should try having him in your head, hearing all your thoughts," Danet grumbled.

"Does that mean you can hear all of his too?" Gehiji's eyes widened in alarm.

"If I tried, I might be able to." She leaned closer to Ceros and added, "But some of us respect the other's right to privacy."

I am trying.

Yes, I know.

"I see." Gehiji cleared his throat. "So what do you need me to do?"

Tell him about the council meeting and ask him to find out what he can about the council members.

"Let me back up even further," Danet said. "In case you haven't figured it out already, we aren't sure Ceros' condition is an accident. Earlier today, I found a thorn lodged in his neck." She pointed to the spot behind her ear to demonstrate where. "I've taken the thorn to my father so he can find out what kind of plant it came from. That should help us determine if it is related to Ceros' condition."

"The queen didn't say anything about a thorn."

"She doesn't know. We decided it would be best to not tell her yet. She's dealing with enough."

Gehiji nodded.

"I doubt it will take Father long to find an answer," she assured him. "Before the queen asked me to tend to the prince I learned two things. First, there is some speculation over the king's death and whether or not it was an accident. Second, there is a high council meeting scheduled to be held in three days. Actually, it's closer to two now. This purpose of this meeting may be to appoint an interim ruler since the prince has taken ill."

"I thought the queen was the interim ruler."

"She is, but only because the prince declared it so until he could make the journey home. But since he is unfit to rule in his present condition, the high council is in a position to appoint another. If they so choose."

"And they choose to do so."

Danet nodded.

"What does Ceros want me to do?"

"He said he needs you to find out what you can about the council members."

"Does he want me to look into his father's death?"

Danet looked to Ceros.

It might help us figure out who could be behind this, Ceros answered.

So you do believe someone might be trying to kill you? she asked.

I think it is a very real possibility.

Danet shuddered. Hearing it from Ceros gave it a new reality. "He said he thought it might help us figure out who is behind this."

"I thought as much."

Gehiji stood and looked down on Ceros. "He's completely vulnerable right now, isn't he?"

"I'm afraid so."

And I hate it.

Danet smiled. "Yes, I'm sure Gehiji can guess how much you hate it."

"I can stay here if you think there is a threat."

"I think he's safe for tonight. The queen hand-picked the guards and I'm here in case he has a life-threatening emergency." She shrugged. "I might not be able to fight off a trained killer, but I would be another witness someone would have to deal with if they did come in."

Gehiji smiled. "I don't know about that. I saw you with that knife when the councilmen burst in earlier."

Knife? What is he talking about? Ceros demanded. Even in her head it sounded as if he growled at her.

Nothing, don't worry about it. To Gehiji she said, "And you shush. You're only upsetting him."

That made Gehiji grin even more. "Am I?"

Don't tell him that. He lives to torment me.

"Okay you two," Danet scolded. "Back to the original topic. I think Ceros is safe for tonight. Any would-be assassin probably thinks they came close to killing him and it could go either way. Surely they wouldn't risk exposure right now."

"You're probably right." Gehiji agreed. "I don't like being so far away. It would take too long to get word to me if something happened."

"Which room did they give you?"

"One halfway down the hall in the southern wing."

"Oh. You are quite on the other side of the palace, aren't you?"

Who decided that? As my honored guest, he should have been put in one of my suites.

"I'll speak to the queen in the morning about moving you. There are guest quarters in this wing but I don't know if they are being used right now."

"I would feel better if you did."

"So would I, quite frankly," Danet admitted. "Once he begins recovering and word gets out, I think he'll be at his most vulnerable."

Don't remind me.

She tossed a look of sympathy in Ceros' direction.

"What'd he say?" Gehiji asked.

"He doesn't like not being able to defend himself, or anyone else for that matter," she answered.

"I can understand his frustration." Gehiji looked to Danet. "Perhaps it is a good thing no one else knows about your ability to speak to him. You might rethink telling anyone."

"The queen is the only one I have agreed to tell. But there are conditions on that agreement."

"I'm just saying, be very cautious with that information. It may endanger your life." He glanced to where the prince lay. "Even more than it probably is."

"Yes, I know," she said with a sigh.

Ceros mumbled something not very gentlemanlike.

CHAPTER NINE

After Gehiji's late-night visit, Danet fell asleep without tossing and turning.

Ceros sensed her tension and the jumble of thoughts streaming through her mind. Thankfully that quieted after talking with Gehiji. He hoped it was because they had the start of a plan and not because of Gehiji.

He knew the moment she woke. She stretched then the seemingly nonstop parade of thoughts began again. How she sorted through everything floating around her mind amazed him.

Good morning, Ceros said. He heard her move around on the lounge.

Good morning.

He sensed her worrying about her appearance. Some things must be universal for all women. *I'm sure you look fine,* he said, trying to reassure her.

Yes, well, you don't have to face an endless stream of royalty before luncheon.

He chuckled.

How are you feeling this morning? she asked.

A little stiff in my back, but otherwise well.

Good. Let's have a look then I'll go freshen up.

Danet checked his temperature and heartbeat. He sensed she was pleased by what she found. Next she checked his neck where the thorn had been.

The redness and swelling are almost gone, she relayed then moved to examine his hands and feet. *It may be me and my wishful thinking but it seems as if there is a little more response in your extremities. I'll do a more thorough check after breakfast, but that's very good news. I hope it means the thorn had something to do with your condition and that you'll continue to improve.*

I'm not worried.

Danet laughed. *Liar.* She patted him on the chest then stood. *I had better make myself presentable before anyone shows up. By the way, what is your favorite song?* she asked.

Why?

I had hoped you could hum it while I'm in the bathing room. Since you're in my head, it feels as if you're standing right next to me. I would feel better having a few minutes of privacy, if you don't mind.

Ceros chuckled. *Very well.*

Thank you.

He heard Danet telling the guards to keep anyone other than the queen or Hesina from entering until she said otherwise.

You can start humming any time now, she reminded him.

He hummed the first thing that popped into his mind. It was a bawdy tavern song he learned while living in Shirghada. Hopefully she didn't know the words.

While Danet washed and dressed, Gehiji snuck in. Ceros listened with half an ear as Gehiji reported what he learned about palace security. Or lack thereof. Knowing Danet was very likely naked in the next room distracted him more than he wanted to admit. He didn't know what she looked like, but had a very active imagination.

He felt her sigh as she admired his oversized tub then held his breath as she debated taking a long soak. Thankfully she decided she didn't have enough time. The thought of her soaking in his tub appealed to him more than it should.

"How did you get in?" Danet asked Gehiji when she returned to the sleeping area.

Gehiji didn't say anything but Ceros guessed he had made some gesture or facial expression that answered her question.

We are trained to get into more secure places than this, Ceros informed her.

She harrumphed. "Did you have breakfast yet?" she asked Gehiji.

"No."

"Would you like for me to have them bring you a tray when they bring mine?"

"Thank you, but no. I will take breakfast in the hall." Gehiji added, "There's a rather pretty girl I keep seeing at meals but I don't know who she is yet. I'm determined to find out before the setting of the sun today."

Remind him the councilmen are of more import than some mysterious woman flitting about the palace.

Danet chuckled. *Somehow I doubt it will be an issue for him to do both.*

No, but the reminder won't hurt him any.

"Ceros asked me to remind you about looking into the councilmen."

Gehiji flicked his hand as if to wave the thought away. "Already working on it."

"But how? We just discussed it last night."

"That's true."

"When did you have time? Don't you sleep?" she asked incredulously.

"Of course I sleep. What of your father and the thorn? I'm guessing you haven't received word yet?" Gehiji asked, smoothly changing the subject.

"No. If I don't hear anything by luncheon, I'll go home to check on his progress. Knowing my father, he stayed up half the night looking for the answer only to fall asleep at his desk before he could write a note."

"I would be happy to escort you home if it comes to that."

"Thank you. I might take you up on that offer. I'm sure Father would love to have a chance to quiz you on Shirghada and triage procedures you might have seen while out on patrols or missions."

Ceros found himself jealous that Gehiji would be spending time with Danet while he remained stuck in a body that wouldn't work.

Are you okay? Danet asked.

Yes, why?

I'm not sure. I suddenly had a weird feeling and I thought it had come from you.

I'm fine.

A knock sounded on the door.

Gehiji whispered, "I'll make myself scarce once I know if it's friend or foe. No need in creating alarm by my presence."

Ceros heard faint footsteps and guessed Danet went to see who had arrived.

He heard Danet thank someone then the echo of the door being shut.

"It's a note from Father." She hurried back to the sleeping area. "He says the thorn is from the Aspenadder plant. A very rare and toxic flower. Your symptoms have been seen in people who came in contact with it, only most people die after prolonged exposure. He adds if it hadn't for your age and excellent physical condition, you might not have survived."

"Remind me to thank Commander Panahasi for working our butts off for the last year and a half," Gehiji mumbled. "Guess it was worthwhile after all."

Does he have a solution for me or am I going to be stuck this way?

"He sends a tonic to help clear the poison from your system. He warns he made it into a condensed solution since he knew you were unable to swallow so it may taste bad and hurt your stomach after a while."

I'll deal with it as long as it helps.

"I bet he wouldn't care if it tasted like eligari excrement if it makes him better."

"That's basically what he just said."

Ceros felt the bed tip and sway as Danet climbed up next to him.

"Do you want to wait until the breakfast tray comes so I can wash it down with some broth? All I have right now is water."

I don't want to wait.

"He doesn't want to wait," she repeated for Gehiji.

"I didn't figure he would. What do you need me to do?"

"Nothing really. It's a slow process of putting small drops in the back of his mouth then massaging his throat until the drops go down."

Danet pulled his chin down and poured in a few drops. Then Ceros felt her tiny hands working along the front of his neck.

Gods, that is foul.

Worse than the broth?

By far. At least I know this should help me. I'm not so sure about the broth.

Danet chuckled.

"What?" Gehiji asked.

"He's complaining about how bad it tastes."

"Medicine never tastes good. Besides, it can't be any worse than some of that crap he cooked while we were on missions."

Ceros laughed. *Tell him he shouldn't criticize.*

"He said you shouldn't criticize," Danet relayed to Gehiji.

"That's probably true." When his laughter died down he said, "I had better go before anyone arrives."

"I plan on telling the queen what we've discovered about the thorn as soon as I can get her alone. I am also going to send a note back to Father asking where that plant can be found. If it's such a rare thing, it might help us identify who is behind this."

"I will check with you two this afternoon and if I can't catch you alone before then, I'll come by again tonight."

"How can I get word to you if I need to?" Danet asked.

Ceros was coming to appreciate how smart Danet was. She grasped the deadly reality of the situation right away without getting upset or having vapors or any of the other annoying things palace ladies often did. She even understood the need for secrecy and stealth.

"For now, have a note delivered to my room letting me know you need me to come by. I'll work on a better way of sending messages today."

"Be careful," she reminded him.

"Ceros, be a good little patient and take all of your medicine now."

Tell him I'd give him a rude gesture but he might take it as an offer.

Danet repeated what he had said, making Ceros realize how crass it was. Gehiji's laughter faded as he slipped out of the room. *My apologies, Danet. I didn't mean to embarrass you with our crude jokes. I forget we're no longer hiking through the wilds and need to turn our manners back on.*

It's okay. I know it's a stressful time and both of you need to blow off steam. I'm not running for the hills just because you were joking with your friend.

It doesn't excuse my poor manners. I really was raised better than that.

Oh, I know that for a fact.

Please don't tell Mother.

She chuckled. *Definitely not.*

He felt unusually comfortable with Danet. They had only known each other a day but already he didn't feel like he had to act like a polished prince. Nor did he want to act like a total barbarian around her. It was a strange mix and he didn't know how he felt about it.

Even more strange was the fact that he didn't even know what she looked like. He'd only had a glimpse of her face. Her green eyes, high cheekbones and dark hair. But what he'd seen of her personality was sparkling and beautiful and most definitely intriguing.

And all of these feelings were for a woman with a lineage that had been outlawed generations ago. Before either of them had been born.

Let's try to get a little more of Father's concoction down, she reminded him.

He groaned. *If taste is an inverse relationship to how well medicine works, I should be sword fighting before dinner.*

Danet laughed.

Suddenly the outer doors of his suite opened and the sound of several pairs of footsteps echoed down the hallway. Ceros felt Danet gather her things and scoot off the bed.

"My queen." The rustling of fabric hinted at the curtsey Danet made. "Did you sleep well?"

"Tolerably so. What about you?"

"Tolerably so," she mimicked the queen's choice of words.

"What is happening with Ceros? I assume since I didn't receive any messages that there was no change through the night."

"I'm afraid not. His breathing remained slow and steady, making me think he slept. My cursory check this morning indicated a slight improvement in his hands and feet."

The queen came to the bed and, as was her habit, brushed his hair off his forehead then slipped her hand into one of his. Ceros was certain she studied his face.

"My queen, if I might have a word with you in private?" Danet whispered.

Not for the first time, Ceros wished he could turn his head so he could see what was happening.

"Girls, I've changed my mind. I would like to take my breakfast in here. Would one of you please go down to the kitchens and have a tray brought up for Danet and me? Tea also. And I believe I would like my sewing basket and journal from my rooms."

"Certainly, my queen," the girls replied. A flurry of skirts and footsteps told Ceros they had left.

Once the door had closed the queen asked, "You have news?"

"I was not completely honest with you yesterday, my queen."

"Oh?"

"I found a thorn in the prince's hairline during one of my examinations yesterday. I removed it and took it to Father to have it identified so we could determine if it had anything to do with the prince's condition. I had a note from Father just moments ago. He identified the thorn as being from the Aspenadder plant."

"I've heard of this plant. It's poisonous, isn't it?"

"Very. Father sent some medicine that should help fight the toxins. He said if the thorn had remained embedded or if the prince not been healthy, his reaction could have been far worse."

"Why didn't you tell me this yesterday?"

Danet lifted her chin. "I didn't want to get your hopes up only to have to dash them again if the thorn had nothing to do with his condition. I knew Father would have an answer for me quickly and that I merely delayed telling you."

You should tell her everything.

Not yet, she insisted.

"I'm not unaware of the power struggle that is going on, my queen," Danet continued. "Nor am I ignorant of the questionable death of King Rashidi. It is entirely possible that someone planted that thorn in hopes of getting Prince Ceros out of the way."

The queen stroked his hand. "You are right as usual, Danet. You always were a quick study."

He felt Danet's concern about the way the queen looked. *What's wrong with Mother?*

She has dark circles under her eyes and looks more tired than I've ever seen her.

Ceros wanted to roar in frustration.

"What do you recommend?" the queen asked.

"My first priority is still to get Prince Ceros well. I've given him a dose of the medicine. I hope to see results before luncheon. However, I think we should keep word of the thorn a secret. Whoever the would-be killer is must not know we found it or that we're treating the prince for poisons."

"How do we explain his recovery?"

She shrugged. "The herbs Darius has ordered and the muscle therapy coupled with Ceros' good health."

"Don't you think Darius will question it?"

71

"Probably. But he isn't so foolish as to raise an alarm over the prince's recovery. Unless someone starts taking credit for it, he'll most likely never say a word."

"You're probably right." The queen sighed. "Now I just have to figure out how to delay this high council meeting until Ceros is better."

Danet sat on the bed next to his mother. "I wish I could tell you the medicine will kick in and everything will be fine by then, but I cannot."

"I know. And I appreciate you not fabricating things just to make me feel better. While I don't like the fact you didn't tell me about the thorn, I understand why you did it."

"Thank you, my queen."

"You have always been a good girl, Danet. From the time you first came into my service I have never doubted your loyalty to me or my family. That is one of the reasons I trust you with Ceros' care." Ceros felt her hand on his chest. "If someone does mean him harm, he is completely vulnerable. Your suggestion to keep the thorn a secret is probably best."

"I suspect that as he recovers and word gets out, you will need to increase his security."

"I agree." The queen stood. Her footsteps sounded as if she moved away from the bed. "I believe I can call upon Gehiji to help with that. He trained with Ceros and appears to be quite capable. He has also offered to assist in any way." She paused. "That may present an issue if you continue to stay day and night. I cannot allow the two of you to sleep in the same quarters."

She's right, Ceros said.

What?

Even though I would know for sure nothing went on between the two of you, no one else would and your reputation would be shredded.

"As soon as Ceros begins moving and regains control of his faculties, we'll need to put you in another room anyway. Probably with a guard of your own," the queen pointed out.

"My queen, may I suggest we take this one day at a time? Let's see how much he recovers through the day then worry about sleeping arrangements this evening."

"You always were sensible." There was a smile in her voice. "I will think about a solution today however."

"If I might make one other suggestion?"

"Certainly."

"If he isn't already, Gehiji should be moved into the rooms next door. The more guards near Ceros the better."

"I'll speak with Hesina after breakfast."

The suite doors opened, heralding the return of the queen's attendants along with servants carrying breakfast trays. Selfishly, it pleased him that Danet chose to feed him before herself. He listened quietly, surprisingly content, when Danet finally went and sat with the queen to enjoy their breakfast.

The remainder of the morning flew by.

By lunch, Danet reported to the queen that she was pleased with Ceros' progress. He could now move all of his fingers and toes and to a certain degree, his eyes. He had even managed to swallow a couple of times.

Danet worked his muscles throughout the day but the nonstop stream of visitors forced her to stop frequently. He picked up on her frustration and desire to have more than a few minutes of peace. Between visitors, family and attending servants, neither of them had any rest and by midafternoon Danet was becoming increasingly cranky.

Perhaps you should lie down for a bit, the prince suggested.

I'd love to but I'm sure that as soon as my head hits the pillow someone else will come in.

Tell the guards to keep everyone out.

I thought about it.

Do it. Blame me if you need to. Tell them you think I need to rest.

Danet chuckled as she curled up on the bed next to Ceros. *I should. I just need a few minutes of peace and quiet.*

Ceros felt her mind relaxing and slipping into slumber. He strained his eyes and his neck, trying to turn so he could see Danet lying next to him. It amazed him how such a wisp of a thing carried so much strength.

Her willingness to defend him when he was unable humbled him. Every time he thought of her placing herself in harm's way his gut clenched.

Now that he had seen her physical beauty, his confusion over why she remained unmated only grew. Her long, brown hair would be glorious when it was unbound and streaming down her naked back. Even more when it was spread across his pillow and her eyes were glazed with passion.

He promised himself that he would see that before the next new moon.

It had become more obvious how much he had come to care for her. Despite their short time together. Rank and station be damned, he would have her. He wondered, however, would she have him?

Living with the royal family was not easy. Danet would know that firsthand. Would she want to be even more a part of it than she already was?

What if the poison left some lingering damage? Would she be able to live with it? He felt certain she could, if she cared for him. He sensed her concerned for his well-being and even her physical attraction to him. His uncertainty came from whether she could ever care for him as a man or would it always be as a patient, or even as a servant would her master? He hoped that more budded.

She stirred in her sleep. He stilled his mind in case his thoughts disturbed her. He certainly didn't want her picking up on those more tender feelings just yet. No need in scaring her off.

No sooner had Danet settled back into sleep than Ceros heard the suite door open and close. The swish of fabric alerted him that someone drew near.

"Oh. The poor dear," the queen mumbled from the foot of the bed.

Danet. We have company. As much as he hated to wake her, he knew she would be embarrassed being caught napping.

Just a few minutes more.

Mother is here.

What? She sat up suddenly. "My queen. I am so sorry. I didn't mean to…"

The queen waved Danet's concerns away. "Don't fret yourself, child. I'm sure you didn't get much sleep last night. And I doubt you've had more than five minutes to yourself today."

"You would be correct," she said as she smothered a yawn.

"It's a few hours until I need to dress for dinner. I can sit with Ceros. Why don't you run home and get some rest? Or you're welcome to find a guestroom and lie down for a bit. I'm always more comfortable in my own bed, however."

Danet looked his way. "I could use another change of clothes," she hesitated.

Go, Ceros encouraged her. *I'm sure you could use the change of scenery anyway.*

"Darius should be coming by any time now. I should stay and give him my report," Danet said.

"I can give it to him," the queen suggested. "Is there anything else you would tell him that you haven't already told me?"

Danet shook her head. "Not that I can think of."

"If he gets upset that you aren't here to speak with him, I'll let him know he should send word next time of when he expects to arrive instead of making you sit around all day waiting on him," the queen said. "Go on. I'm sure you want to check in with Sebak anyway."

"Yes, actually I do." Danet grabbed her bag from the floor next to the desk. "I won't be long." She bowed her head to the queen. "Thank you, my queen."

"You're welcome."

I will return shortly, Danet reassured Ceros.

You'd better, he teased.

"Oh, and Danet," the queen stopped her as she moved toward the door. "Take an escort with you, please, and have them wait for you. There's a reason we have them, you know."

"Yes, my queen."

Would you have listened if I had suggested that? Ceros asked.

Hard to say.

We need to talk about your willfulness.

If I remember correctly that's not the first thing you've said we needed to talk about, and it most likely won't be the last. How about if I start a list for you?

He sighed. *What am I going to do with you?*

Her laughter rang in his head even after the door to the suite clicked shut.

CHAPTER TEN

As when she made her previous trip home, Danet's father and Ryana greeted her at the door.

"You two worry too much," she said as she hugged Ryana.

"I think we worry the exact amount we should." Ryana looked her over from head to toe. "Well, you don't look tortured or worked half to death, so I suppose they're treating you fairly at the palace."

"I'm a little tired, but fine," Danet assured them both.

"Are you here for the evening or just a short while?" Ryana asked.

"Only a short time, I'm afraid."

Ryana nodded. "I'll pack a sack of goodies for you to take."

"Any sweetbread?"

"I promised you I'd save some."

"You're wonderful."

"Would you like tea brought into your study?" Ryana asked Sebak.

"I believe so, thank you," he replied.

"Speaking of tea, Ryana, would you mind packing some of Mother's tea with the sweetbread?"

Ryana seemed surprised by the request but didn't question it. "Certainly."

Almost on cue, Danet and her father turned and entered his study. "How is the prince?" Sebak asked.

"I have seen a marked improvement since he began taking your tonic. He has movement in his hands and feet as well as his eyes. He was even able to swallow a couple of times."

"Good. Very good."

"Where does the Aspenadder plant grow? Or where can it be found?"

"The Aspenadder has almost died out. For such a poisonous plant, it is surprisingly delicate. Too much water can kill it but so can too little." He pulled a book out of the stack on his side table and flipped through a few marked pages. "The closest location the plant has been seen is the Nightshade Oasis."

"The one north of the city?"

"Yes. That's right."

"I thought I heard someone saying the prince had stopped at an oasis to meet a welcoming party, but I'm not sure which one," Danet mumbled. "I could ask Gehiji."

"Who is Gehiji?"

"One of Ceros' friends. He accompanied Ceros to Licosia."

"Ceros?" Her father's eyebrow lifted in question. "You've been given leave to address the heir apparent, the prince of Licosia, by his given name?"

The blood drained from Danet's face. "Did I just call him that?"

"Yes, you did."

Danet sat on the edge of a nearby chair. At what point did she begin thinking of him so informally? Surely she didn't refer to him that way to the queen. She would have said something, just like Father had.

"It's all right, Danet," her father said gently. "I was mostly teasing you."

"But it's not all right, Father. I'm trying to think of when in the last day and a half I stopped thinking of him as the prince, the prince whom I serve, and starting thinking of him as a friend. I need to correct that in my own mind before it slips out again with someone who would not understand."

"I agree only because it would be embarrassing for you. However," he said as he put the book he had been reading aside, "because of the connection the two of you share, you will never again be able to think of him formally."

"Gods. I'm going to have to leave Licosia, aren't I?"

Her father chuckled. "I suggest you let this play out before you start packing your bags."

"But, Father, there is no way I could work in the palace and be near him. That would be far too intrusive for both of us. Especially once he takes a bride." She shuddered. "That would be…"

"Unthinkable?"

Danet's stomach hurt at the thought of Ceros with another woman. "To say the least."

"Actually, the thought of a destined mate with another should make you either ill or jealous and angry enough to take on a wild boar."

She put a hand over her stomach. "Lovely."

"If you are truly destined, he will feel the same and want no other."

The question she dared not ask, not yet, was, what happened if they really were destined? How would they make it work?

Afraid to dwell on the thought, Danet stood and took a deep breath. "I need to get some clean clothes and I thought I would lie down for a bit." She smiled regretfully. "I haven't been able to get much rest at the palace and the queen suggested I might rest better at home."

"You do look tired, Daughter." He smiled. "I'll tell Ryana to save the tea for later. Do you want someone to wake you in an hour or two?"

"That would be perfect. And would you mind writing down every place the Aspenadder may be found? I'd like to take that list to Gehiji. He might be able to find out who had access to the plant and therefore who tried to kill Ceros."

"I will have it ready for you when you wake."

Even though her father rarely displayed signs of affection, she hugged him. "Thank you."

He patted her shoulder awkwardly. "Go get some rest."

Danet hurried up the steps to her room. She tossed her dirty clothes on the floor beside her dresser and pulled a couple of clean outfits out of the drawers. The thought of a long shower where she was guaranteed privacy flitted through her mind, but the lure of an hour of sleep in her own bed overrode it.

As expected, it only took a few minutes after she curled up in her pillows to fall asleep.

~~ + ~~

The beast was waiting for her.

She found herself in a brightly lit room. The walls were covered in gold, amplifying the natural light. Across from her sat an oversized bed covered in white sheets and draped with sheer white fabric. The drapes fluttered in an imaginary breeze.

In the center of the bed lay her beast. She still marveled at his golden body. Powerful muscles rippled beneath a velvety smooth surface. The mane around his head was the same gold color but thick and soft. Danet loved to sink her fingers into it.

As she approached, he lifted his head from his massive paws and watched her.

"You are well then, I see," she said to the beast. "I feared whoever had been hunting you in my previous dream might have succeeded."

She sank to the floor in front of the bed and studied his eyes. It had been many years since she feared her beast, but his size and strength still overwhelmed her. She knew he could strike her down with one blow of his mighty paw, but felt comfortable he wouldn't.

Danet crawled up onto the bed so she could stroke his mane.

The beast turned and pushed his head into her hand, silently asking for more.

She smiled and gladly complied. As she petted her beast, she recalled her day for him.

"I have been asked to help our prince. He has been poisoned and cannot move. Father found a medicine to help rid his body of the toxin, but I worry for his safety." She noticed an unusual fog had crept in and now surrounded them. "He is vulnerable. If his enemy were to return to finish the job the poison didn't, he would not be able to defend himself."

A rumble in the beast's chest made her think he didn't like what she had said.

"I think I need to dig out Mother's journals. I remember her telling me stories as a child about some of the wondrous things her mother and grandmother had done to heal people, but I know so little of our gifts I wouldn't know what to attempt."

Her beast rolled onto his side and made a pulling motion with one paw on her arm.

Danet lay on her side, facing her beast's massive chest. She ran her fingers over the velvety fur, letting her fingernails drag lightly as she pulled them back and forth.

Her beast made a purring noise in his throat, letting her know he enjoyed her affections.

"I wish to help our prince but I am afraid once he sees what I am and what I can do, he will fear me. Maybe even force me to leave Licosia. That would embarrass Father and maybe even endanger his work. I can't be the cause of that."

Her beast looked at her solemnly then his giant tongue darted out to lick her hand.

"Are you saying I worry too much? Father tells me that all the time." She sighed. "Perhaps I do."

She put one arm around her beast and lay her head against his ribs. His heart beat steadily inside and the sound comforted her.

"How I wish you could talk. I feel you have many of the answers I seek." She stroked her hand down his back. "In all the years you've been in my dreams, you've never said a word. But then, you don't really need to. I usually know what you are saying."

She turned her head and rested her chin on his side. "Isn't that odd?"

Her beast made a grunt then took a deep breath and exhaled as he lay his head back down.

They lay there, soaking up the peace and quiet until he sat up suddenly, forcing her to do the same. He looked at a particularly gray tendril of the fog as if he heard something.

Danet's eyes darted between the creeping mist and her beast and she tried to determine what he had seen or heard. Her heart had not yet slowed but she knew her beast would protect her against anything that might step out of the mist.

Suddenly he roared loudly and rolled away from her. She scurried off the edge of the bed, watching him. He seemed to be favoring one paw, but she didn't know why. She eased closer so she could take a look and try to figure out what had happened or what had caused him pain.

His chest heaved as if he had run around the city twice. Every time she stepped closer, her beast took a step back. He kept shaking his head as if he needed to clear it.

Before she could reach him, he ran around her and charged into the fog. As she debated whether to follow, she heard Ceros call to her. *Someone here… Come back…*

His voice was too faint for her to understand everything he said. Her anxiety spiked and she willed herself to wake up.

Danet!

CHAPTER ELEVEN

Danet jerked awake and found herself sitting up in the middle of her own bed. Based on the way the shadows were forming on her wall, she knew it was nearing dusk. She must have dozed for at least an hour.

She scampered off the bed and grabbed her bag of clothes. Just before she left her room, she remembered to grab her mother's journal. She tucked it safely in her bag then rushed down the stairs. Using her fingers, she quickly smoothed her hair and retied the ribbon.

"Father, I need to go," she said as she burst into her father's study.

"Why? What's wrong?"

"I—" She gulped in a mouthful of air. "I heard Ceros in my dream. Something is wrong."

"Then you must go. Here," he grabbed the piece of paper he had been writing on and handed it to her. "It's the list of places the Aspenadder can be found. If I learn of any more, I'll send word."

"Thank you."

"And Ryana packed that for you." He pointed to a small sack sitting near the door.

"Give her my thanks also." She grabbed Ryana's treats as she rushed to the entryway.

"Be careful," he shouted as she ran to her escort.

The return to the palace took longer than she cared for. Even though the crowds weren't thick, Danet had no patience for anyone standing between her and her destination.

She needed to see Ceros and know everything was okay.

As they passed through the palace gates, she tried to reach him. *Ceros? Are you there? Is everything all right?*

There was no response. She tried to tell herself he could be sleeping.

Panic made her rush through the hallways. When she reached his chambers, she found the queen on her lounge, speaking with Darius.

She forced herself to slow down and catch her breath. Nothing could be amiss as far as this crowd was concerned.

"My queen." Danet bowed her head. "Master Darius." She looked at Ceros. He appeared to be in the same position as when she left. "How is the prince?"

Her heart still drummed against her chest.

"I was hoping you would arrive before I left." Darius stood. "I have concerns."

"About?"

"Yesterday, when I examined Prince Ceros, I saw improvement in his movement and his responses. But today he seems to be worse than when he first arrived."

"He is?" Danet set her bag of clothing on the floor and the sack of Ryana's goodies on the desk. She hurried to the prince's side.

She took his hand in hers and placed her fingers at his wrist where she could feel his heart beating. It was slower than this morning. Next she felt his brow. He felt warmer than normal. His face was paler than before she left.

Ceros? Still, he didn't respond.

"Something is wrong." Danet looked to the queen. "What happened while I was away?"

"Nothing that I know of. Aleric and those councilmen insisted Master Darius bring them to see Ceros and give them an update. After they left, Ceros stopped moving but I assumed he had fallen asleep. What's wrong?"

Darius spoke before Danet could. "His heartbeat is weaker and he may have a fever." To Danet, he asked, "He wasn't like this before you left?"

She shook her head. "No. His color was good. His eyes were clear and seemed to focus occasionally on objects. His heartbeat was steady and strong. Did anyone give him any herbs?"

The queen glanced at Darius, but answered, "Not that I noticed."

Darius drew himself up to his full height. "I did not order a change to any of the herbs he should have been receiving with his broth. And I never dispense them to my patients."

Helping patients with medicines would certainly be something Darius considered beneath him.

"What about broth or water? Did anyone give him anything while I was away?" Danet asked.

The queen shook her head. "You are the only one who knows how to get him to swallow anything. It would be pointless for anyone else to attempt it."

Danet nodded. "Perhaps it is simply a setback or his body trying to shake off the last of whatever caused the issue." She turned to Darius. "I will monitor him closely through the night for elevated fever. I assume you will wish to be notified immediately if he worsens?"

"Most definitely."

"Would you like for me to attempt to continue the water and the broth as well?"

Darius hesitated. "The water, yes. But only small quantities."

"I have successfully used cold water-soaked linens at major junction points to treat fevers. If his takes a sudden turn for the worse, do you wish me to proceed or would you rather examine him first?"

"Without knowing how quickly I can get here, proceed with the linens. They can do no harm and may help until I can arrive."

"Very well. Is there anything else I can do for him?"

"No. I believe that will be all."

She dipped her head to Darius respectfully, even though it galled her to do so. "I am sure you have other patients to see before you return home. I hope the rest of your evening goes well, Master Darius."

"Yes, actually I do now that you mention it." He gathered his robes and made a bow. "My queen. As always, at your service."

"Thank you, Master Darius. I bid you a good evening. We will send word at once if we need your services."

He made one more bow and scurried out.

After the door clicked shut behind him, the queen turned to Danet. "All right, what's going on, Danet?"

"I don't know but I do not like how he looks." She pulled the sheet back to reveal Ceros' chest. It was still a rather magnificent chest to look at. Only now it appeared paler and covered in perspiration. "I want to check him again for thorns."

"I thought you said you extracted it."

"I did, but someone could have put another in, or used something else poisonous on him. I won't know until I check."

"What can I do?"

"Have Hesina bring a few more lamps. The sun is almost set and I'm going to need as much light as we can get."

"I will have them here in moments."

"My queen. Do not forget that this must be done quietly. There are a great many reasons to not let word get out."

The queen stiffened but then nodded. "Of course. I will be cautious."

Once the queen left, Danet took Ceros' hand in hers and concentrated on reaching him through their connection. *Ceros? If you are there, please wake up. You are scaring me.*

Still nothing.

She opened her mind and tried to sense what he was feeling or thinking or, well, anything. So much of her time had been spent building a barrier between their minds to avoid intruding on his feelings and memories it felt awkward to drop it.

She sensed the thread of connection and tried to follow it but each time she did, the strand would simply dissolve.

Something was very wrong.

Ceros? Her voice echoed as if she were standing in a hollow chamber. As annoying as it had been to know he could hear her thoughts, this scared her more than she wanted to admit.

She calmed herself and opened her eyes. The sight of his large hand in hers comforted her and reminded her of what she needed to do.

Gently she opened his palm and looked closely at each finger. Every bump, blemish and line was inspected. She also checked under each fingernail and in the webbing between the fingers. Nothing. She continued up Ceros' wrist to his elbow then to his shoulder. Still nothing.

Before she could finish checking through his hair, the queen returned followed by two of her attendants. They were all carrying lamps. Danet directed them to place the lamps about the room near the bed.

"We need to get a message to Gehiji," Danet whispered to the queen.

The queen nodded. "I'll write a note and have one of the girls deliver it."

After her attendants left, the queen came to stand next Danet. "What's wrong?"

"I'm not sure."

"You look more worried than when I left. Why?"

"I…" She couldn't tell her the truth about her connection with Ceros. The queen was unlikely to believe her and with Ceros being unresponsive, she had no way to prove it. "I don't like his lack of response. After making so much progress this morning and now almost nothing, I am worried."

The queen patted her shoulder. "You'll figure it out."

"I'm also worried about what I might find when I do."

The queen nodded. "What do you need me to do?"

Danet knew she needed to give the queen a task. One thing she had learned while working in the clinic was, most mothers tended to hover in the way because they were so worried. It was usually better to give them something to keep busy. "You can check his other hand while I check his hair. Just be careful. If you find something that feels like a large splinter, let me know. If there is another thorn, it is poisonous and shouldn't be handled with your bare hands."

"All right."

They fell silent as they worked.

Danet instructed the queen check his arm and shoulder. They finished about the same time. Together they examined Ceros' feet.

There were no thorns or any marks on his skin. The queen helped Danet turn Ceros onto his side so they could check his back.

Still nothing.

With a deep breath, Danet sat on the side of the bed and looked at Ceros. The queen sat on the other side and held his hand.

"I felt certain his reaction had been due to more toxin. Which would mean another thorn."

"Is there any other way to give him the poison?" the queen asked.

"Yes, but they would need extensive knowledge of the plant and how to extract the poison from the thorns."

"How else could they give it to him? Maybe we're not thinking of something."

Danet shrugged. "I would have to confirm with Father to be sure, but they could probably make a tonic that could be added to food or drink."

"He didn't have anything to eat or drink that you didn't give him."

"I suppose they could try to pour a liquefied version of the toxin on his skin, but his reaction would more likely be a rash or skin irritation than this. I didn't notice anything like that."

"I didn't either. What else?"

"Maybe a poultice. But again, that would have to be added to food or drink to do anything." She considered the possibilities. "Unless..." Danet scooted closer, thinking of the places she hadn't checked.

"What?"

"I didn't look in his mouth." She looked to the queen. "Can you grab that lamp and hold it over his head for me?"

Danet said a prayer of thanks the queen didn't mind dropping formalities and helping. She pulled Ceros' jaw down and peered inside. There was nothing on his tongue. That would have been way too easy.

When she pushed his tongue aside, she found a small thorn pushed into the soft underside.

"There you are," Danet whispered.

"You found something?"

"I'm afraid so." Not bothering with a linen, Danet pulled the sleeve of her tunic over her hand as protection and slid the thorn out. She examined it in the light.

"Is it the same kind as before?" the queen asked.

"I believe so, but Father will have to confirm."

Danet took the thorn to the desk and put it on a piece of parchment. She folded the edges of the parchment around the thorn to secure it and tucked it into a pocket of her bag.

"While I'm glad you found it, I'm very disturbed someone was able to get to him and leave it."

"Who came in after I left?"

The queen grimaced. "Several people, I'm afraid."

"We need to let Gehiji know who." Danet rummaged through

the basket she used for supplies and found the bottle of medicine her father had made to get rid of the poison. Next she grabbed a couple of clean linens and the pitcher of water.

"Do you need help with anything?" the queen asked.

"Not that I can think of. I am going to rinse out his mouth to make sure there are no lingering poisons from the thorn. But I have to be careful because I don't want him to swallow the water. Unfortunately I can't think of anything to put on the puncture that wouldn't be bad for him to ingest."

"What is that?" The queen pointed to the bottle in Danet's hand.

"It's what Father sent to counteract the toxins from the thorn." She lifted the glass decanter up to the lamp. "Thankfully there is enough left to get him through the night. I should probably send a note to Father to have him make some more just in case."

"I can write the note while you take care of Ceros."

Danet nodded. "Thank you."

The queen went to desk and searched for parchment and ink while Danet set the things she needed on a small table next to the bed. It was surprisingly difficult to push aside her fears for Ceros and concentrate on what she needed to do.

Deciding it would be easier to keep the water from pooling at his throat, she rolled Ceros onto his side then added a few linens beneath his head and neck. She swabbed his mouth out with a damp rag to make sure there were no large particles then poured a bit of water in from the side as a rinse.

He had to be pushed onto his back again in order to give him the antitoxin medicine. As she spooned in the first few drops she remembered how much he complained about the taste. Maybe the bad taste would be enough to jolt him out of his stupor.

She hoped anyway. Right now his complaints would be a blessing.

The process of getting the medicine down went slowly. Gehiji arrived before she finished. He came to the bed and looked down at Ceros. "He's a lot more pale. What happened?"

"I'm not entirely certain. I went home to check in with Father and get clean clothes, and quite honestly, to have a nap." Danet's guilt over her nap hung heavy about her neck. "When I returned he was like this."

"He took a turn for the worse?"

Danet nodded solemnly. "A lot worse." She let her expression convey her meaning.

Gehiji glanced at the queen, who was still busy writing the note to Sebak. "Is he still responding?"

"No. His responses are gone. No blinking or communication of any kind."

"Even with you?" he asked quietly.

She shook her head.

"Do you think it's just a relapse? Or maybe a temporary setback before he shakes off the last of the poison?"

"No." She shook her head again. "I found another thorn. This one had been hidden under his tongue."

Gehiji's expression turned grim. "We need to know who had access to him while you were away."

"The queen and I were talking about that earlier. I believe she was here the entire time but that may be an assumption on my part. She said there were several people in and out of here though."

He laid a reassuring hand on her shoulder. "You concentrate on making him well. I'll worry about finding the person trying to kill him."

She nodded mutely.

In the back on her mind she was aware of Gehiji crossing the room and speaking to the queen, but Danet didn't pay any attention to what they were saying. Her focus remained exclusively on Ceros.

It hurt to look at his handsome face and not hear his voice. Even though she hadn't seen him animated, her imagination filled in the details. His feelings and his sense of humor came through loud and clear when he spoke to her.

Despite the fact it had only been a couple of days, she already missed having him there. In her head.

Her father was right. It was a special connection. A powerful one, too, given the way she felt about him already. Letting it go when this was all over was going to be hard and she dreaded it.

Once she had coaxed enough medicine into him, she took her time cleaning his face and neck. Being able to touch him and feel his warmth and his breath on her skin comforted her. At least he was alive.

"Danet? Are you finished?"

"Yes, my queen." She looked over her shoulder to where the

queen and Gehiji sat.

"Come. We have things to discuss." The queen waved to the nearby chair.

"We do?" Danet asked as she gathered her supplies. She dropped the dirty linens on the floor not far from the bed, left the pitcher of water on the table then joined them.

"We need to make plans about how to best protect Ceros," Gehiji added.

Danet sat on the end of the lounge near the queen. "Agreed."

"I see now that despite the security I have put in place, he is not safe even in his own chambers," the queen said.

"Do we know who is behind this?" Danet asked.

"Not yet, but I have a list of potentials based on who had access to him both times," Gehiji said. "Unfortunately, that list doesn't mean that person or those persons are who is actually behind the acts. There could be someone else behind the scenes directing people."

"So even if you catch the person doing the deed, the real criminal could still be out there and could strike again in another manner at a later date," Danet guessed.

"Exactly. That's why we need to make sure we cut the snake's head off, not just its tail," he said.

"What do you suggest?" Danet asked.

"This is where I will excuse myself." The queen stood.

Danet looked up at her, questioning.

The queen reached for Danet's hand. "I cannot be privy to any plans you two come up with. I need to remain here and see to Rashidi's funeral. We cannot put it off any longer. The people of Licosia need to grieve and pay their respects. Then I must play the role of concerned mother. It will be more plausible if I do not know what you're doing." She squeezed Danet's hand. "But know that I trust the two of you to keep him safe and bring him home again healthy so he can assume his rightful place on the throne."

"Yes, my queen." Danet pulled their linked hands to her forehead. "I will do everything in my power to heal him and bring him home to you."

"I know you will, child."

The queen turned to Gehiji. "If you are half as capable as Ceros said you are, I know he will be safe under your watch. The things you have asked for will be delivered within the hour."

"Thank you, your Majesty."

"Send word through Hesina or Danet's father if you need anything. If I learn of anything, I will send it through Hesina," the queen said. "Be safe. All of you."

"You as well," Danet and Gehiji said at the same time. They watched as the queen swept out of the room.

Danet took a deep breath. "Now what?"

"Now we do what must be done to protect Ceros and his throne," he said.

CHAPTER TWELVE

Within the hour, a tea tray arrived, delivered by Hesina herself. "My queen said you needed a few things to protect our young prince with." She set the tray on the desk. "She also mentioned you may need a little help doing so."

Danet stood to greet her friend. "I'm sorry you have to be dragged into this tangle, Hesina. Have you been introduced to Prince Ceros' friend, Gehiji?" Danet asked with a wave of her hand in Gehiji's direction.

He stepped forward.

"I've seen this handsome devil lurking about my dining room," Hesina said, "but no, I have not yet been introduced."

"An oversight, I am sure. It is certainly my honor to finally meet you." Gehiji bowed over Hesina's hand. "I understand you are the one who keeps the palace running in tiptop shape."

"You are a charmer, aren't you? No wonder my girls have been all aflutter this week," Hesina said with a grin.

With a jerk of his head in the direction of the desk, Gehiji asked, "I assume the queen sent more than just tea and cookies?"

"I believe you will find everything you need is there." Hesina added, "Oh, and these as well." She pulled two pouches from her apron pockets. The clanking of coins gave away what they contained as Hesina handed both to Danet.

Danet looked to Gehiji. He nodded in affirmation that he expected them. She transferred the pouches to her own pockets.

"My queen said you needed a way to send and receive

messages," Hesina said.

"That's right. Will it be a problem?" Gehiji asked.

"Not at all. If you needed to send word from outside the palace, my boys come and go frequently, so it would not be unusual for either of them to be here."

"Are they still working at the Metalworks?" Danet asked.

To Gehiji, Danet said, "The Metalworks is in the center of town. There are a lot of people in and out, vendors included, so a stranger is not an unusual sight."

"Perfect," Gehiji said.

"Now, messages to and from your father might be more difficult. I think catching him at his clinic would be best," Hesina suggested.

Danet nodded. "You're probably right."

"I have a young cousin with an ailing leg. He helps me with the herbs out back from time to time. But it wouldn't be unheard of for him to pop into your father's clinic for medicine."

"Excellent. Now for the hard part," Gehiji said. "We need to get Ceros out of here, unseen."

Hesina took a seat. "The hard part is going to be getting him past those two." She pointed to where the guards stood on the other side of the main chamber doors.

"Agreed. There is never less than one at the door at all times," Gehiji added.

"And you'll not find one who isn't loyal to the queen and, by extension, the prince. So bribery won't work and drugging them will only raise the alarm," Hesina informed them. "About the only thing that would draw them away from their station would be if the palace were under attack."

"That could be arranged." Gehiji grinned. "But it would take a couple of days."

Danet and Hesina stared openmouthed at Gehiji for a moment.

Finally Hesina shook her head. "It's too bad we don't have a big batch of laundry," she said thoughtfully. "He would probably fit in one of the carts we use to haul linens out to the drying lines."

"What would it take to justify bringing one in?" Danet asked.

"If we were to change all of the bed linens," Hesina looked around the room, "and the draperies in the wing, I doubt anyone would notice the cart. But how would you justify changing everything while the prince lay ill?"

They threw a few more ideas around but everything they came up with had too many flaws.

"We're just going to have to do it the hard way and carry him out a window during the night," Gehiji declared. When Danet started to argue, he held one hand up to stop her. "If we can get him to Hesina's area before daybreak we could sneak him out of the palace in a cart even if it's light."

Danet looked to Hesina. The older woman nodded once. Resigned, Danet said, "All right. What do you want us to do?"

After reviewing Gehiji's plan, Hesina said, "I best be getting back to the kitchens. I need to make sure everything is properly cleaned then I'll make sure the carts are gathered up and stored outside the garden wall."

"Excellent," Gehiji said. "I'll be down to check the area so I know which paths to take."

Hesina stood. "Send word if you think of anything else you need."

"We will. Thank you, Hesina," Danet said.

After she had left, Gehiji asked, "Is he still unresponsive?"

"I think so." Danet frowned. "I've called to him a time or two as we were talking with Hesina but he didn't respond. Let me try concentrating on connecting with him again."

"Yes, do," Gehiji encouraged.

She walked to the bed and sat on the edge of the mattress. She took his hand and rubbed her thumbs on the back as she cleared her mind and focused on finding their connection.

It was there, glowing in her mind like a beacon. When she reached for it, she heard a loud roar. It echoed around her, making her jump back. It sounded like her dream beast, calling out a warning.

She opened her eyes and found Gehiji watching her. "What's wrong?"

"I'm not sure." She shook her head to clear it. "I heard something."

"What did you hear?" He moved closer.

"It's my, well… I don't know what it is. I just call it my beast."

Gehiji's brow lifted in question.

"I've been having dreams of a beast for almost half of my life. This beast is large with golden fur and long, shaggy hair about his face." She shrugged. "He looks rather ferocious but he has always been very gentle with me."

He sat forward in his seat and leaned his elbows on his own thighs. "Does your beast have large paws and a narrow tail?"

She frowned. "Yes, how did you know that?"

"Do you know what an omegamorph is?" Gehiji asked.

She shook her head. "No. I've heard the word, but I'm not sure what exactly it is."

"An omegamorph is a person who has supposedly been blessed by the Gods with the gift of transformation. Usually that person can only transform into one form but there are legends of some who could transform into whatever shape needed."

Danet racked her brain trying to remember where she had heard similar stories.

"Supposedly there are only a handful of omegamorphs at any given time," Gehiji continued. "They are charged with protecting the people of the Gods and ensuring peace and prosperity in the world."

"No small chore," she mumbled.

"No it isn't. But each omegamorph is given a helpmate. One who has also been blessed by the Gods in some way."

The way he said that made Danet look up to study his expression. He stared at her intently, as if trying to make her understand something. "So what does this legend have to do with my dream beast?"

"I think your dream beast is an omegamorph."

She shook her head. "In all the years I've dreamed of him, he's never been anything but the beast. He's never transformed into anything else."

"Perhaps the Gods didn't want you to see his true form. You may not have been ready to know."

"Know what?" Her confusion and frustration rang in her tone.

"Ceros is an omegamorph."

Danet's mind reeled.

"His alternate form is a beast much as you described. A large gold-colored beast who walks on four legs with massive paws and a thick, full mane of hair about his face. His roar has been enough to make grown men, full-fledged warriors, wet themselves in battle."

She shook her head again. "My beast is not aggressive. He is gentle and comforting. Especially when we walk together. It can't be him."

"I may get into trouble for telling you, but Ceros told me about some of his dreams. He said he often found himself in beast form in a beautiful oasis-like place and a girl would come and sit with him. She spoke to him and usually petted him. He could never see her face, but she always wore a simple white gown or dress with no jewels or adornments."

Danet's breath caught in her throat.

"He said it soothed him to see her in his dreams," Gehiji continued. "He always felt at ease when he woke and he wondered who she was and why she came to him so frequently."

She stared at Ceros' face. "Gods. If what you say is true, it is him, isn't it? He's my beast."

"Probably in more ways than one," Gehiji said gently.

"Wait. If he really is my beast, then I was dreaming of him when he was poisoned again."

"You were?"

Danet nodded. "Yes. I took a nap at home. In my dream I was petting him and talking to him as I usually did when he suddenly roared out in pain and jumped away from me." She focused on the image in her mind. "He tossed his head about as if he were shaking something off." She looked up at Gehiji. "That might have been the thorn in his mouth. But he also limped on one paw as he charged into the mist."

"His paw?"

Without saying anything more, Danet grabbed Ceros' hand. The one the queen had checked earlier. She found nothing on the surface of the front or back, but when she spread his fingers apart, she found another thorn stuck in the soft webbing between two of them.

She used the sheet to pull the thorn out then held the fabric open for Gehiji to see. "No wonder he hasn't come around. He was still being exposed to the toxin."

His face drew into a frown. "That's small. I'm surprised it affected him so much."

"It's probably due to repeated exposure and his body not having healed yet," Danet explained. "I hope this wasn't in so long it creates lasting damage."

"Is that possible?"

"I'm afraid so."

"We need to get him out of here before they strike again. He's got to shake this off so he can go to that council meeting and prove he's fit to rule."

"When do you want to try to move him?"

"We need to wait until it's fully dark." He looked to the windows. "The sun has nearly set. I had best go down to the gardens and have a look around. Will you be okay here alone with him?"

"Yes. I will be fine." She laid the thorn on the bed. "Let me get something to put that in," she pointed to the offending thorn, "and then I'll treat the place I removed it. Now that we know for sure there is a threat, I won't let anyone near him."

She went to the desk and rummaged around in her basket of supplies. She found her medicine and something to store the thorn in and took them back to the bed. After she scooped up the thorn and set it aside, she treated the wound.

When she returned her things to the basket, Gehiji approached. "Here." He handed her a small knife in a protective casing. "Keep this hidden in your pocket. It's extremely sharp. If you use it, be aware that it will cut whatever or whoever you get it close to."

Danet nodded and tucked the knife into her pocket.

"I will return shortly."

"Do you need me to do anything while you're away?"

"Other than heal him?"

She nodded.

"Make sure you have everything you need packed. Your medicines and herbs, I mean. We won't have room for much else, I'm afraid."

"I require very little," she assured him. "But I will pack the tonic Father made for him and a few basic supplies."

"You might pack some of the food Hesina brought too."

She glanced at the tray they had not yet touched. "All right."

"I'll return after nightfall but I won't come through the suite doors."

"Be careful."

He gave her a boyish grin. "Always."

With a sigh, she returned to Ceros' side. Sitting on the edge of the bed, she watched the rise and fall of his chest. Could he really be the beast from her dreams? Gehiji seemed convinced of it.

That could be what made their connection so strong.

It embarrassed her to think about what she might have said

when she talked to him in her dreams. Things from her day. People she treated in the clinic. He probably got bored listening to her.

She shook off the thought.

While she had the room to herself, she needed to pack. The items they had to have went into the basket next to the desk. Using the spare tunic she'd brought from home, she covered the contents to make it look like a pile of dirty clothes.

When she lifted the largest cover on the food tray she nearly dropped it when she found weapons instead of sweets. Many of which she couldn't identify. Those needed to be hidden before anyone looked for snacks.

She stashed a few things into her baskets of supplies, another in her personal bag along with a partial bag of coins. Another went into the desk drawer and the last couple she hid in the bathroom.

When she was satisfied she had everything she could think of, she returned to Ceros' side.

I don't know if you can hear me or not. I'd like to think that you can because that would mean you were getting better. And I pray you are healing.

The doors to the suite opened and closed and brought Danet to her feet. She slipped her hand into her pocket and clutched the knife. When she saw Ceros' younger sister, Femi, she relaxed.

"Oh good, you're here," Femi said in her usual upbeat manner. "How is he?"

"Still unresponsive."

"Oh." Her usual bubbly personality dimmed slightly. "I had hoped he just needed to rest for a while."

"I would like to think so as well, but at this point, I don't think that is the case. But we're still watching him and trying to figure out what's wrong."

Femi stood at the foot of the bed with Danet and looked at Ceros, each lost in their own thoughts.

Finally Danet turned to Femi and said, "I know this is a tough time for the family, but I've been so focused on Prince Ceros I haven't been able to check on anyone else. How is everyone holding up?" Danet asked.

"As well as can be expected, I think." Femi turned to Danet. "We all miss Father and mourn his passing, but I think we're more worried about Ceros." She grimaced. "Especially Mother."

"How is she, really?" Danet asked. "She puts on a strong front for everyone, but this has to be hard on her. I worry for her."

"I do too. If the worst happens to Ceros, I'm not sure she'll be able to handle it. Especially so soon after Father."

"That is my fear as well."

Femi lowered her voice. "Mother says someone may be trying to kill Ceros. Is that true?"

"I'm not certain but there have been enough indicators to make me take precautions."

"But who would want to kill him?"

"Anyone who thought they stood a chance of getting the throne," Danet said without preamble.

"So you don't know."

"No, I don't. I wish I did." She grimaced and scratched her head. "I say that, but I'm not sure I really do."

"Why not?"

"The possibility that someone I know, or might have come in contact with, is capable of killing another person for power or money or whatever their reason is, is unnerving. This person probably looks normal on the surface and yet doesn't mind taking someone else's life for selfish purposes." She shook her head. "I just don't understand it."

Femi took Danet's hand in hers. "I see what you mean. It is a little frightening, isn't it? Especially for you. Someone who spends her days trying to heal people or alleviate their pain."

"Maybe that is why it bothers me so much." Danet looked at Ceros.

"You didn't know him before he left for Shirghada, did you?" Femi gestured for Danet to follow her to the seating area.

"No, I didn't. It would not have been appropriate for me to spend any time in his company."

"You are one of the few who let propriety stop her," Femi mumbled.

Danet felt her cheeks heat.

"I don't mean to that in an insulting way. We all think a lot of you, Danet, and that is probably one of the reasons we do." Femi sat back on the lounge. "When Ceros left for school, he was very much full of himself. Girls and full-grown women were constantly throwing themselves at him. He excelled at his lessons and at sports and bested everyone at everything. There was little that didn't go right for him." Her eyes got a faraway look in them. "Then he left for Shirghada. When he came home after his first year, you could tell a huge difference in him."

"How so?"

"He was still quite confident, but not quite so arrogant. The next year when he returned he was even more changed. He was bigger, stronger and more," Femi waved her hand as she searched for a word, "graceful, I suppose. But he was also quieter. He watched and listened more. In some ways, he had become more like Father."

"What did he do while in Shirghada? Did he attend some kind of training or learning?"

"I remember Father saying he thought it would be good for Ceros to see how an elite military ran from the inside. I think he expected Ceros to come home after a year or two though." Femi shrugged. "We were all surprised Ceros stayed as long as he did."

"Why did he?"

"I'm not sure, really. I know Ceros and Father disagreed about many things before Ceros went away." She grinned. "Of course, you know, the royal family never got into fights. That would be disgraceful."

"Of course." Danet smirked. She could well imagine those two very strong-willed men, father and son, clashing over things as simple as what kind of meat should be served for dinner.

"Mother said she thought Ceros had found himself or a focus for his life while he living in Shirghada. Whatever he found, changed him. Significantly. For the better. And I think that man will be an outstanding leader and king." She looked to Ceros. "I just hope we get a chance to see what he's really capable of."

"So do I, Femi." Danet sighed. "So do I."

CHAPTER THIRTEEN

Even though she had far too much nervous energy to sleep, Danet finally instructed the guards to refuse admission to any more visitors, except the queen, for the night. Since she didn't know when she might have another opportunity, she took time to bathe and wash and braid her hair. Instead of a nightdress, however, she changed into a clean tunic and leggings. Her boots were waiting by her basket of supplies so they would be easy to find in the dark.

Knowing it would be a few more hours before Gehiji returned, Danet pulled out her mother's journal and curled up on the bed next to Ceros. Instead of focusing on the printed words, her attention returned to the man lying beside her.

His hair hung limp on his pillow and was becoming duller in color. The poison was taking its toll even on the shimmer that used to be there. Of its own accord her hand reached out to trace the ridge of his cheekbone and the arch of his brow. The rough texture of his jawline tickled the pads of her fingers as they eased toward his lips.

He truly was a beautiful man.

There was very little she wouldn't do to try to heal him.

Throughout the day, she'd had a nagging thought, a memory really, that mystics had the ability to connect their life force with others and heal them. Her mother had done it with her own father after he had caught a fever. Danet has been just a child at the time, but her father related the story many years later. From what she had read it was a risky undertaking and the mystic often absorbed some of the other person's illness in exchange for healing energy they supplied.

Making the connection with the other person was also difficult. The bond between mates made it easier but it wasn't something that could be achieved with just anyone. Danet wondered if her connection with Ceros was strong enough to make it possible.

In the pages of her mother's journal, she looked for passages that spoke of that type of healing. What her mother might have done to prepare or what she did to connect their life forces. The entries about his illness were glum. Danet never knew the mystic healing had been their last desperate hope.

Thankfully there were a few pages where her mother had written about her research into the healing. It described glimmering threads of the soul that needed to be found. From what little information she had, it sounded as if she simply needed to touch their "threads" together and the healing energy would pass between them.

It sounded easy but Danet knew that could not be the case. Especially when it was more than a week before the next entry was made in her mother's journal after the healing. With a sigh, she closed the book then stood and put it back into her bag.

She turned down all but one of the lamps and returned to Ceros' side. She knew she wouldn't sleep, but curled up next to him on the bed to rest.

The next thing she knew, Gehiji was shaking her awake. "Danet. It's time to go," he whispered.

His voice cleared the fog in her mind in record time. "Okay. I'm ready. I just need to put my boots on."

"Is everything packed?"

"Yes." She rubbed her eyes as she stumbled off the bed. "Except for the two larger weapons. I hid them in the bathroom under the stack of linens. There's one in the desk too."

"Very good." Gehiji headed to the bathroom and returned without making any sound. "Show me what you're planning to take with us."

Danet pointed to the two baskets of supplies.

"That's all?" he asked with surprise.

She nodded. "Oh, and my bag also." She patted the small, well-worn bag on the end of the desk.

Gehiji made a quick inspection of all the contents then moved a few things around, eliminating the need for one basket. From his own bag, the one strapped around his chest, he pulled out a dark cloak. "Help me put this on Ceros." As they worked, he asked, "Have you heard anything from him?"

She shook her head.

Gehiji nodded curtly. "Here's what we're going to do. I'll carry Ceros. You follow as close as you can, making as little noise as possible. Understand?"

"Yes."

"If I stop suddenly, I need you to watch this hand." He held up his right hand. "I may have to signal you with it."

"Okay."

"This," he made a fist, "means stop and be silent. If I point in a certain direction I mean for you to pay attention to that area because either someone is coming or there is something you need to see. If I want you to go ahead of me in a certain direction, I'll do this." He held up his first finger, swirled it in the air then pointed. "Got it?"

"Got it."

"Good. Ready?" He extinguished the lamp next to the bed.

"Wait. What about our supplies?"

"If you think you can carry the basket and your bag easily without making any noise, then do so. If not, carry what you can and we'll have Hesina send whatever is left."

Danet slipped the bag strap over her head and around her body then tested the weight of the basket. It wasn't significantly heavy since it wasn't full. She shrugged and said, "I can carry it."

He nodded. "One more thing. If we're discovered, I'll do what I can to distract them so you can slip away and return to the room."

"Why? Wouldn't it be best if we stayed together? I can probably convince anyone in the palace that we're going to get help or something."

"You're his best chance for healing. I don't want to risk you being banished from his care. The queen won't be able to protect you if this goes wrong."

She swallowed the fear that bubbled up. "I understand. But I still think I would be a credible witness to what you are doing."

He sighed. "Just promise me that if we're caught and you can get away easily and unseen, you will."

"Depends on who it is," she said stubbornly.

He shook his head. "We need to go." Gehiji extinguished the last light then scooped Ceros up. He hung Ceros over his shoulder like a sack of grain and whispered, "Put a few pillows under the sheet so it looks as if he's still lying there."

Danet nodded and did as he suggested. Then she grabbed the basket and followed Gehiji to the adjoining chamber. That secluded sitting area had rows of bookshelves and an open balcony overlooking the family gardens.

Even in the dark it appeared to be a comfortable room. One she hadn't explored but now wished she had.

Gehiji walked to the edge of the balcony and checked the one across from them and the area below. He gestured for her to come closer as he put Ceros in a nearby chair. "I'm going to lower you to the ground first. When you reach the bottom I want you to look in every direction to make sure no one saw you. You also need to make sure there is no one nearby."

"All right."

He unwound the sash that circled his waist and crisscrossed his chest. It had been made from a fabric she had never seen before. The narrow width allowed him to wrap it multiple times around his body without it being bulky.

When he had loosened all of the fabric, he wrapped it around her waist and legs in a strange fashion and knotted it before she realized his intent. Good thing she'd worn leggings instead of a dress.

"Climb up on the rail then turn and stand on the edge, facing me," he instructed.

Her eyes were probably as large as saucers. The drop to the ground below them might not be enough to kill someone on impact, but a fall could certainly cause injuries. The thought frighten her.

"I won't let you fall." He showed her the ends of the fabric bunched in his hands.

"But is the fabric just as confident?" she mumbled.

He chuckled. "It will hold you."

Doubt lingered, but seeing no alternative, she climbed over the rail and faced Gehiji. "Now what?"

"I want you to hang on to the fabric here." He showed her where to put her hands. "Then lean back, keeping your feet flat against the balcony ledge or the wall below it. I'm going to slowly let out more fabric. As I do I want you to walk backwards down the wall."

She gulped in air. "All right. Sounds easy enough."

"It is, actually, for you. I'll be doing all the work up here."

Keeping her eyes locked on Gehiji, she took a deep breath then leaned back.

"That's right. Good." Even though he whispered, he didn't sound as if he strained to hold her weight. "Now take a step back."

She did, hesitantly, afraid to look down.

"That's right, now another," he encouraged.

She took another tentative step.

"Good. Keep going."

The tightness in her chest eased. Now that she knew she wouldn't plummet to the ground, her remaining steps were smoother and less jittery. When she drew close enough, she stepped off the wall and put her weight onto her feet on the ground.

She checked the area around her to make sure no one had come near then looked up at Gehiji. He had leaned over the railing.

"I don't see anyone," she whispered as loudly as she dared.

He indicated he had heard her then gestured for her to unwind the fabric from her body. He pulled the material up as soon as she'd freed it.

Their basket of supplies floated down from the balcony at the end of the makeshift rope.

She quickly untied it and set the basket behind some nearby plants. It took several moments before she heard rustling from the balcony. When she looked up, her breath caught as she watched Gehiji climb over the railing. He had Ceros draped over his shoulder once again.

It felt as if their descent took an eternity. Her heart pounded in her ears and she prayed they didn't fall.

Once they were on the ground Gehiji set Ceros down then quickly freed himself from the binding. With a few jerks and tugs he somehow freed the fabric from whatever he'd secured it around on the balcony.

Danet checked on Ceros while Gehiji finished.

Ceros? Can you hear me?

Her heart ached when she heard no reply.

"Is he all right?" Gehiji asked as he knelt beside her.

"As far as I can tell, yes. But he's still not responding." She looked to Gehiji. "I don't suppose I have to tell you how much this concerns me."

"I know. I can see it in your face. It will be fine. He's been through worse than this."

Her eyes widened in alarm. "I don't think I want to know."

"No. You don't." He stood and checked the area around them. "Come. We need to move quickly while the guards are still on the other side of the fountains."

She nodded then retrieved the basket from where she had hidden it. Once Gehiji had Ceros in position again, over his shoulder, he motioned her to follow. He moved silently along the perimeter of the building, using the shadows to stay hidden. Each time they crossed a span not hidden in shadow, she worried everyone in the palace could see them. Even though it was very dark outside.

When they reached the kitchen gardens Gehiji stopped at an ancient doorway that looked as if it had been installed when the palace had first been built. He knocked twice on the faded wood. In response, they heard a scratch then one knock down low on the door. Gehiji responded back with three quick raps. She heard the sound of the bolt sliding then the door eased open a fraction.

Gehiji pushed it open and stepped through. Danet followed but was surprised when she didn't see Hesina or someone else waiting for them. Gehiji slid the bolt quietly back into place to secure the door then put his finger to his lips to indicate she should remain quiet. They waited in the semi-dark as Gehiji listened to the sounds around them.

Danet? A groggy voice whispered in her head, startling her.

Ceros? Are you okay? She reached out to grab Gehiji's sleeve.

Don't know... I...

Gehiji looked at her with a questioning expression. She pointed to Ceros then held up one finger to ask him to wait.

Ceros? She paused for a response. *Ceros? Are you awake?*

Her shoulders slumped and she shook her head for Gehiji's benefit. Ceros' contact gave her a ray of hope. She reached out and pushed his hair away from his face even though it was pointless given the way he hung over Gehiji's shoulder. It made her feel better to touch him.

Voices from across the garden caught her attention. She tensed and turned to Gehiji. He looked as if he had expected to hear them. Next she heard the slam of a heavy door. The voices were gone and Gehiji's posture relaxed.

"Should be clear now. Come on," he whispered then turned to follow the path opposite where the men had gone.

Danet followed but found herself frequently looking back to make sure no one snuck up behind them.

When they came to a shed built in the corner of the wall, he gestured her to come closer. "Look inside on the shelf," he whispered. "There should be a stack of clothing. Grab what's there and bring it with you."

She eased the shed door open and cringed when it squeaked in protest. There was even less light inside than what she had become accustomed to, making it difficult to find the shelf. Thankfully the area was clean and organized and she found the clothes easily when she ran her hands along the wall to the shelf.

She latched the shed door closed and joined Gehiji and Ceros in the shadows near the wall. "Now what?" she whispered.

"Now we find the cart Hesina had brought around."

Gehiji led them to a door that was a mirror image of the one they had used to get into the garden. He slid the bolt as quietly as possible then gestured for her to precede him.

She stepped to the side so Gehiji could pass through with Ceros. As he did, Gehiji pulled the wood door closed behind them.

"Where do they store the supply carts?" he whispered.

"Behind the stables, I believe." She pointed to where the stables were. In case the smell of eligari excrement wafting toward them hadn't been enough to give it away.

"Lead on then."

She blinked in surprise then rallied herself and showed him where to go. When they rounded the corner, she startled when she found Hesina's son.

Danet turned to whisper to Gehiji over her shoulder. "It's Ptah. Is he supposed to be here?"

"Hesina said someone would come to drive the cart." Gehiji shrugged. "Could he be the one chosen to do it?"

"Maybe. How about if I talk to him and verify this is where we're supposed to be and ensure no one else around?"

Gehiji frowned but finally nodded. Before she walked away, he grabbed her arm. "If something looks wrong or you feel uncomfortable for any reason, I want you to say something, anything, about the color red. Understand?"

"Yes. The color red." Danet squared her shoulders and headed to Ptah. As quietly as possible, she walked closer.

When Ptah saw her approaching, he hopped off his perch on the edge of the cart and greeted her. "Mistress Danet." He took her hands in his then bowed his head and brought their joined hands to his forehead in a gesture of the deepest respect. Keeping his voice low, he said, "I'm glad you made it." He looked around. "You didn't come alone did you?"

"No, Ptah. My friend is trailing nearby. I came to make sure the coast was clear for them."

"I haven't seen anyone since the watch made its last round. Won't be much longer until the next pass."

"How long have you been waiting?" she asked.

"Not long. I waited until little Ptah went to bed before coming. Apris tucked the little ones in bed with her so it wouldn't be a problem to be away."

Danet smiled at the family picture his words created in her mind. "How is little Ptah?"

"He's a dandy. Getting taller and stronger every day. Won't be long now 'til he's able to run on that foot again."

"Good. I'm very glad to hear it. I know it's tough to keep little boys off their feet at that age."

"Yes, but if it meant tying him to his bed so he didn't lose that foot, we'd have done it."

Danet patted him on the shoulder. "I know you would have but I'm glad you didn't have to." She chuckled. "And I'm sure little Ptah is too."

"I know I've said it before, but I don't know what we would have done if you hadn't helped him."

"I'm just glad I was able to. And that we were able to save his foot. I wouldn't wish that on any child." She looked around. "Do you think it's safe for my friend to come out and load our things in the cart?"

Ptah looked up at the moon then at the palace walls. "If he can move quickly, we can get them into the cart before the next pass of the watch. We'll have to resettle things once the watch is past."

"All right. Let me go tell him."

"Hurry."

She quickened her pace and darted around the corner, nearly running into Gehiji. "He said he hadn't seen anyone since the last pass of the watch but that we'd need to hurry."

"All right. Grab the basket."

Danet did as instructed and followed Gehiji to the cart. Ptah held the tarp up to allow them to climb in. If he was surprised by their cargo, he didn't indicate.

Once Danet and Gehiji climbed into the cart, Ptah handed Ceros to Gehiji and their basket of supplies to Danet then pulled the tarp into place. "I'll leave the corner flipped back to let in some air. As soon as the watch has passed out of sight, I will let you know."

"Thank you, Ptah," Danet said.

Under the canvas, Danet crawled next to Ceros. She kept her movements slow so as to not rock the cart.

"Did he say something to you earlier?" Gehiji asked softly.

"Yes. But it was very brief and then he was gone." She placed her fingers on the pulse on Ceros' neck to count his heartbeats. "And no, I haven't been able to reach him again."

"From your expression, I guessed that was what happened but I didn't want to risk setting him down or asking questions just then."

She looked to where Gehiji sat. She couldn't see his expression, but he had to be tired after carrying Ceros so far. "I know. And there was little we could do right then. I don't think it would have mattered even if we had been in his room." She shrugged. "The movement might have been what brought him around. It's hard to say either way." Danet reached across and patted Gehiji on the arm. "Why don't you rest while you can? Ptah will warn us if anyone comes near."

He chuckled. "Shouldn't I be telling you that?"

"Perhaps it's good advice for both of us."

Danet let her head fall back against the side of the cart. For safe measure, she took Ceros' hand into hers. As she listened to the sounds of the night she let her eyes fall shut. It would be for just a moment, she promised herself.

The jolting of the cart startled Danet awake.

"It's all right," Gehiji reassured her. "Ptah is hitching a couple of eligari to the cart."

"So we'll be off soon?"

"Yes."

She rubbed her eyes. "How long did I sleep?"

"An hour or two, I would guess."

It didn't feel as if it had been that long. But then again, given the stiffness in her neck and backside, it was possible. "Apparently the watch passed without incident."

"Umhmm. I heard Ptah speaking to someone from the stables a little while ago but he didn't let on we were here. Right after that he brought the eligari."

Ptah appeared at the back of the cart. "It's time. I'm going to put the tarp back in place to cover you. I know it'll be dark and maybe even warm, but as soon as we clear the gates I'll stop and loosen the corner again. Okay?"

Danet and Gehiji spoke at the same time. "We understand." "Do what you need to do."

"I recommend not speaking again until we're past the gates," Ptah added.

"Agreed," Gehiji answered for both of them.

The flap of the tarp flipped closed, throwing the cart into total darkness. Danet didn't realize how helpful the little light they'd had before had been.

When the wagon lurched forward, her heart raced. The possibility of being discovered at the gate buzzed through her mind. Worry for her father, Gehiji and Ptah threatened to send her into a panic as she sat in the dark, enclosed cart.

Danet...

Her name whispered through her mind.

Ceros. I'm here. We're taking you someplace safe. She waited for him to say something else. *Can you hear me?*

When he didn't respond, she wondered if she was hearing things. She turned his hand and touched the pulse at his wrist. It beat slower than she liked but was steady. Somehow it calmed her. She intertwined her fingers with his and forced her mind to brighter things.

An image of the oasis she frequently saw in her dreams floated though her thoughts. She concentrated on the flowers and trees she usually saw there. The colors and scents and sounds. Before she knew it, the cart slowed then stopped.

She held her breath and listened for voices.

One corner of the tarp lifted, letting in a hint of light along with a wave of fresh, cool air. Danet filled her lungs.

"To the address you told me?" Ptah asked.

"Yes. No problem at the gate then?" Gehiji asked.

"Not even a second look," Ptah said.

"Good."

Danet felt the cart dip as Ptah climbed back onto his seat. "Where are we going?" she asked Gehiji.

"I made arrangements for an alternate place to stay as soon as I saw there trouble brewing with Ceros."

"Just in case?"

He shrugged. "One can never be too careful."

"I suppose not."

"Now we need to figure out how to get Ceros inside without drawing attention."

"It's still early, isn't it?" she asked.

"Yes, but as soon as the sun breaks there will be people about. We'll need to move quickly when we arrive."

"All right."

Gehiji cocked his head to one side and stared at Danet. "You've done very well tonight, Danet. I'm impressed. And that's not an easy thing to do."

"Thanks," she said, somewhat puzzled.

"Most of the women we've been around over the last few years are either war- weary cast-outs or pampered court birds. You are neither."

"What kind of birds?"

"Court birds. Women who flock to court to see and be seen by those they believe to be important enough for their attentions."

"Ah." She nodded. She'd seen enough during her years with the queen to avoid them. "I never had the time or the patience for such nonsense."

"Not even if meant a chance at snaring a brave warrior to care for you? Or perhaps even a prince?"

"I know my station and my place." She relaxed her grip on Ceros' hand and let it fall back onto his thigh. "My work fills a very large place in my life. Father and the people who come to the clinic need me. I have no need to sit before a dressing table for hours on end, waiting for a servant to make me beautiful in hopes that someone will ask me to dance or expect me to fill their bed. Only to have them move on to the next pretty face. That life is not for me."

"You are a remarkable woman, Danet."

"No, I am just a woman, Gehiji. But thank you for the thought."

They fell silent. Danet felt the cart make several turns through the streets. She guessed they were in the heart of the city but couldn't tell where exactly. Finally they came to a stop.

Ptah pulled the flap over the cart open more. "This is where you said to bring you."

"Is there anyone about?" Gehiji asked.

"Not that I see on the street in either direction."

"Stay hidden until either I or Ptah tells you to come out," Gehiji said to Danet then he climbed out of the cart. He laughed as he stumbled then slapped Ptah on the shoulder.

From his suddenly slurred speech and his mannerisms, she guessed he was pretending to be drunk. When they reached in to pull Ceros out, she slid farther into the shadows on the other side of the cart.

CHAPTER FOURTEEN

Danet waited for Ptah's return. Every creak of the cart and flutter of the tarp was amplified louder than normal. They were close to removing Ceros from danger and she was anxious to attempt the healing.

It would be both scary and exciting. She'd never attempted it before but felt certain it would work. Particularly if she and Ceros were destined mates.

How much deeper would their connection be after the healing? It was a very intimate form of healing that required her to merge their souls. It would be hard to force them apart later.

She simply couldn't think of later right now. He needed her and she believed this would be the best way to heal him in such a short span of time. Consequences would have to be dealt with.

"Mistress?" Ptah asked when he finally returned.

"I'm here, Ptah."

"I'm to drive to the end of the street then return on the other side of the building. Master Gehiji said when I stop, you need to climb out as if you've done this a hundred times before."

"I can do that," she reassured him.

A few minutes later, Ptah stopped the cart and rapped on the side.

With as much grace as she could summon, she crawled out of the back of the cart with the basket. "Thank you," she said politely.

Ptah grunted and pulled away.

Danet scanned the nearby dwellings. She found Gehiji standing at the entrance of a darkened alley not far away.

When she reached his side, he took her arm. "This way."

He led her to a small courtyard then to a tidy home with a brightly painted door. Gehiji held the door open and allowed her to enter first.

The interior had been designed simply. The furniture was plain but functional and there were few decorative items.

Gehiji led her to a bedroom at the far end of the hallway. Ceros had been placed on one side of the bed. She went to him and felt his skin then found his heartbeat. Steady but still a little slow.

Ceros? she instinctively called to him, but received no response.

"Is he awake yet?" Gehiji asked.

"No," she said, shaking her head.

He had taken the basket from her as soon as they entered the house. He sat it on the small table next to the bed. A pitcher of water and a basin along with linens waited in the corner.

"What will you need while we are here?"

"For now, rest." She removed her bag and set it next to the table. "There is a healing that I want to try on Ceros that I haven't done before. I need to be able to focus so I need some rest and then some quiet time with him."

"I sent messages to a few friends of ours. I expect them before luncheon. Until then, I will stand guard. You rest and then let me know what you need to do this healing."

"Gehiji, I need you to understand something." She rubbed the side of her face as she thought about how to explain. "It's not traditional healing."

"Okay."

"It is something that most people would have trouble believing in even if they saw it happening."

"And?"

"And I don't want to worry or alarm you."

"Unless you're planning to drain all of his blood or hang him upside down by his privates, I doubt anything you do is going to worry me." He put his hand on her shoulder. "Obviously you and Ceros have some kind of connection if you can talk to each other in your heads. And I can see that you care about him and are trying to help. I don't believe you will do anything to deliberately harm him."

"By doing this, I will be revealing to the next king the extent of my gifts. Once he's well, he will have to send me away or order my execution."

Gehiji frowned. "Ceros wouldn't do that."

"He'll have no choice. As king, he cannot ignore royal decrees."

"Believe me when I tell you he will find a way to make it work out for everyone." Gehiji stopped her pacing by reaching for her arm. "Trust me." With a jerk of his chin in Ceros' direction he added, "Trust him."

She searched his eyes and found nothing but sincerity. She nodded. "Do you think he'll see me as an oddity later, when this is all over?"

"Ceros is able to shift into some kind of animal. I've seen one of our friends walk through and control a raging fire with only his thoughts. Another friend has an uncanny knack for finding water, even in the middle of the desert. And I can sense a lie before it leaves a person's lips." He smiled. "No, I don't think he'll see you as an oddity later."

The knot in her chest eased. "Thank you."

He stood. "Get some rest. The alarm will be raised soon and they will start looking for Ceros in earnest."

"All right." Danet smiled. "I won't need much. Just enough to clear my head."

"Take whatever time you need." He approached the door then paused and looked back. "I'm assuming you'd feel better staying here with Ceros. However, if you want a room to yourself, you may use one of the others."

"No, you're right." She blushed. "I'll rest easier here. Thank you though."

He nodded once then shut the door behind him as he left.

Danet extinguished the lamp. Traces of yellow from the rising sun rimmed the bottom of the window.

Exhaustion set in as she climbed up onto the bed. She curled onto her side, facing Ceros, then laid her hand over his heart. The last thing she remembered before she fell asleep was counting his heartbeats.

She dreamed of the oasis. Everything looked the same except she didn't see her beast. She sensed he was there somewhere but couldn't find him even after making her way around the spring.

With a sigh, she sat on a rock next to the water and dipped her toes into the cool liquid. Her beast's reflection shimmered on the surface. She looked up, but he was still nowhere to be seen.

Her heart ached.

In the distance, she heard his roar. She gathered her skirt and ran in that direction. She still couldn't find him.

Frustrated, she called out. "Ceros? Are you there?"

A growl sounded nearby. She spun around but couldn't see through the thick foliage.

"Ceros?"

She jerked awake. It took a moment to remember where she was. Seeing Ceros next to her calmed her.

The urge to touch him had become a powerful thing. She gave in and stroked his cheek then took a deep breath and sat up on the bed.

It was time. She needed to prepare.

From the basket of supplies, she removed her special tea and set it aside. She'd have Gehiji boil some water while she conducted the healing.

Using water from the pitcher in the corner, she washed her face and hands then climbed up onto the bed next to Ceros. Gehiji had removed the robe they had put on him before leaving the palace, making it easier for her to bathe his face and neck. She pulled the sheet down and washed his chest and arms too.

It was a cleansing process but also served to prepare her to connect with Ceros.

She returned the bowl of water to the table and set the dirty linens aside. Before she returned to the bed, the door burst open. A large, dark-headed man stepped in. He had a sword strapped to his side and some kind of weapon in his hand. Something about him warned Danet he was a trained killer.

Without hesitation, she put herself between Ceros and the stranger and called on every form of protection she could remember. She raised a magical shield between them then aimed a burst of wind toward the stranger. He staggered backward but steadied himself at the door.

"I won't let you harm him," Danet shouted.

"Who are you?" The man's voice thundered in the small room.

Danet prepared herself to summon a heat flare when Gehiji pushed his way into the room.

"What's going on?" Gehiji looked from one to the other. "What's all the shouting?"

"What is she doing?" the stranger demanded.

Danet felt the heat in her hand surge.

"Danet. Stop." Gehiji held both hands up, palms facing her. "This is Runihura. He's a friend."

Danet glanced at Gehiji. "A friend?"

"Of mine and Ceros," Gehiji reassured her.

She struggled to calm herself and bank the fire she had stirred inside. Finally she lowered the shield.

Gehiji stepped closer and gestured to Danet. "Runihura, this is Danet. She's a healer and a close friend of Ceros' family."

"If she's such a close friend, why did Ceros never tell us about her?"

"Because we never actually met until he returned." She tucked a strand of hair behind her ear. "I served the queen and Ceros' sisters."

Runihura grunted. "And you are loyal to him as well?"

"I am," she said with a lift of her chin.

"Are you ready to do your healing then?" Gehiji asked.

"I was preparing when he came in." She gestured to Runihura.

"Did you think of anything you need?" Gehiji asked.

"Not for the healing." She retrieved her tea and handed it to Gehiji. "But can you make a pot of this tea? I'll need it afterward."

"I can do that," he assured her.

"Thank you."

"We will leave you to your work then," Gehiji said as he pushed Runihura to the door.

Runihura gave her a slight bow and followed Gehiji.

One of them closed the door, leaving her alone with Ceros once more. She took a deep breath, shaken but determined to at least connect with Ceros even if she couldn't complete the healing.

Thinking it might help, she climbed up onto the bed and knelt beside Ceros. She placed one hand on his chest and another on his forehead then closed her eyes.

Ceros? Can you hear me?

In the scattered debris that was their consciousness, she searched for the thread of their connection. In the distance she saw something gold sparkling with tiny fragments of light. She drew closer then reached for it and held tight.

Ceros? Are you there?

The thread began to dissolve and she fought to hang on. She

remembered the fire she had been forced to bank when Runihura had startled her. Drawing on the warmth and passion of her feelings, she pushed energy through to Ceros.

His consciousness flickered.

Come on, Ceros. Help me find you.

Here.

She heard his faint response and it gave her hope. She pushed more energy to Ceros and the connection snapped into place.

Danet.

There you are. She sighed in relief.

What's going on? Even in her head, he sounded weak.

You've been unconscious for most of a day. I haven't been able reach you. We've all been very worried. Do you remember anything?

Not really. The last thing I clearly remember is you talking to me. You said you were going home to see your father.

That's right. I left and while I was gone someone came in and stuck you with two more thorns. We didn't find one of them for hours. I'm sorry.

It's not your fault, Danet.

I shouldn't have left.

It's not for you to guard me. He sighed. *I assume Mother has increased the security around my room.*

Well...

Danet. His tone held all kinds of warning. *What did she do?*

Your mother did nothing, really, just let Gehiji and me do what we felt was best.

And that was?

We kidnapped you.

He fell silent.

Are you still there? she asked.

You and Gehiji kidnapped me, the prince, from the palace while I was unconscious.

Yes.

You realize they will send all of the guards after you, don't you?

Gehiji is aware of that.

And your plan is what exactly? He sounded more tired than angry.

I'm to heal you. Gehiji has asked some friends of yours to come help. Some big, scary-looking man named Runi-something showed up a few minutes ago.

If he sent for the people I suspect, I won't worry nearly as much. The palace guards will never get near you if they're here.

Are the others as intimidating as this one?

They will be skilled in their own way, but Runihura is a bit frightening at first glance.

Just a bit. Okay. While we are connected and before any more big, scary men show up, I want to try something. A healing. But it isn't a traditional healing method. It's something my mother wrote about.

Some of your mystic abilities?

Yes.

All right.

You're okay with trying it?

Will it harm either of us or anyone around us?

Not if everything goes the way it should.

Then what's the problem?

It's a very intimate form of healing. I have to merge our life forces in order to push the poison from your body. The connection we share now will probably intensify after this healing. You need to be sure that you want that. That you can handle knowing I've glimpsed into your very soul.

If you had been unable to reach me to ask me what I would want, what would you have done?

I would have attempted to do it anyway.

Then why do you ask now?

Because I see it as the ultimate invasion of your privacy. I won't do it if you tell me no. If I hadn't been able to reach you very soon, I would have taken it as a sign that you were too far gone and possibly in a life-threatening situation.

I'm not seeing where the situation is all that different. Do whatever you think is best to heal me. I trust you, Danet.

Thank you. I just hope you remember that when you can hear my thoughts from across the city and know that I can hear yours.

We'll deal with that later.

She took a deep breath. *Okay. Let's see about pushing that poison out then. I need you to relax and let me in. All of your defenses must come down, Ceros. I give you my word that I won't pry or dig into memories. But I need to be able to come all the way in.*

How will you know it worked?

I suspect we'll both know.

In the space she occupied within their joined consciousness, she saw a room surrounded by a golden curtain. She walked up to but couldn't find an opening. She ran her hands over the silky fabric, searching before realizing the entrance would not be one a physical body would use.

She closed her eyes and sank against the billowing panel. As she did, it gave way and allowed her to seep through. She took a large step and felt the feather light caress of the silk over her entire body. When she opened her eyes, she was in the same room she had dreamed of the day before. Gold walls. The raised platform bed. Glistening white sheets covered the bed and iridescent sheers fluttered about the posts.

She expected to find her beast lying on top of the bed. Instead, it was empty.

Gazing around the chamber, she became vaguely aware of light reflecting off the gold that surrounded her. She was far more interested in finding Ceros. Or her beast. Or perhaps both.

"Am I dreaming again?" a voice from behind her asked.

Danet turned slowly. Ceros stood across the room. His golden hair fell in waves down the back of his neck. He wore a simple white cloth around his waist and a gold band bearing his family emblem about his upper arm. His bare chest glistened in the light as if it had been bathed with oil. The sight of him stirred something deep within her. "You have been here before too?"

He moved toward her, but not directly. He circled the perimeter of the room as if he were stalking prey. "Yes. And not long ago."

She turned to keep her eyes on him. "Were you alone?"

"No, I was not."

"Were you beast or man?"

He stopped circling and asked quietly. "Why do you ask me this?"

"In my dream, the last time I was here, my beast was too." She took a step in Ceros' direction. "But he was attacked by something I couldn't see and he ran from me. I should like very much to know if beast and man are one."

Ceros took a few steps closer. "The last time I found this place, it was as a beast. And my lady of light comforted me. Something disturbed my dream and forced me from this place and from my lady."

"And do you sometimes find your lady in a lush oasis in your dreams?" she asked, taking another step closer.

"I do." He took a couple steps in her direction. "We walk. She tells me her secrets and sometimes she sings. It brings peace to my troubled heart and mind."

"And the great beast is always gentle with her. He offers her comfort and companionship in her lonely existence."

He reached for a lock of her hair. "Is it possible that you were the girl turned woman who has haunted my dreams all these years?"

"It is possible but I don't understand the why." They stared into each other's eyes, both unsure what to say or do.

Suddenly Ceros' legs buckled. Danet moved to catch him. "What's wrong?"

He shook his head. "A moment of weakness." He touched his head. "And a bit of dizziness."

"You should lie down." She steered him to the raised platform.

"I've been lying down for days," he groused. "I shouldn't need to in a dream." Thankfully he was able to climb the platform with nothing more than a little steadying.

He sat on the edge of the bed and she helped raise his feet to the mattress. "We need to do the healing before this gets any worse or you may not recover."

"At the moment I'm not inclined to argue. What do we need to do?"

"The only information I have is from my mother's journal. She performed it on my father when he became sick with an unshakable fever."

"And?"

"She didn't say exactly what she did." Danet blushed. "But she left enough information that, as an adult, I believe they had an intimate encounter and that was the catalyst for their merging."

His brows lifted in surprise. "An intimate encounter?"

"Not that I'm suggesting we do the same thing," she stammered.

"Well, now I'm disappointed." He gave her a half grin.

"Oh stop. You know you're attractive. And I'm sure you've traipsed around in my head enough to know I'm not immune to your appeal. But I don't want you to think I'm making this whole thing up just to get into your bed."

He sat up and leaned closer. "I don't believe that anyone, much less you, could be deceitful enough to pull this off." He gestured to the room they were in.

"I suppose it would be difficult to create all of this." She smiled ruefully.

Ceros lifted her chin until she looked at him. "I've been in your head, Danet. I trust you. And I believe you sincerely want to help me. So, what do you suggest we do to trigger this merging?"

"Touch is probably important," she suggested.

"I believe touch is very important."

Danet hesitantly placed one hand over his heart. She looked up into his eyes, seeking confirmation that he was not offended by what she did.

The warmth of his skin flowed up her arm and into her chest.

He cupped her face in his hand then slid his fingers into her hair. When he reached the back of her head, he pulled her forward, slowly. Their eyes were locked on each other until their lips met.

She felt as if she were floating on air.

Ceros fell back onto the bed and pulled her with him. Their tender kiss quickly turned into one of hunger and need. She may be inexperienced, but she knew what she felt and she knew she wanted Ceros. He teased her lips with the tip of his tongue, daring her to follow him.

She took his challenge.

He slid his hands up and down her back, pressing her body even closer against his rock-hard form. His erection pressed into her hip, making her both anxious and excited.

Soon they were both breathless.

He gripped handfuls of her gown and slid the thin material up her back until she felt the cool air on her backside. Using one knee, he parted her thighs then set her back on her haunches, forcing her to straddle him.

With her hair falling about her face as she leaned over him, her weight on her hands at either side of his shoulders, she felt downright hedonistic.

"We probably shouldn't be doing this," she whispered.

"I'll stop if you tell me to."

"But I don't want you to stop."

"Good. Because I don't want to stop either."

He pulled her down for another kiss. This one she felt down to her toes. Then he rolled her to one side so they were facing each other. When he pulled her knee up onto his hip his erection pressed against her. The only thing separating them was the cloth wrapped around his waist.

Her hips surged in response.

Ceros tugged at the clasp at her shoulder and the front of her gown fell open. His work-roughened hand palmed one of her breasts. He flicked his thumb across the pink bud, making her moan.

He pushed her back against the bed and leaned down to take the delicate tip into his mouth. Using his lips, his tongue and even his teeth, he teased and tormented first one then the other nipple until she writhed beneath him.

She grasped his head, trying to pull him closer.

When he slipped one hand between her thighs, her breath caught in her throat. His fingers caressed her then drove her to the brink of madness. The intimate invasion was more than she could take. She thrashed about, afraid of the intensity of the feeling building inside her, but he used his body to prevent her from fleeing.

She felt as if she were a spring and he was winding her tighter and tighter with each flick of his fingers. In her haze of sensation she became vaguely aware that he had repositioned them. Without warning, he locked his lips onto her core. When she remembered to breathe it came in short gasps. The things he did with his tongue wound that spring even tighter, overriding her instinct to run and hide in embarrassment.

Her hands gripped the silky sheets and she tried desperately to hold on to something solid while her body writhed under his ministrations.

Then it happened. A dam burst inside her. She saw lights behind her eyes and she felt as if her body had turned into a river of water that now rushed off a rocky mountaintop. The sensation of falling continued until Ceros wrapped her in his arms.

When she opened her eyes he was leaning over her.

"There you are."

"Here I am." She smiled and ran her hands up his broad back to his shoulders.

"I wanted to make sure you were with me when we were joined." He shifted his hips and aimed the tip of his cock at her entrance. "Tell me you want this, Danet. There will be no going back once we do. Our joining will mark you as mine."

"I want this, Ceros," she whispered and urged him to kiss her.

"Thank the Gods," he groaned as he captured her lips and her body in one swift motion.

His invasion made her stiffen in resistance, but his kisses and the flicks of his thumb across her breast distracted her. Her instincts flared to life, urging her to wrap her legs around his thighs. She arched her back, encouraging him to show her more. Slowly he began to move, creating a delicious friction between her legs.

It didn't take her long to join his rhythmic movements.

She clung to his back, silently begging for more. In the haze of her mind she became aware of Ceros' grip on her hip and his heavy breathing.

The tension quickly built inside her until the fluttering where they were joined began. She arched her back and let go of all that she knew.

Ceros called her name as the starburst went off in her head.

Instead of the free fall sensation she expected, they were surrounded by a pulsing white light. It beat in time with their combined hearts and pounded a rhythm in their ears. Still they clung to each other as they floated in nothingness.

Danet was beyond speech. She got lost in Ceros' gaze as she caressed his chin and the base of his throat with the pad of her finger.

It was peaceful there, hovering above any physical plane of existence, locked in each other's arms.

But something called them back to reality.

Danet felt their bodies being pulled back to the bed, then from the gold room and through the frail curtain.

She tried to call out to Ceros but had no voice.

As she became aware of her body, her physical body, she realized how heavy her limbs felt. She forced her eyes open and found herself slumped against Ceros' chest. It took considerable effort to lift her head to check on him.

Relief swept through her when his eyes opened. She said a prayer of thanks for having been able to remove enough of the poison from his system.

"You," he whispered when his eyes landed on her. His voice was rough but didn't sound as weak as she expected. "You did it." He lifted a hand to stroke her cheek. "Thank you."

"I'm just glad it worked." She let her head fall onto his chest. Exhaustion weighed heavily on her.

"Are you all right?" he asked as he tilted her head back. A frown formed a little V in the middle of his forehead.

"Just tired." She smiled at him.

He gently slid out from underneath her then rolled her onto her back. He kissed her and said, "I feel as if I could drink all of the water in the Genoa River."

Danet sighed against his lips. Despite her exhaustion, her blood still ran hot for Ceros. She wished she had the strength to physically do what they had just done in spirit form.

"You rest. I need to see Gehiji."

"Be careful getting up," she cautioned him. "You haven't used your legs for several days." Even to her own ears, her voice sounded weak. She knew there would be a price for doing the healing and right now she felt as if she could sleep for the next five moons.

"I will go slow." Ceros' words faded as she succumbed to her body's demand for rest.

CHAPTER FIFTEEN

Ceros sat on the edge of the bed, watching Danet sleep.

Curled on her side, she rested her hand where his body had been. As if she reached for him, even in her sleep.

What an amazing woman. Whether she understood what he had meant or not, she was now his. She would be his bride and his queen. There could be no other for him. He would deal with any court politics that came about.

No stranger to injury and recovery, Ceros followed her advice and took his time getting up. It was good he hadn't been down any longer than he had and felt certain his strength would return quickly. A few rounds of training would probably help him sweat out the last of the poison.

Now he needed to find out who was behind it.

He paused at the door to take one more look at Danet. His body burned with unfulfilled desire. Their joining gave him a feeling of completion, but his physical need remained. He promised himself he would have her in his bed without the threat of someone trying to kill him hanging over their heads.

And it would be soon.

He stepped into the hallway and softly closed the door behind him. He listened for sounds to determine which way to go.

Before he had taken two steps, Runihura blocked his path.

"Ceros." Runihura seemed surprised. And that was a hard thing to do. "We thought you were near death."

Ceros smiled and leaned against the wall for support. "I might have been."

"Let's get you to the kitchen before you fall over and that little lady comes after me again." Runihura offered his assistance.

Ceros declined his help but used the wall to steady himself. "Again?"

Gehiji laughed as he turned the corner and stepped into the hallway. "Our big friend here startled Danet when he arrived unannounced. She was just about to call down the heavens on him when I came in and stopped her."

Ceros didn't know which he surprised him more, Runihura's discomfort or the fact she defended him so fiercely. "What did she threaten you with? One of the poisonous thorns?"

They both shook their heads as Runihura helped him take a seat at the small kitchen table.

"I don't know what she was doing or what she is capable of doing but her eyes glowed and I swear she had smoke coming from her fingertips," Runihura said. "I've never seen anything like it."

Gehiji chuckled. "It's the first time I've ever seen him ready to leave a fight."

"You would have too if she'd been looking at you that way," Runihura said defiantly.

"True. But she wasn't, so it's funny," Gehiji jested with Runihura.

Runihura made a less-than-polite hand gesture at Gehiji.

Smoke? Ceros was stunned. He needed to learn the extent of her abilities. Abilities that she had somehow kept hidden from the world, until now.

Gehiji turned serious. "So how is it that an hour ago, you looked as if you were ten steps from death's door and now you're walking around?" He grabbed Ceros' shoulder. "Even if you aren't walking steady, it's more than you've done for days. What did she do to you?"

"I'm not entirely sure." He wasn't about to disclose everything that occurred between them but he couldn't lie. Especially not to Gehiji. "She connected her soul with mine and somehow that joining forced the poison out."

"Where did the poison go?" Runihura asked with his usual bluntness.

"I don't know." Ceros frowned. "Out, I guess."

"It couldn't have just vanished. It's a tangible thing," Runihura reasoned. "It had to go somewhere."

"Maybe she burned it up?" Gehiji suggested with a grin.

Runihura gave Gehiji a dark look.

"Where is Danet?" Gehiji asked.

"She fell asleep," Ceros said.

"The water is hot enough to make her tea. Do you think I should take it in or wait 'til she comes out?"

"What tea?" Ceros asked.

Gehiji shrugged. "She asked me to make it for her. Said she'd probably need it after the healing."

"I suppose I should take it to her if she asked for it. It may have herbs she needs."

"I'll take the water off the fire and add the tea. That will give it a chance to cool first." Gehiji went to take care of it.

"What have I missed the last couple of days?" Ceros asked. The three of them took up more space than the tiny kitchen was meant to accommodate.

"Don't ask me. I only know what he," Runihura pointed to Gehiji, "has told me." "After you went down, I monitored your immediate area," Gehiji said. "When I saw your mother had things under control, I expanded my watch to the palace in general." He grinned. "Found a helpful little thing in the dining hall who provided me with insight into your staff."

"Did you learn anything other than someone is smart enough to put the pretty girls in the dining hall as opposed to the sleeping quarters?" Ceros asked.

"Some. After Danet said you wanted me to look into the council members, I started digging."

"Are they as stodgy as I fear they may be?" Ceros asked with a grimace.

"Stodgy isn't the right word. I couldn't place my finger on it, but my alarms went off anytime I heard the top members speak. They just ooze lies."

"Wonderful," Ceros mumbled. "What about Danet?"

"You have nothing to worry about there. From what I could tell she is well-respected at the palace by both servants and the queen. By your sisters too. Haven't learned much on her father yet, but it hasn't been a priority." He gave Ceros a meaningful look. "I can step up the efforts if I need to rush it."

Ceros waved his answer away. "No, not yet."

Gehiji made a harrumph sound. "Back to the council. I did learn who their top picks would be if the council were to have to choose the next ruler."

"Who?"

"A man named Shenti and your cousin, Aleric."

"Aleric?"

"Apparently there is some belief that he would be a natural choice since he is the closest male relative through your father's line," Gehiji said.

"He would be the closest male relative but I've never had any indication to make me think he would even be interested in sitting on the throne."

"People change," Runihura reminded them.

"True," Ceros said, a frown forming between his brows. "What do you know about Shenti?"

"He's a third-generation council member. Not a very strong personality. Easily led. If the council wants a figurehead sitting on the throne, he would an ideal choice."

Ceros grunted. "So he's not someone who could or would orchestrate the poisoning?"

"Highly unlikely," Gehiji said. "And given his preference for cleanliness and the pampered life, I don't see him getting his hands dirty gathering thorns from a hard-to- find plant."

"What do you think the next move will be?" Ceros asked.

"They're going to want to seat their own man on the throne," Gehiji speculated. "If not on the throne, at least in a position of power. The council meeting will give them that chance. We need to make sure you are there. And healthy. You will have to demonstrate you are able to rule."

"Thanks to Danet, that won't be a problem," Ceros said proudly.

As usual, Runihura pointed out the obvious. "We still have to get you into the meeting."

"Mother will know where it will be held."

"We'll just need to keep you away from thorns until then," Gehiji joked.

Ceros?

I'm in the kitchen with Gehiji and Runihura. Are you all right? I woke and you were gone.

Everything is fine. I'll come back in a moment.

"Danet is awake," Ceros relayed. "I should take her tea in."

"Can you carry it?" Gehiji asked with a lift of his eyebrow.

"I think so. My energy has been returning even as we talked."

"How about if you only take the cup instead of the whole pot. Just in case," Gehiji suggested.

Ceros grinned ruefully as he stood. "Perhaps that isn't a bad suggestion."

"I'll send a note to your mother asking for the information on the council meeting."

"Good idea." Ceros took the cup of tea from Gehiji. "I'll be out shortly."

"Take your time," Runihura said. "You're going to need the rest."

"I didn't know you cared," Ceros teased.

"I don't want to have to carry your sorry ass into the council meeting," Runihura said gruffly. "Extra weapons would be more helpful."

Ceros shook his head as he turned toward the hall, tea in hand. Behind him he heard Gehiji chuckling.

When he opened the door to their room, he found it much lighter than when he'd left. The sun now shone brightly since there nothing shielded it in the window. Yet somehow Danet was able to sleep.

Danet? he called softly.

Her legs moved under the sheet. She slid one arm over her face and burrowed deeper into her pillow.

I have your tea. Gehiji said you thought you'd need it.

Ceros? She sounded exhausted, even in his head.

He sat on the edge of the bed. "I didn't know how long I should let you sleep."

She peeked from underneath her arm. "You look better. How are you feeling?"

"A little wobbly but good. Whatever you did worked. Remarkably well."

Even with her face half covered, he could see her cheeks turn pink. Recalling their intimate encounter made him harden instantly.

He set the cup on a nearby table. "Here." He reached to help her. "Let's sit you up so you can take your tea."

"Oh, my prince," she mumbled. "There's no need for you to do that. I can do it. I just need a moment."

"Danet," he said her name softly and waited until she looked him in the eye. "Please don't 'my prince' me. After everything we've been through the past couple of days there should be no formality between us."

"But my—"

He placed one finger over her lips. "I'm quite serious. Unless you are using it as an endearment, you will only anger me. It's Ceros." Her eyes widened at the mention of endearment. "But not 'my prince'. Never again. Do you understand?"

Ceros held his breath until she slowly nodded her agreement. He removed his finger from her lips without giving in to the temptation to trace the outline, and reached for her tea.

"Drink," he said, lifting the cup to her delicate pink lips.

She automatically tried to take the cup from him, but he refused to relinquish his hold. Her tiny hands covered his and guided the cup.

He was mesmerized by her mouth, especially when her tongue darted out to catch a wayward drop of tea.

The red staining her cheeks contrasted against the paleness of her skin.

"Thank you," she mumbled.

He had to clear his throat to speak properly. "I assume this is some kind of herbal tea."

She nodded slowly. "Yes. It was my mother's recipe. I use herbs from the garden at home."

"It smells pleasant."

"You are welcome to try it. There should have been enough for a whole pot."

He turned the cup and took a sip from the exact spot she had been drinking from. Her eyes widened once again at the intimacy his action implied.

"Not bad," he said without dropping his gaze. "I doubt I'd want it every day, but it has a soothing taste."

"I, uh…" Danet blinked, as if trying to clear her mind before speaking. "It's not meant to be an everyday tea. I only have it when I've overdone it at the clinic or with my studies."

He held the steaming mug out for her to take another sip. Her hand closed around his wrist and she guided the cup to her mouth.

"Gehiji has been catching us up on what happened over the last day or two," he said as he watched her take several small sips in a row. "As soon as you feel rested, I'd like for you to come listen. You may have some thoughts we hadn't considered." He shrugged. "Besides, you know the palace and the schedules people keep better than any of us."

She seemed surprised by his invitation but quickly recovered. "Yes. All right."

Ceros put one hand on her shoulder to make her stay reclined against her pillows. "But not until you are rested."

Danet's lips lifted in a half grin. "So you're the physician now instead of the patient?"

"Something like that," he answered with a half grin of his own.

She took a few more sips. "Ceros, about this connection—"

The one where I can hear your thoughts and you can hear mine?

Yes, that one. She continued, "I need to explain something."

"Yes, you do, but not now."

A frown creased her brow in a charming way. "But there's something you need to know."

"I'm sure there is, but it will have to wait. We need to make plans to get into the high council meeting tomorrow. This," he touched a finger to his forehead then touched hers, "isn't going away and neither are you. But I need to focus on the council meeting. We will talk after."

Ceros silently gave thanks that Danet was intelligent enough to grasp the importance of what they needed to accomplish. Despite her instinct to argue, she relented and simply nodded.

"Rest as long as you need. Gehiji will keep your tea warm."

"What about you? Shouldn't you be resting too?"

If he didn't know how tired she really was, he would think she offered him more than concern. One part of him wished that were true. "As a matter of fact, Runihura suggested the very same thing." He shook his head. "You don't want to hear the rest of his thoughts on it, though."

"I can well imagine." She looked around the room. "Do they have another room for you or am I in your bed?"

"You are welcome to climb into my bed any time you wish," he said with a wink then waited for her cheeks to turn that delightful shade of pink again.

She didn't disappoint. "Now you're trying to embarrass me."

"Absolutely." He grinned shamelessly.

"I can move to one of the other rooms so you can rest." She

tugged the sheet aside to get out of the bed.

Once more he put his hand on her shoulder to stop her. "You will rest here with me."

She shook her head. "I can't do that. It wouldn't be proper."

"I don't care what's proper and what's not." He pushed her back against the pillows as she tried to rise. "I will not relax if I don't know you're safe and sleeping comfortably."

"What will Gehiji think?" She tried to sit up once again.

"He'll know that we're resting, as we both should be, and he'll think nothing more than that."

"I am an unmated woman and you are an unmated man. We cannot share a room, much less a bed."

"People do it all the time and think nothing of it."

"I'm not most people." She crossed her arms over her chest.

"I like that about you."

"And neither are you." Danet caught him by surprise by sitting up then poking him in the chest. "You're the prince."

"A fact I am well aware of," he mumbled as he rubbed the spot on his chest where she had poked him.

"You can't just go around sleeping with anyone you want to." Instead of replying, he lifted one brow.

"Yes, well," she became flustered and waved her hand back and forth as if to brush away what she had just said. "You know what I mean. Propriety must be maintained."

"Propriety be dammed," he growled. "I'm not letting you out of my sight unless I know you are safe. So, lie down so we can both get some rest."

Her mouth fell open in shock but she recovered quickly. She took a deep breath as if to argue but he narrowed his gaze in warning.

He could tell she struggled to comply. Finally she flopped back against the pillows and crossed her arms over her chest again.

Ceros got up and walked around to the other side of the bed. It wasn't as large as his, but it would do. Besides, it forced them to lie closer to each other.

He lay down then rolled onto his side so he faced her. She squeaked in alarm when he reached across her waist and pulled her snug against him. The faint smell of berries wafted up from her hair. He closed his eyes and took a deep breath.

Unfortunately one part of him was attuned to the fact that

Danet was in his arms. And that part now pressed against her hip. Given the way she stiffened and held still, she was aware of his discomfort.

"Relax, Danet," he mumbled. "We both need to rest."

It was a gradual process, but eventually she softened and fell asleep again. In her sleep she burrowed closer. A telling sign of her trust and level of comfort with him.

Why then did she seem so anxious to go to another room? After making love to her in their minds, he was ready to do it with their bodies. Meanwhile, he was loath to let her get very far away until he could claim her.

She indicated she was concerned about propriety, but there was no one around except Gehiji and Runihura. She may not realize it but they would never call anyone out by claiming a lack of decorum. There had to be more that worried her.

Sleep crept over him as he held Danet. His reality faded into dream.

CHAPTER SIXTEEN

The sun had ridden high in the sky but their oasis was lush and green without a hint of the desert heat.

Danet turned her head to the side when the shadow of a swaleena bird flying over the water caught her attention. She let her fingers trail across the carpet of lush grass she lay on and wondered if Ceros would appear as himself or as her beast.

As if thinking of him summoned him, his shadow fell across her body.

She allowed herself the luxury of drinking in his beauty. Sunlight glistened on the hard lines of his body. The linen he wore draped around his waist hid little from her view. Not that she was complaining. In this dream world Ceros was a man, not a prince or patient.

She marveled at how godlike he appeared. Gold sparkled in his hair. His skin glistened with freshly applied oil. Perhaps he had been touched by the Gods when they gifted him with the beast.

"It's strange how I could never see your face until now," Ceros said.

Danet shrugged. "The Gods must have had their reasons for hiding it."

Ceros dropped to his knees next to her. "Perhaps."

She sat up then mirrored his kneeling position. Her eyes roamed across his shoulders and chest. Before she could stop herself, she reached out to touch him. It mesmerized her to see muscle ripple beneath her fingertips.

She didn't make it as far as his shoulder before he grabbed her wandering hand and brought it to his lips. He held her gaze as he turned her wrist and pressed a kiss to her palm. She shivered as his tongue skimmed across the surface up to the tip of her middle finger.

Ceros didn't give her a chance to catch her breath before he reached for her and pulled her against him. His desire burned hot in his gaze. He gave her no time to think before laying siege to her lips.

Her insides turned to putty as he deepened their kiss. With the tip of his tongue he teased and tantalized. She was helpless to resist his urging.

It had been years since she had been with a man, but her body instinctively knew what it wanted. The thin layer of silk covering her breasts was no barrier to the heat rolling off Ceros. Her fingers trailed across the ridges of hard muscle in his arms as they moved up his shoulders to his neck.

The urge to lose herself in his kiss was great but she held out, wanting to memorize every inch of him while she had the chance. Her palm scraped against Ceros' cheek and chin. The rough patch tickled, making her fingers curl into a light caress.

She hooked one hand around the back of his neck and pulled herself even closer against him. Their breaths mingled into one. Each fed on the other. Their lips stroked, nipped, pulled and soothed.

Shifting her weight backward, she showed him what she wanted. What she craved. He followed readily, but caught their joined weight before he fell upon her. Slowly he lowered himself onto her body.

Danet reveled in the feel of his hard, masculine form above her. It shielded her from the sun and the grasses blowing nearby in the breeze. Everything except him.

The silk wrap she wore felt heavy against her skin. She wanted no barriers between them. Nothing except the combined sweat from their bodies. She squirmed and tried to get closer.

She freed her leg from the fabric and wrapped her foot around Ceros' calf.

His hand cupped her breast. He squeezed gently then flicked his thumb across her nipple.

She arched her back, silently begging for more.

Ceros shifted his body and kissed his way down her neck to her breast. He suckled her through the silk.

Danet moaned and sank her fingers into his hair, trying to hold him in place.

He moved to the other breast, pulling the silk aside as he did. His warm breath sent shivers down her spine. When his lips clamped around the nipple, quivers rippled through her lower belly.

He lifted his head. "You know this isn't real, don't you? That we're dreaming again."

"It is real. We just aren't using our physical bodies." She squirmed beneath him, urging him to continue.

"I want more, Danet. I want you. All of you."

He captured her gaze. His need for her was clearly written on his face and in his eyes. She sensed there was more to what he was feeling than physical desire. It mirrored her own needs.

Danet knew it was pointless to resist. She was destined to make love with Ceros. She would deal with any consequences later. For now, she would gather these precious memories and hold them close to her heart.

Reaching up, she touched her hand to his cheek. When she lifted to press her lips against his she whispered, "Then wake, my prince, and take what you want of me."

Darkness fell around her like a curtain.

When she woke, it was to the feel of Ceros' hand cupping her breast as he nuzzled her neck. She arched her back, forcing her breast farther into his palm and her rear into his crotch. His erection pressed against her.

She smiled knowing he was awake too.

His hand slipped beneath her tunic then found her breast again. Anxious to feel his skin against hers, she wiggled and pulled the bunched fabric over her head.

Ceros rolled her to her back. Leaning up on his forearm, he admired her bared breasts. She blushed under his scrutiny. Almost reverently he caressed first one and then the other.

"So beautiful," he murmured.

When his lips closed around her nipple, her breath caught in her throat. The flicks of his tongue alternating with suction drove her wild with need. She pulled helplessly at his shoulder, trying to draw him closer.

His hand slipped beneath the waist of her pants and found the delicate folds between her legs. The dual sensations fractured her thoughts and sent her desire spiraling higher.

Her hips jerked when his finger found her sensitive bud. With slow, deliberate strokes he drew small circles on and around the peak. Danet's breath came in short gasps.

She moaned his name.

He kissed his way down her ribs to her belly then lifted his head and adjusted his position. Danet opened her eyes a fraction and saw him kneeling next to her. He reached for her pants and pulled them down to her thighs. She raised her knees to help him slip the garment the rest of the way off.

As soon as he dropped the pants to the floor, he grabbed her leg that was closest to him and drew her ankle up to his shoulder. Turning his head slightly, he licked and kissed a trail down her calf and thighs. Before she could catch her breath, he buried his face in her curls and found her clit.

His talented tongue danced over the sensitive nub, making her writhe on the bed. Her fingers dug into the sheets beneath her as she struggled to hold on to reality.

Ceros pulled her legs over his shoulders then he raised her hips off the mattress. Blood rushed to her head when he lifted her even higher and increased the laps against her clit. When he sucked the swollen nub into his mouth, Danet stiffened and a hundred stars burst inside her head.

The last of her mental shields dropped and her pleasure flooded Ceros' mind.

He groaned then grabbed her behind the knees and pulled her legs around his waist. He aimed his cock at her entrance and slid into her silky depths.

The feel of him buried inside her made her want to weep with joy. The friction from his cock sliding in and out reset her orgasm and sent her spiraling upward again.

Ceros came down on top of her, changing the angle of his penetration. He dropped his own shields, allowing her to feel how close to the edge he was.

Their blended passion was more than she could process. Danet clung to Ceros as the stars fell from the heavens once more. This time she didn't fall alone. Ceros groaned then collapsed against her.

Afterward, they both struggled to catch their breath as they tiptoed around the oddness of having another person in their heads at such a vulnerable moment.

As soon as he was able, Ceros rolled to the side to take his weight off her. He collapsed on the mattress then reached over and pulled her into his arms.

She snuggled against his chest and listened to his heart beating against his ribs.

Her exhaustion weighed heavily upon her and she struggled to keep her eyes open.

With the last of her waning strength she touched the edges of his mind, curious to know if he enjoyed their coupling half as much as she. She felt a deep sense of satisfaction and calm. Beyond that feeling she thought she detected a low rumble.

A sound much like a purr.

She smiled to herself. Apparently her beast enjoyed it as well.

CHAPTER SEVENTEEN

Ceros used the rest of the water in the basin to clean both of them. After he dressed he held a hand out to Danet. "Have you recovered sufficiently or do you need to rest longer?"

She took a deep breath then slipped her hand into his. "I suppose I can get up if you can."

He smirked as he helped her sit up. "Why does that sound somewhat insulting to me?" He brought her hand to his lips and placed a gentle kiss on the back.

The faint blush that stained her cheeks was charming.

"I only meant that you've been ill for the last three days." She tugged the sheet tighter around her ribs. "Even I'm surprised you've recovered so well."

He moved in closer, forcing her knees apart as he stepped between them. "It's all thanks to you, you know," he said softly as he leaned in for a kiss.

"Oh, I didn't do—" He stopped what she started to say by pressing his lips to hers. "I just..." She bit her lip.

What was it about her that made him feel like grinning from ear to ear? "Just say you're welcome."

"I didn't hear you say thank you," she pointed out.

His smile broadened. He leaned closer but maintained eye contact with her. When he was only a breath away, he whispered, "Thank you, Danet." He gently touched his lips to hers. "Thank you for saving me."

"You're welcome."

Ceros caressed her cheek. "Come. Let's find out what Gehiji and Runihura are planning."

She nodded. "Okay. Give me a minute to get dressed."

He picked her discarded tunic and pants up off the floor and set them on the bed beside her. "I'll wait for you."

She ducked her head and shifted nervously on the edge of the mattress. "You realize I'm not used to anyone watching me as I dress, don't you?"

He placed one hand on the mattress on either side of her thighs and leaned in until they were eye to eye. "You realize I plan on seeing a lot more of you as you dress and undress, don't you?"

Danet's eyes widened and she swallowed loudly enough for him to hear. "You do?"

"Yes. I do." He gave her a quick kiss on the mouth. "Now. What can I help you with?"

"I, uh." She picked up her tunic and held it against her chest. "A brush would nice. Would you mind digging around in my bag for one?" She pointed to the corner. "It's the brown one with multicolored birds."

He took his time locating the bag and the brush to allow her a chance to dress in relative privacy. He wasn't so callous that he didn't recognize her discomfort, but he had no intention of letting her out of his sight any more than necessary. Some instinct declared she was his to protect and demanded he keep her nearby.

When the rustling of fabric stopped he held up the brush. "Is this what you wanted?"

"Yes, that's it." She took it from him with a smile.

It soothed him to watch her take down her hair then run the brush through the strands. When this was over he planned to spend several nights running his fingers, and maybe a brush too, through her silken tresses.

Even watching her weave the long mass into a single braid fascinated him.

"Okay. That will have to do," Danet said as she put her things back in her bag.

"You're beautiful," he said as he caressed her cheek then reached for her braid.

She blushed. "Thank you for thinking so."

"You don't believe me?"

She shrugged. "I'm just me."

"And you are beautiful." He put one finger on her lips. "We can argue about it later. Let's get out there and see what's going on."

From behind his finger, Danet nodded her agreement.

He took her hand and led her to the kitchen. Ceros stopped at the edge of the room when he found yet another of his friends, Mdjai, slouched over a cup of tea, reading a book. His oversized form looked out of place at the table.

Mdjai turned and looked over his shoulder at them. The beads in his dark braids glinted in the light as they fell across his shoulder.

"About time you crawled your sorry ass out of bed."

Ceros cleared his throat and gestured to Danet with his head.

Mdjai rose from his chair and took a step in their direction. He gave a short bow and clarified, "I meant his sorry ass, not yours, my lady."

Ceros closed his eyes and briefly shook his head. "Mdjai. As always, it's a pleasure to see you." They clasped hands and slapped each other on the shoulder. Ceros gestured to Danet. "This is Danet."

Mdjai took her hand and bowed over it as he mumbled a greeting in his native language.

Ceros gave a silent prayer of thanks Danet didn't understand Mdjai had just given her what amounted to a royal greeting. "Danet, this is Mdjai, yet another of our brothers in arms."

"It's very nice to meet you, Mdjai. It's very good of all of you to come so far to assist Prince Ceros."

"Assist?" Mdjai grunted. "I came because I heard a little wisp of a lady had set Runihura back on his heels." He leaned down until he was eye level with Danet. "That wouldn't have been you, now would it?"

Danet's cheeks turned pink again. "I, uh…" She looked from one of them to the other. "I don't think I did."

Ceros nodded.

Mdjai burst into a full belly laugh, making the cups on the counter rattle.

"Speaking of Runihura, where is he?" Ceros asked as he gestured for Danet to take a seat at the table.

Once Mdjai got his laughter under control, he waved to the door at the far end of the room. "He said he would be the lookout on the roof. Something about getting familiar with his surroundings."

"Hmm." He probably wanted to get away from Mdjai. Obviously Gehiji had shared the story of Runihura meeting Danet. And Ceros was certain Gehiji didn't paint Runihura in a flattering light. "What about Gehiji?"

"That weakling said something about needing sleep. Said to wake him if anything interesting happened."

"We were up most of the night last night getting Ceros out of the palace. He has to be tired," Danet said, trying to stick up for Gehiji.

Mdjai raised an eyebrow then glanced at Ceros.

Ceros shook his head to cut off any unflattering remark Mdjai might have made. Danet wouldn't know they were trained to go for days without sleep.

"Danet, would you like another cup of your tea?" Ceros asked to distract her. He looked at the empty cup on the table in front of Mdjai. "That is, if Mdjai hasn't consumed it all."

"That weak batch of herbs?" Mdjai jerked his chin to indicate the pot on the counter. "I thought it might be some of that foul brew you like so well, Ceros. At least it has some kick to it."

"We'll hunt up some java just for you when we go for supplies," Ceros promised. To Danet, he asked, "Would you like some?"

"Yes, please." She smiled as she took the seat he offered.

She must have been tired to sit without arguing about who should be fetching tea for whom. Ceros found a clean cup then checked the pot to make sure it had stayed warm.

"There's fruit." Mdjai pointed to the end of the counter. "And Gehiji said there was a loaf of bread and a bit of cheese too."

Ceros looked to Danet in question.

"Perhaps a little bread," she said then her expression turned to surprise when she remembered who she spoke to. "I can get it."

Ceros waved her back to her seat. "I'll get it." He placed her tea on the table in front of her. "I want a little as well."

"You need to take it easy with what you eat. You haven't had much of anything for the last couple of days," she reminded him.

Mdjai watched them with open interest. "How long have you two known each other?"

"Not long." "A couple sets of the sun," they answered at the same time.

Mdjai grunted. "Then why do you two sound like a bonded couple?"

Danet choked on the tea she had just sipped. Ceros patted her back until she waved.

Gehiji came around the corner. "Oh good. You're up." He sat down in one of the empty chairs.

Ceros put a plate of sliced bread in front of Danet.

"Thanks," Gehiji said as he grabbed the largest piece.

Ceros frowned at him then returned to the counter for a couple more pieces. While he had the knife out, he sliced some cheese then added them to the plate in front of Danet.

"Eat," he ordered as he took the last chair.

When Gehiji reached for a piece of cheese, Ceros stabbed it with the knife he still held. "That's not for you," he growled.

Danet's eyes were wide as she looked back and forth between them.

Gehiji smiled and winked at Danet. "Gotta keep him on his toes."

Mdjai swiped an unstabbed piece before Ceros could protest. "And humble."

The two men laughed when Ceros grunted.

A knock on the front door brought Ceros and Gehiji to their feet. Mdjai simply looked in the direction of the door with a placid expression on his face.

Ceros pulled Danet out of her chair and slipped around the corner into the hallway. He pushed her behind him and listened as Gehiji went to see who it might be.

After closing the door, Gehiji called out, "Just a messenger."

As Gehiji broke the seal on the parchment, they each returned to their places at the table. Except for Mdjai, who never left his seat.

"It's from the queen," Gehiji informed them.

Ceros held his hand out for the message.

Gehiji glanced at Ceros' hand then promptly dismissed it. "It's addressed to me, not you."

Ceros rolled his eyes.

Runihura came through the back door. "I saw a messenger. What's the word?"

Ceros reached for Danet and pulled her onto his lap.

She squeaked in protest. "What are you doing?" she whispered.

"He needs a chair." Ceros gestured to Runihura. "You can sit on my lap and he can use yours."

"But this isn't proper at all," she hissed.

"In case you haven't figured it out yet, we aren't a formal group," Ceros said.

"Not at all," Gehiji agreed without lifting his eyes from the paper.

"Besides, if you don't let him mark you as his territory, he's bound to do something really stupid like peeing on the floor around you," Runihura said.

Danet looked at Ceros. "Is that what you're doing?"

Ceros shrugged and reached for a slice of bread.

"And you don't want the big baby," Mdjai jerked his thumb in Runihura's direction, "to start telling stories of old battle wounds that make his leg hurt when he stands too long."

The others grunted in agreement.

"What did Mother say?" Ceros asked when Gehiji refolded the note.

"The council meeting will be held before high luncheon tomorrow. She's been asked to meet them in the throne room at the palace." Gehiji reached for another slice of bread.

"How difficult will it be to get in?" Mdjai asked.

"Is it an interior room?" Runihura asked.

Ceros and Gehiji described where the room was located in the palace. Ceros described what he remembered of windows and doors as well as possible access from the roof. Gehiji reviewed what he'd learned of security and patrols around the palace.

When Ceros turned to Danet to clarify something, she asked, "Why don't you just walk through the front doors? No one should stop you from entering the palace." She shrugged. "Your mother can verify who you are if anyone questions if you are really you."

The three men looked at each other with similar expressions. Part surprise and part disappointment. Like him, they were probably hoping for a stealthy, in-depth plan of action. To simply walk in seemed anticlimactic.

"Well, damn. I had hoped to use at least one explosive on Ceros' house," Runihura grumbled.

"And that is why we don't want women in the field with us," Mdjai said, shaking his head.

Ceros chuckled. "Maybe next time, Runihura."

They're just teasing you, Ceros reassured Danet through their connection when she began to chew on her lip.

Should I have just kept my mouth shut?

No. Thank you for being the voice of reason. We might have gotten there eventually, but not before wasting time on a lot of highly destructive ideas.

Oh. She blushed prettily. *You're welcome then.*

"So who do you want to go with you?" Gehiji went to the sideboard and sorted through the fruit in the basket.

Ceros shrugged. "Why not everyone?"

Danet shook her head. "There is no reason for me to be there."

Ceros frowned. "I want you there."

She leaned back. "But the meeting has nothing to do with me. All you will do is raise eyebrows by dragging me along." He started to argue, but she continued. "Besides, you need to focus on the council and any tricks they may try to pull. I'd rather not be something they could use against you."

He frowned harder.

"She has another good point." Gehiji set the fruit he selected in the middle of the table.

"If I can't blow anything up, I don't mind staying with her until the meeting is finished." Mdjai pulled out a wicked-looking knife and cut one of the wakaloi fruits in half.

"Actually, I was thinking of going home after everyone leaves for the palace," Danet said as she eyed Mdjai's efforts.

"You can't wander the city alone." Runihura looked at her as if she were a simpleton.

"I do it all the time when I go between patients," Danet protested.

Runihura joined Ceros' frowning.

"But now word has probably spread that you were involved in the prince's disappearance. It may not be safe," Gehiji pointed out.

It was Danet's turn to frown. "Well, what am I supposed to do, just sit here and wait?"

The three men exchanged glances. "Yes." "Sounds about right." "Afraid so," they said at the same time.

This time, surprisingly, Runihura was the voice of reason. "Or one of us can go with her."

"I already said I didn't mind staying behind." Mdjai shrugged. "I can escort her to her father's, if that is where she would prefer to be."

Danet looked to Ceros expectantly.

While he liked the anonymity of their current abode, she had been away from the comfort of her own home for several days. It would only be fair to let her return for a while.

"I would prefer if you went with us." He squeezed her and cut off her protest. "But I agree with your point as well. So if Mdjai doesn't mind going with you, then I don't think it will be an issue for you to return to your home."

She dipped her head in acknowledgement.

"However." He let the word hang in the air before continuing. "I will expect you at the palace as soon as this matter with the council is settled."

Danet frowned. "Why?"

"Because I want you there." And that was all the reason he needed.

She blinked in surprise.

"Is that all the queen had to say?" Mdjai asked.

"Not quite," Gehiji said hesitantly. He looked to Ceros.

"What's wrong?" Ceros asked.

"She sent word that your father's pyre had been lit this morning," Gehiji said quietly.

Ceros' chest tightened.

Danet's tiny hand slipped into one of his. He squeezed it to acknowledge her silent offering of support. All four pairs of eyes were on him as if waiting for an answer. "I should have been there."

"Do you wish to go this evening and pay your respects?" Gehiji asked.

He took a deep breath. "Yes, actually I would."

"If we wait until full dark, I believe we could blend in with what few citizens stream in. You've been gone long enough now that if you wear a hooded cloak, it's doubtful you'd be recognized," Gehiji speculated.

"Runihura and I could go with you since no one at the palace would know us. Gehiji could stay here with Danet," Mdjai suggested.

Ceros nodded.

"Unless you want to go as well?" Mdjai asked Danet.

"No. Too many people would recognize me. I can go tomorrow, after all of this is over," she said.

He gave her hand another squeeze in thanks.

"Now, what about the evening meal?" Runihura said, trying to turn the conversation to something lighter.

Ceros smiled but his mind remained lost in memories of his father.

CHAPTER EIGHTEEN

The next morning, Danet gathered her things as she reminisced the night spent in Ceros' arms.

Ceros returned late but assured her they had gotten to the pyre without incident. His mood, as one might expect, had been solemn. When he crawled into bed with her, he pulled her close and held her for the longest time.

Their lovemaking had been sweet and slow. It had branded his touch on her body and her heart in a way that would never fade.

A sigh escaped as she finished packing then she went in search of Mdjai. She found him sitting near the front window with a knife and a small piece of wood. At first she thought he was sharpening the blade but then she realized he was carving something. Even though the wood held his attention, she suspected he knew exactly what went on outside the window.

"What are you making?" she asked as she approached.

He shrugged. "I don't know yet."

"Then how do you know where to put the knife?"

"I just know."

Part of her wanted to scoff at his response but his voice held only sincerity. Besides, who was she to criticize anyone's talents? Healing was much the same way for her. Herbs and their uses as well as symptoms for common illnesses had been part of her learning. However, diagnosing what ailed a patient fell to her intuition more than book learning.

She watched Mdjai work the wood. The steady strokes of the

knife were oddly soothing. Finally she spoke up. "I'm ready to go whenever you are."

He nodded once. "I'll have another look around and ready my mount."

"We're riding?"

He slipped his knife into the sheath strapped to the side of his thigh and the wood into a small pouch at his waist. "Of course. I'm not about to leave Amisi with a stranger."

She frowned. "I don't know why I didn't realize some of you might have brought your own."

"Ceros probably didn't. The beast inside him spooks most eligari." Mdjai stood. "Besides, he prefers to run for some reason." Mdjai shook his head. "I've never understood that."

Danet smiled and filed that bit of information away. "I'll grab my things. Should I wait for you here or meet you outside somewhere?"

The look on his face indicated how foolish he thought the question was. "Here." Without another word, he fled out the door.

Danet returned to the room she had shared with Ceros. The bed only reminded her of what had passed between them. Heat spiraled through her body as images of the two of them together flashed through her mind. Ceros had certainly made it memorable.

Probably a good thing since it would likely be her last intimate encounter with him. Once Ceros regained his place on the throne, not only would he not have time to spend with her but it wouldn't be appropriate. Sneaking through the palace hallways to be with him would be asking for trouble. However, the thought of being with anyone else after sharing such intimacy with Ceros made her heart ache.

She shook off the depressing thoughts and picked up her bag. At the door, she hesitated when she spotted Ceros' robe lying across the back of a chair. He probably wouldn't even miss it if she took it. And it would be nice to have something of his to remind her of him.

Lifting the fabric to her face, she inhaled his scent. The smell of his soap and his natural musk rippled through her senses like a gentle breeze.

To make sure no one saw what she was doing, she quickly stuffed the robe into her bag and returned to the front room to wait. Her backside had just landed on the seat cushion when Mdjai returned.

He looked at her bag, the floor then the nearby seats. His brows drew together in a frown. "Where are the rest of your things?"

"This is all I brought." She lifted the strap of her bag. "Everything else was supplies."

"What woman doesn't travel with two trunks and an assortment of satchels?" he asked with a scowl.

"This woman," she said, pointing to her own chest.

He grunted. "Well, don't complain later if you left something behind. I'm not coming back to get it."

She shrugged. "Fine."

"Let's go," he said gruffly.

Danet rolled her eyes and followed him out the door. A woman had obviously made a bad impression on him at some point in his life.

When they stepped out onto the street, Danet saw the sun had risen high in the sky. It was the busiest part of the day so the streets were fairly crowded. She pulled her scarf over her hair to partially shield her face as she followed Mdjai to a stable on the other side of the neighboring dwelling.

He stopped just inside the small structure that housed animals. "Wait here while I get Amisi out of her stall."

Every time one of Ceros' men gave her an order she had to bite down on her impulse to tell them what she thought of their brisk manner. Only the knowledge that they were protecting both her and Ceros kept her from saying something she probably shouldn't.

She might have grown up serving the royal family but they had always treated her with respect and didn't order her about. When she finished her learning, she obtained a status that garnered respect from almost every class of citizen. It made her extremely uncomfortable having three men she barely knew telling her where and when to go.

Mdjai led a massive creature from a stall in the far corner. It looked much like an eligari but with a thicker body and legs and a longer but finer coat of hair. The thing looked as if it could pull three wagons and not breathe hard.

"You named that massive creature Amisi? It certainly doesn't look like any kind of flower I've ever seen," Danet said as she looked up at its giant face.

Mdjai held the reins. "The woman who used to own her told me that Amisi chose her own name."

Her eyes widened in surprise. "Your mount chose her own name?"

"She did. Now are you going to stand here all day asking questions or are you going to get into that saddle?"

Danet glanced at it. "The only way I can get up there is if you give me something to stand or climb up on."

Mdjai sighed loudly as if he were being extraordinarily inconvenienced. "We'll do this another way then." He climbed up into the saddle with ease then reached a hand down to Danet.

"What?" she asked.

"Give me your hand and I'll pull you up." When she hesitated, he asked, "You're not afraid to ride, are you?"

"No," she said incredulously.

"Then give me your hand."

Danet pulled the strap of her bag over her head so it lay across her chest instead of on her shoulder then put her hand in his.

With one swoop, Mdjai pulled her up and set her in the saddle in front of him. He steadied her then said, "Now swing around and sit behind me."

A task easier said than done, but Danet made it without unmanning him. As she put her hands around his waist, she wished it were Ceros she rode behind. Mdjai was a handsome man also. He was more rugged in appearance and darker than both Ceros and Gehiji. The unmated women at the palace who hadn't lost their minds over Gehiji would probably be tripping over themselves now.

The journey through town was uneventful other than the few people who stopped and stared. She wasn't sure if the stares were due to the large beast they rode or if the townspeople were on alert because of the prince's disappearance. Either way, Danet feared word would spread to the palace. She just hoped they reached her home before anyone tried to detain them. Almost as fervently, she hoped Ceros would be able to settle the matter with the high council quickly.

Danet answered Mdjai's questions about where things were located around the city. She even pointed out a few of her favorite places as she showed him how to reach her home.

As a precaution, she kept her scarf in place to cover her hair and face until they reached the gates to her father's property. She directed Mdjai to the small stables behind the main house and introduced him to the young man who tended the few animals they kept.

The stable worker was hesitant to lead Amisi to a stall but relaxed when he realized she could and would follow simple commands once Mdjai instructed her to do so.

"Come. I'll introduce you to my father." She grinned, knowing what was in store for Mdjai. "Father will be very happy to meet you."

"Does the wall circle the entire property?"

Danet rolled her eyes. These guys were always on alert, weren't they? "Yes, it does."

He grunted. "How many people do you employ?"

"Here it's just Father, myself and Ryana. Ryana runs the house and makes sure Father eats on a regular basis."

"Is your father an invalid? I was given the impression he was quite active as a healer."

Danet chuckled. "No. He is not an invalid but he does tend to get wrapped up in his research and forgets to eat."

"Ah. More scholar than social."

"That is an apt description." She grinned as she led him through the back patio entrance. "Ryana has a couple of girls who come during the week to help with the cleaning and laundry. Other than the girls and Ryana's son, whom you met at the stable, we don't employ anyone else. We consider Ryana family rather than staff. She's been here since before my mother's death."

As if speaking of her conjured her out of thin air, Ryana came in, wiping her hands on a towel. She quickly ran an assessing eye over Mdjai then wrapped Danet in a hug. "Thank the stars you're all right." She stepped back and put the fist holding the towel on her hip. "What have you gotten yourself into the middle of? I hear the palace is in an uproar over the prince but nobody is saying why. What's happened?" She flicked a hand in Mdjai's direction. "And who is this giant of a man?"

"Ryana, this is Mdjai, a friend of Prince Ceros. He's supposed to be guarding me while the prince takes care of some royal business."

Mdjai tipped his head and murmured a greeting but Ryana cut him off. "Guarding you? Why?"

Danet grimaced. "Let's go find Father so we only have to tell this story once."

"He hasn't returned from the clinic yet. Should I send for him?" Ryana asked.

Danet looked to Mdjai.

"It would probably be best," he advised.

Danet put one hand on Mdjai's arm. "Could he be in danger?"

"It is unlikely at this point."

"Then yes, would you please send word to Father that he should come home as quickly as he can? But don't say anything of my being here."

Mdjai nodded his approval.

"I'll send for him right away." Ryana hurried off to complete her task.

Danet took a deep, cleansing breath and caught a hint of baking bread. "Are you hungry? Ryana makes the best sweetbread in this world."

"Why don't you finish showing me around first?"

She nodded then led the way to the front of the house. "This is the main entrance. Father's library, workroom and bedroom are at this end." She gestured in that direction. "The formal dining room, which rarely gets used, is here." She indicated the room from the doorway then continued to lead the way through the house. "The kitchen, pantry and washroom are at the far end of the house, but I'll show you those in a bit. Upstairs," she said as she led the way up the main stairway, "are all of the bedrooms." When they both reached the top she pointed to the left, down the long corridor. "Ryana's room is at the far end. There is another staircase just outside her room that leads down to the kitchen. There are a couple of guestrooms here," she turned to the right, "and one more at this end."

"And yours?"

"Is here." She pointed to the doorway closest to them.

"Any access to the outside from any of these bedrooms?" Mdjai asked.

"Other than windows, you mean?"

He nodded.

"The guest suite," she pointed to the one room behind them, "has a small balcony. The doors may or may not be locked."

"I assume the balcony overlooks the back of the house and the gardens."

"That's correct." She swept a hand toward the door. "You're

welcome to take a look."

He shook his head. "Not necessary." With his hands behind his back, he turned to face her. "Now, about that sweetbread."

Danet grinned. "Follow me."

She led Mdjai to the kitchen and waved him to the stools sitting next to the large window. "Pull a couple of those up to the counter. If you don't mind, we'll eat there instead of getting the table dirty."

"Fine with me. That's what we used to do at my grandmere's."

Danet dug around in the bread pantry for one of the sweetbreads. Ryana could always be counted on to save one for her. Danet grabbed a bowl of butter and a knife and put them on the counter in front of Mdjai along with the bread. She pulled a large mug out for Mdjai and a smaller glass for herself then grabbed the jug of cider from the chiller. "Do you mind pouring while I slice the bread?" she asked Mdjai.

"Not at all," he said as he reached for the container.

"I thought I heard someone rummaging through my kitchen," Ryana said as she came through the side door from the gardens.

Danet looked up from her task of slicing bread. "I hope you don't mind that I took the last sweetbread."

"Of course I don't mind." Ryana wagged a finger at Danet. "But you'll not want your supper if you eat too much." She looked at Mdjai and mumbled, "You, I'm not so worried about."

Mdjai chuckled. "No, mum, it's unlikely a bit of your bread will dampen my appetite."

That was the first time Danet had seen him laugh. It brightened his face so much she had to take a step back.

"So you will be here for supper then?" Ryana pressed.

Danet looked to Mdjai for an answer.

"That is the most likely scenario, mum," he said.

Ryana wiped her hands on her apron. "I'll add a few more portions to the meal then." She glanced at Danet. "That will please your father. He's been worried about you."

"I didn't mean to upset him."

"I know you didn't, child." Ryana reached across the counter and patted Danet's hand. "But you can't stop a parent from caring, no matter how old his baby gets."

Ryana added a few things to the pot simmering over the fire then returned to the garden. Danet passed a couple of slices to Mdjai then sat next to him to enjoy her portion.

"You know, I believe this is the best I've ever had," Mdjai said as he chewed thoughtfully.

Danet smiled. "I told you." She chuckled. "Ryana always makes it when I've been sick or studying hard or when Father or I have had a particularly difficult patient. It's my comfort food."

"Needing some comfort today, are you?"

"A bit."

"I imagine it's been a difficult week for you, getting thrown into the middle of a royal power struggle. Not to mention being responsible for the royal prince's health."

"It's definitely been one of the more engaging weeks of my life," she mumbled.

"Cheer up. At least no one is throwing knives or firebombs at you yet."

Danet choked on a sip of cider. Mdjai pounded on her back to help her clear it. She waved a hand to let him know she was okay before he broke a rib.

"Do you really think it'll come to that?" she rasped out.

"Probably not." He actually sounded disappointed.

The sound of the front door slamming had both of them turning around.

"Danet?" Sebak called out from the front entryway.

"In the kitchen, Father," she yelled back.

Mdjai relaxed his stance and put the wicked-looking knife he had drawn back into its sheath.

Sebak hurried in then stopped when he spotted Mdjai. "Are you all right?" he asked Danet.

"Yes, I am well." Danet crossed the room and gave him a hug.

"Ryana's message said it was urgent I come home." He looked at Mdjai again. "What's going on?"

"Father, this is Mdjai," Danet gestured to the oversized warrior. "He's one of Prince Ceros' closest friends. They trained together. The prince has asked him to keep an eye on me while he meets with the high council."

"So he recovered enough to meet with them, then?" Sebak asked.

"From what I understand, he made a rather remarkable recovery." Mdjai shot a very pointed look at Danet.

She blushed in response. "Yes. He was doing very well when he left with the others. The meeting should be going on as we speak."

"The others?" Sebak asked.

"Gehiji sent word to some of us who trained with Ceros that he needed assistance." Mdjai shrugged. "So we came."

Sebak approached Mdjai with a look in his eye that told Danet his researcher's mind whirled with questions. He extended his hand to Mdjai. "I didn't mean to be rude when I came in. Allow me to properly introduce myself. I am Sebak. You are very welcome in my home. And I thank you for your protection of my daughter and our prince."

Mdjai shook Sebak's hand. "I am honored to be of assistance," he said equally as formally.

Sebak pulled another stool over to where they had been sitting. "Please, sit." He waved to their stools. "Finish your refreshments and tell me what has been happening."

Danet relayed what she and Gehiji had done to smuggle Ceros out of the palace. She tried to generalize what she had done to heal Ceros but Sebak wouldn't let it drop. His curious nature needed to know what she had done.

"Do you think the serum I mixed for him finally worked?" Sebak asked excitedly.

"It was working until someone slipped in two more thorns," she informed him.

"Two more? Gods, if he had been exposed to that amount of poison, it should have killed him."

"I'm sure that's what they were hoping for," Mdjai mumbled.

"I found one thorn fairly quickly, but the other took longer." Danet inhaled a deep breath. "I didn't find it until after I realized your serum wasn't working."

"Does he have any lingering side effects?" Sebak's brow drew into a frown.

"Not that I could tell, other than he acted a little tired." Mdjai said, looking to Danet for confirmation.

She nodded her agreement.

Sebak studied her, making Danet uncomfortable with his silence. Finally he asked quietly, "You performed a healing on him, didn't you?"

"A what?" Mdjai asked.

"Yes," she said. There was no point denying it. She would do it again in a heartbeat to save him.

"You know what this means, don't you?" Sebak asked.

"What what means?" Mdjai tried to interject again.

"I do." She raised her chin. "And I'm willing to live with the consequences."

"What consequences?" Mdjai asked a little louder.

Sebak cocked his head to one side. "Does he know what it means?"

"No." She stood. "Once this is over, I'll tell him. If he asks. Otherwise, as I said, I'm willing to live with the consequences. At least he is well."

Before she embarrassed herself by bursting into tears, Danet slipped out the back patio doors. She felt certain Mdjai would demand her father explain what they were talking about and she didn't want to see his expression as he did.

CHAPTER NINETEEN

For the tenth time in less than an hour, Ceros caught himself looking at the doorway. The council had been far more accepting of him than he expected once they realized he was indeed healed. Of course, he had been forced to submit to an exam by Darius.

Naturally, Darius had taken full credit for the quick recovery, but Ceros had seen the wonder in his eyes. As he left the room, Darius was still muttering to himself about how he couldn't believe it.

The council voted to proceed with the crowning ceremony as originally planned. No interim ruler would be needed. The crowning would take place with the rising of the new moon.

Ceros turned to Gehiji so he faced away from the pressing crowd. In a lower voice he said, "I'm ready to get out of here."

"Runihura could set a fire in the far corner. That would clear the room quickly," Gehiji suggested.

"I wouldn't even need to search for small pieces of wood," Runihura said matter-of- factly.

Ceros had to fight the lift of his lips. "And damage my home? Perish the thought."

"Then you're stuck smiling and playing the role of prince for a bunch of people you don't know," Gehiji pointed out.

Ceros grumbled to himself and forced away thoughts of what Danet might be doing at that moment. And whether or not she was fully clothed while she did it. Whatever it might be.

When the last of the council members filed out the door, his mother swept in. She very nearly knocked him over as she captured him in an enveloping hug.

"Oh my son, I can't begin to tell you how pleased I am to see you." She squeezed him once more then pulled back. "And looking as well as you do."

"Thank you." Ceros squeezed her hand. "I'm happy to see you too."

The queen wiped a tear away from the corner of her eye. "The last time I saw you I was not sure you would be standing here. Ever again."

"I've been told how very fortunate I am." He chuckled. "Of course they also hinted that the only reason I healed was because I was just too stubborn to die."

His mother sniffed. "Whatever it takes to keep you with us." She looked around. "Speaking of which. Where's Danet?"

"Mdjai took her to her father's."

"Ah." She nodded. "I'm sure the poor girl needs some rest. She's been taking care of you since you arrived."

"I understand I have you to thank for securing her care."

"No need to thank me. I knew you needed the best so I made sure you received it." She harrumphed. "That pompous ass, Darius, may be taking credit for your recovery, but I know it was really because of Danet."

"There is no need for everyone to know that, however," he said with a meaningful look.

"No, you're probably right. If word gets out that she healed you so well, every one of the gentry will be signing up to get Danet as their personal physician. We'll never be able to get her back to the palace."

"I'll get her back to the palace, Mother, don't you worry."

"Oh? And how do you plan to do that? Offer her a position as the palace physician?" She shook her head. "You know Darius will cause problems if you do."

"The position I have in mind won't conflict with Darius."

The queen frowned. "Then what are you thinking of doing with her?"

Ceros' smile bordered on wicked. "I plan to take her as my mate and make her my queen."

His mother's usual composure slipped and her mouth fell open.

A voice from behind asked, "You're to be bound?"

Ceros whipped around and found Aleric stepping between the curtains draped over the doorway in the wall behind them. Aleric looked as stunned as the queen. "Aleric, I didn't hear you approach."

"I, uh…" Aleric cleared his throat as he glanced warily at the frowns on the three warriors' faces. "I circled back so I could tell you how glad I am about your remarkable recovery. But now it sounds as if congratulations are in order as well," he said smoothly.

"I assume I don't have to tell you that information is not widely known." Ceros nodded to the queen. "I was just breaking the news to Mother so I would appreciate you not saying anything to anyone else."

"I understand." Aleric tipped his head in a partial bow. "Since I am obviously interrupting I will leave you to your conversation." He bowed again to the queen. "My queen."

Ceros turned to his mother. She had regained her calm and asked, "Am I to take it that the time you spent with Danet brought this," she waved her hand in Ceros' direction, "news about?"

"Partially." He had no intention of going into details about his reasons.

She stepped closer and lowered her voice. "Son, I like Danet. More importantly, I respect her. However, I don't want you to feel as if you are expected to bond with her just because you've spent a lot of time alone with her. Despite her unmated state, her position and reputation will prevent others from thinking ill of her."

"That is not why I want to bond with Danet, Mother." When she started to speak, he held up his hand. "Not now. Not here. I just wanted you to know first."

"Answer one thing for me now. What did her father say?"

Ceros took a deep breath. "Nothing. I haven't spoken with him about it."

The queen's brows drew together.

"She doesn't know it yet either," he mumbled.

Her mouth fell open again but she quickly recovered and snapped it shut. She studied his face and seemed to come to some decision. "I expect you know what you're about so I won't tell you what a muddle you're about to make of this if you don't have a conversation with your intended very soon."

She leaned forward and lifted herself up on her toes so she could press a quick kiss to his cheek. "You can tell me about it later as I suspect you want to be off so you can gather up your mate-to-be." She patted him on the chest. "Bring her to me once you two have come to an agreement."

Ceros smiled down at his mother. "I will."

He watched as she regally swept out of the room, her handmaidens falling in place behind her. Once the doors closed again, Ceros turned to Gehiji.

"Before we go get Danet and Mdjai, I need to meet with the chancellor on a couple of issues that need to be addressed right away. I'd also like to talk to Hesina about having a few things moved into my rooms for Danet. And we need to make sure rooms have been prepared for you and Mdjai." Ceros pointed to Runihura.

"I thought I saw Hesina listening to the proceedings from the back of the room. I'd bet my favorite eligari she's already taken care of a room for Runihura," Gehiji said.

"Probably, but she won't know about Mdjai and I don't want to worry about it later." Ceros grinned. "I suspect I'm going to have my hands full placating Danet."

Runihura snorted.

"There's no point asking if you meant what you said about being bound to her." Gehiji made it a statement rather than a question.

"No point at all. She is my one true mate. I have no doubt of it."

Gehiji smiled and offered his hand to Ceros. "Then I wish you both all the joy in the world, my friend."

They clasped wrists. "Thank you. Now I just have to convince Danet."

"I thought every woman dreamed of bonding with a prince?" Runihura clasped wrists with Ceros.

"I suspect I found one of the few who aren't enamored with the idea," Ceros mumbled.

Runihura chuckled and slapped Ceros on the shoulder with his free hand. "Then enjoy the chase. And don't let her forget what you went through to capture her either."

"Thank you." Ceros grimaced. "I think."

"Come," Runihura said. "I'm anxious to see how many circles that little lady makes you run in."

Gehiji chuckled as the three men left the hall.

After the doors closed a shadowy figure moved along the edge of the wall not far from where Ceros and his men had been standing. The shadow blended further into the darkness then the sound of a door latch echoed through the room.

CHAPTER TWENTY

Danet's aimless wandering led to her mother's fountain in the center of the gardens. She could always count on the calming effects of the water when her troubled mind ran amok.

She slipped off her sandals and sat on the edge. For a moment she watched the play of colors from the setting sun in the clear pool and let the sounds and scents wash over her. She'd always believed there was something magical about the space her mother had created so long ago. It soothed her in a way that defied explanation.

Trying not to disturb the tiny garah that lived in the basin, she eased her feet into the cool water. The garahs' bright-blue bodies twisted and swam away, only to float back where they started.

She tried to gauge the time of day based on the position of the sun. It had already dipped near the horizon but still cast shadows on everything it touched.

It had been some time since Ceros and the others left. She wondered how the council had taken his sudden recovery. Surely the meeting wouldn't last very long. Those old men could be stubborn, but there was nothing to argue about. Either Ceros was fit to rule or he wasn't. And given the fact that he had full control of his mind and body, they shouldn't be able to label him incapable.

The temptation to touch his mind and find out what was happening weighed on her, but it seemed rude to do so without permission. Even if she managed to make the connection while they were so far apart, she didn't want to risk interrupting him during a critical point in the meeting. Nor did she want to distract him.

A few times this afternoon she thought she had felt him brushing up against her mind but dismissed it as wishful thinking. He would be far too busy to do that.

As she watched the garah swim around her toes, a shadow fell across her lap. Assuming it Mdjai or her father had come to find her, she didn't bother to look up. "I know I shouldn't have run away but I needed to clear my head."

When she received no response, she turned to see who was there. Before she had even a glimpse, someone grabbed from behind.

Danet struggled against whoever held her and tried to free her hands. She opened her mouth to scream when she recognized the smell of a familiar drug pressed against her nose. The last thought she had as she sank into darkness was that Ceros was still in danger.

* * * * *

Across town, in the palace, Ceros was jolted into awareness.

It sounded as if Danet had called his name but it had been faint and rather weak.

He closed his eyes and focused on her. Her face, her smell, the feel of her in his arms. He even tried to remember what it felt like when they spoke in each other's minds.

"What's wrong?" Runihura asked.

Ceros held up one finger, silently asking for a moment, as he tried to call out to Danet.

Nothing. He tried again. Still no response. Not even the fluttery sensations he had felt earlier when he'd tried to connect to her.

Gehiji approached. "What's going on?"

Ceros shook his head. "I'm not sure. I just suddenly had the feeling that Danet had tried to call out me. It felt as if she had been scared or alarmed by something."

"Are you sure you weren't imagining things?" Gehiji asked.

"No. I'm not sure." Ceros ran his fingers through his hair in frustration. "This connection with her is too new. And I'm not sure that it works when we're this far apart." He paced away. "But it felt real. For a few seconds I felt scared and I have no reason to be. There is no immediate threat to me."

"Do you want me to go to her father's house and find out for sure?" Runihura offered.

Ceros looked around the room at the stack of documents on his desk and at the progress the staff had made in his room.

"No." He reached for his sash and quickly tied it around his waist then buckled his sword and belt over it. "Let's all go."

The other two grabbed their own weapons and followed. As the three marched through the hallways to the exit, Ceros' father's chancellor ran to catch up with them. Actually, the man was now his chancellor.

"My prince? A word, if you please?"

"Not now," Ceros called over his shoulder without breaking stride.

"But my prince, it will only take—"

Ceros stopped and faced the aging politician. "I will ring for you when I am ready." His expression brooked no argument.

The man swallowed nervously and clutched the stack of documents he held against his chest. "Ye-yes, my prince."

Ceros resumed his march to the door.

The expression on his face was fierce enough no one else dared impede their progress. When they reached the stables, they didn't bother the stable hands. It was faster to saddle their mounts themselves. More than one mouth fell open to see the prince readying his own eligari.

Ceros called one of the young stableboys to his side and asked where he could find Mistress Danet's home. Thankfully the boy knew.

To avoid any alarm, Ceros forced himself to slow down after passing through the palace gates. The crowded city streets tried his patience. It felt like an eternity before they reached Danet's home.

They dismounted. Runihura took all three sets of reins while Ceros hurried to the entrance. He banged on the heavy wooden barrier and fought the urge to burst through.

Mdjai opened the door. "Ceros." He looked past Ceros to where Gehiji and Runihura stood. "What's wrong?"

"Where's Danet?" Ceros asked as he pushed his way inside.

"Out back in the garden. Why?"

"I need to see her." Ceros scanned the various doors and

entryways, looking for something that might be an obvious way to the gardens.

A tall, gray-headed man wearing dark-brown robes came from one of the rooms to the right.

"Is there a problem?" When the man's eyes lighted on Ceros, he dipped his head in a bow. "Prince Ceros. I'm glad to see you've recovered so well."

"Thank you." Ceros hesitated. "You look familiar."

"This is Sebak, Danet's father," Mdjai said by way of introduction.

"Ah, yes." Ceros crossed the room to shake Sebak's hand. "I remember you from when I was a boy. I hurt my arm and you splinted it." Ceros cocked his head to one side. "Don't take offense, sir, but Danet doesn't look anything like you."

Sebak released Ceros' hand. He smiled sadly as he removed his eyeglasses. "No offense at all for I know she doesn't. She is very nearly a mirror image of her mother." He rubbed the lenses with the edge of his sleeve. "It's startling sometimes."

"Yes. I could see where it might be," Ceros mumbled. He shook the thought off. "I don't mean to be abrupt, but can you show me where to find Danet?"

"Certainly." Sebak gestured for Ceros to follow.

"Gehiji, why don't you go with them? I'll help Runihura with the mounts," Mdjai suggested.

Gehiji nodded and followed Ceros and Sebak.

Sebak led the way through a well-tended garden. The sound of water reached his ears before he noticed the magnificent fountain. If this was one of Danet's favorite places, he could see why.

Unfortunately he didn't see Danet.

"That's strange. I would have sworn this was where she was headed." A frown creased Sebak's brow as he glanced up and down the adjoining paths.

"Where else might she be?" Ceros tried to remain calm even though tension gripped him.

"She might have gone up to her room while Mdjai and I were in my study, but I think we would have seen or heard her."

Gehiji stepped closer to the fountain. To the untrained eye, it looked as if he were simply admiring it but Ceros recognized he was studying the area. "Ceros," Gehiji said quietly.

Ceros moved in next to Gehiji to see what had caught Gehiji's eye. Inside the pond a skid mark had been made in the moss covering one of the larger stones near the edge.

It looked as if someone had either slipped on the rock or had suddenly been pulled away from the pond. Given the amount of sediment still stirred up in the bottom of the pool, it happened recently. Some of the plants growing next to the wall of the fountain had been pulled and dropped on the rock below.

Gehiji and Ceros exchanged looks of concern.

Sebak leaned over the pond. He looked at Gehiji then Ceros. "Something has happened to her, hasn't it?"

"It's hard to say for sure," Ceros said.

"But you think so, don't you?" Sebak said quietly.

Ceros took a deep breath. "As much as I don't want to believe it, my guess is yes."

"Where's the closest exit?" Gehiji asked.

"There's a gate in the wall, just there." Sebak pointed to a dark spot in the wall. "It's never used and should be locked."

"I'll check." Gehiji sprinted to the wall.

Ceros closed his eyes and tried to reach Danet through their connection. *Danet? If you can hear me, say something. It's very important.* He paused and listened. He didn't know how to yell without a voice, but he put everything he had into the bellow. *Danet!*

"Were you able to connect with her?" Sebak asked.

Ceros' eyes popped open. "What did you ask?"

"Danet. Were you able to reach her?" Sebak asked again.

"She told you about our connection."

He nodded. "But don't worry. She didn't repeat anything said between you. She only mentioned the connection was there."

"And you believed her?"

"Of course." Sebak sat on the nearby bench. "Her mother and I shared a soul-bond and could communicate in a similar fashion."

"What kind of bond?"

"A soul-bond." He gestured that Ceros should sit with him. "It's a type of bonding that goes deeper than a set of vows said before witnesses. Once a mystic finds and bonds with his or her mate, there can be no other." He smiled sadly. "The bond transcends even death."

"How does a mystic recognize her mate?" Ceros asked, even though he felt he already knew the answer.

Sebak lifted one shoulder in a half-shrug. "There are many

signs. A feeling that you knew each other before you met. A sense of ease or comfort whenever you're together. But the most obvious is the couple's ability to share thoughts."

Ceros hung his head. "I'm really going to have to talk to her about keeping information from me."

Sebak chuckled. "She always did what she felt was right or best for everyone. Even at her own expense."

"Well, I suppose this soul-bonding makes things easier for me."

His brows rose in surprise. "How so?"

"I was already trying to figure out how to get her to accept my offer to be my mate. Doesn't this mean she can't refuse me?"

Sebak shook his head. "Afraid not."

"Why not?" Ceros' voice rose.

"Danet knows that even as rare as a soul-bond mate is, she still has a choice. She could choose someone else and maybe even live a satisfied life. It would never be as fulfilling as a life with her soul-bond mate but she could still find happiness."

At the thought of Danet with someone else his beast roared. Ceros struggled to not transform but from the expression on Sebak's face, he must not have succeeded at completely hiding his alternate form.

Instead of running in terror, however, Sebak simply tilted his head to one side and watched. "Interesting," he said in a thoughtful manner.

"My apologies," Ceros murmured as he gripped the edge of the bench.

"I didn't realize, my prince, that you had been gifted by the Gods."

Ceros chuckled. "I'm not certain I would call it a gift, but yes." He sighed. "Very few people know, but as we are soon to be family, you might as well. I am an omegamorph."

"I see." Sebak continued to study Ceros. "Does Danet know?"

He was a bit taken aback by Sebak's calm acceptance of the news. "Yes. She has met the beast in dreams."

"But not in reality?"

Ceros shook his head. "No."

"And the beast has accepted her?"

He looked Sebak in the eye. "Even before I knew who she was."

Sebak nodded. "This is good."

"It is?"

"Legends say that, like a mystic, every omegamorph has a destined mate. One they will recognize instinctively. The mate will have the ability to soothe the beast in ways the vessel would have never been able to on his own."

"I see," Ceros said. He sensed this about Danet. With her gone, his beast stirred close to the surface. It took considerable effort to remain in control.

"I've also read that omegamorphs and mystics were able to share energy. It was quite common for an omegamorph to seek out and include a mystic in his inner circle. If you'll forgive my forwardness, if you and Danet are soul-bond mates, you would be in a very unique and fortuitous position. Neither of you would have to worry about illness or injury. Only of creating a bit of pain or discomfort for the other."

"What do you mean?"

"In healing, like the one that Danet did with you, it is an exchange. She passed her healing energy to you and took some of the illness, or in your case, poison, into herself."

"She did what?" Ceros jumped to his feet.

"Did you not sense her weakness?" Sebak asked calmly.

"Yes, but she acted as if it were normal. I assumed it was because of the effort she made, making the deeper connection with me. She said she had not been taught the ways of mystics. Did she know what would happen?"

Sebak nodded. "She hasn't been taught but her mother and grandmother and even her great-grandmother left journals. She has studied almost every word written in those books. I feel certain she would have known the risk of completing the healing."

Ceros muttered to himself about hardheaded women.

Sebak smirked as he rose to his feet. "Perhaps we should return to the house."

"What about Danet? Aren't you worried about her?" he asked incredulously. It occurred to Ceros that Sebak may be one of those people who were really smart but didn't have a lot for skill with people. But Danet was his daughter. He should be showing a bit more concern than he was.

"Yes. I am quite worried about her." Sebak turned so his whole body faced Ceros. "By now your friend," he pointed in the direction Gehiji had gone, "has assessed the gate and the surrounding area, perhaps even followed any trail that had been left. After that he mostly likely circled back to the house to tell Mdjai and your other friend what has happened. I would guess that between the three of them they have completed a search of the house to determine if Danet is truly missing. Shortly your friends will be coming to report on all they have found and ask when you'll be ready to return to the palace to await a message from whoever is behind this. Am I missing anything about the situation?"

Sebak's ability to not only figure out what most likely happened to Danet but also what they were doing to investigate was impressive. "Not that I can think of." He gestured for Sebak to lead the way back to the house. "You are remarkably calm for someone who's just figured out his only daughter has been kidnapped."

"Believe me when I tell you that my insides are churning. But I realize giving in to my fears will not help any of us." He glanced back at Ceros. "I also suspect that if anyone can find her and bring her back safely it is you and those friends of yours. And if you'll forgive me for assuming anything about such a newly forged bond, but based on your earlier reaction, I also believe that you will do almost anything to find her."

"Once again you are correct," Ceros said with deadly assurance.

"Then I'll only ask what I can do to assist your efforts."

"Let's find out what has been discovered first."

Just as they reached the patio area, Gehiji and Mdjai came out of the house. "We were just coming to find you," Gehiji explained.

"Perhaps we should go into my study where we might have some privacy?" Sebak suggested.

"That would probably be best," Ceros agreed.

The four filed into the room and Mdjai shut the door behind him. Ceros scanned the room but opted to stand instead of taking a seat. His beast was too keyed up to be still. "Where's Runihura?"

"Tracking," Gehiji said.

Ceros nodded his approval. "What did you learn?" he prompted.

"She's nowhere to be found in the house or on the grounds," Mdjai reported.

"All signs indicate there were two people who entered through the far gate." Before Sebak could ask, Gehiji added, "The lock on the gate was broken and they didn't try to hide their exit." He shook his head. "Very sloppy. Not warriors."

"Did she put up any kind of fight or did she go with them willingly?" Ceros asked.

"My guess is she was unconscious. There was no struggle except for a very minor one at the pond. And the footprints on the way out were deeper than those coming in, as if they were carrying a load."

Ceros exchanged a look with Sebak. "That would explain why I cannot connect with her."

Sebak nodded his agreement.

"What else?" Ceros prompted.

"There were three eligari outside the gate. One of them pulled a small cart." Gehiji told them.

"Where does the alley lead?" Ceros asked Sebak.

"To a side street. There you can go any of three directions. None of which are very populated," Sebak added.

"So it's unlikely that anyone saw them leaving the alley," Ceros mumbled.

"Correct," Sebak agreed.

"Did you talk with the staff to find out if they saw anything?" Ceros looked to Gehiji and Mdjai.

"Not yet," Gehiji answered.

"We don't have a large staff here," Sebak interjected. "Most days it's usually our housekeeper and one or two others."

"To run a house this size?" Ceros frowned.

Sebak smiled. "We live simply. Danet and I both spend more time away than home so there's little to be done for us." He shrugged. "And quite frankly, we both value quiet time to think."

"Good to know," Ceros mumbled. To Mdjai and Gehiji he said, "Find out what you can without alarming anyone."

When the two moved to spring into action, Sebak held up one finger. "If I might make a suggestion…"

Mdjai's brows rose and both he and Gehiji paused.

"How about if I call Ryana in so you can ask your questions? She will be able to tell you who else is in the house today and where you can find them."

"An excellent suggestion," Ceros said.

Sebak went to find Ryana and returned shortly. All they were able to discover was that Ryana had been working in the kitchens to prepare dinner when the incident occurred. Only one other girl had been present and she had been in the kitchen as well.

They called the girl in but she hadn't seen anyone other than Danet, Sebak and Mdjai that day. Ceros thanked Ryana and the girl for their help. Sebak sent them back to the kitchens with a promise to Ryana to explain after the prince had left.

"I don't think there is anything else we can do here. And I strongly suspect I will be hearing from whoever is behind this instead of you." He looked at Sebak.

"I fear you may be correct." Sebak frowned. "Who knew that you intended to bond with Danet?"

"Other than these guys? No one except Mother. I told her right after the council meeting this afternoon."

"Could anyone have overhead you?" Sebak asked. "A servant perhaps?"

"It's possible, but unlikely. We were in the throne room. Servants remain near the main door."

"Your cousin did," Gehiji reminded him.

"Aleric?"

"Yes, that's him." Gehiji nodded. "He came in through that hidden door while you were telling the queen."

"He wouldn't have anything to do with this though."

"How do you know for certain?" Gehiji pressed.

"After my uncle was killed, he came to live with us. He always looked up to Father. He even declined the offer to go to Shirghada to be trained with me because he felt he could help Father and Licosia more by staying and joining the council." He rubbed a hand over his face. "Aleric never gave the slightest hint he had any aspirations of being king. And he certainly never displayed any hostility toward me, much less Father."

Gehiji's face indicated he didn't necessarily agree with Ceros' statement. "Even if it has nothing to do with him, there is still a hidden door that anyone could have stood behind while you were talking."

Ceros closed his eyes and took a deep breath. The thought of Danet in danger because of him was unbearable. Part of him was afraid of finding out who was behind this because he didn't know what he would do to them.

His beast wanted blood.

At this point he didn't know if he would be able to stop the beast from taking what it wanted.

When he opened his eyes, all three of the others were watching him. Warily.

"What?" Ceros growled.

"Your eyes are doing that glowing-gold thing you do right before you transform," Gehiji cautioned.

Mdjai tried to ease some of the tension. "Calm down before you get big and hairy on us."

"We'll find her," Gehiji reassured him.

"I'd tell you to change and run off some of your irritation, but I don't think that's a good idea," Mdjai said, thinking out loud.

Ceros shook his head. "I'd only end up scaring half the people in town."

"And half the eligari." Mdjai sounded as if he found the idea funnier than Ceros cared for.

"All right," Ceros groused. "Let's get back to the palace so we can find who the bastard behind this is."

"You will send word as soon as you hear something?" Sebak asked even though it sounded more like a statement than a question.

"Yes. And if by chance you hear from her, send word immediately." The four headed for the front entrance. "It probably wouldn't be a bad idea to stick close to home for a while," Ceros suggested to Sebak. "At a minimum, avoid going anywhere alone until this is resolved. I will send a guard from the palace." With his hand on the door latch, Ceros asked, "Unless you would be more comfortable coming with us to the palace?"

"No, thank you, my prince. I don't believe that will be necessary. It is highly improbable I am a target and I would rather be here if word is sent or Danet returns on her own." He bowed his head. "But I appreciate your offer."

Ceros nodded then turned to follow Gehiji and Mdjai out the door but Sebak stopped him.

"One more thing, my prince. Do not forget that Danet is a strong and capable woman and she is not without defenses. She may not have been properly trained to use all of her gifts, but she will not simply give in to whoever has taken her."

Ceros grimaced. "I don't expect she would and that's part of what frightens me."

With that thought weighing on his mind, Ceros hurried to his waiting eligari.

CHAPTER TWENTY-ONE

Danet struggled to open her eyes but her head ached and her stomach protested any movement she made. She tried to swallow but her mouth felt as if it had been stuffed with linen.

The cool stone or tile floor she lay on actually helped with the nausea.

Since her need to know outweighed the pounding in her head, she forced her eyes open.

She was in a tiny room. Boxes were stacked along the wall across from her. The door was not far from her feet. The window in the wall across from her let in what remained of the sunlight.

To distract herself from her rolling stomach, she assessed her situation.

She had obviously been drugged and kidnapped by unknown persons. Her hands were bound behind her. She had been left in some kind of storage room and the sun had nearly set.

She had no idea where Ceros was or what happened with the council.

Ceros.

She needed to tell him what had happened. If she could reach him.

Before she could relax to try to reach out to him, she heard voices outside the room. She struggled to hear what they were saying.

"She was still out the last time I checked."

The doorknob rattled as someone put a key into the lock.

Danet closed her eyes and willed her heartbeat and her breath to slow so she could pretend to be unconscious. The sound of footsteps grew louder as the person came closer. As much as she wanted to know who it was, she didn't dare open her eyes.

"Yes, she's still out," the man informed whoever else had been there.

"What did the fool do to her?" the second voice groused.

"He said he knew of some medicine that would knock her out."

"Did you pay him already?" the second voice asked as the two moved away.

She lay still and listened for a moment after the door closed before deciding the two had walked away. When she opened her eyes, she took in more details of the room and tugged on the ropes holding her hands. They were securely bound. Without being able to see the knot she doubted she'd be able to free herself.

She needed to tell Ceros. If she could reach him, that is. Their connection was still new and she didn't know how far apart they could be and still reach each other. Since she didn't know where she was, she could only hope.

A couple of deep breaths helped her calm her racing heartbeat and focus on what she needed to do. Ceros' handsome face sprang easily into her mind and she concentrated on him.

The tingly sensation in her forehead that she felt when they had connected before started and gave her hope.

Ceros?

She paused then gave her thoughts another push. *Ceros? Are you there?*

Danet?

The sound of his voice in her head startled her. It sounded unexpectedly strong and clear.

Are you all right? His question weighed heavily with concern.

She smiled. *Yes. I am all right.*

Thank the Gods. Where are you? he demanded.

I don't know.

What do you mean you don't know? he growled. *Why don't you know?*

Because I'm tied up and I haven't been able to get up to look out the window.

His beast roared through her mind. Oddly enough, instead of startling her, the sound soothed her.

I'm okay, she reminded him calmly. *It's just my hands that are bound.*

175

I felt dizzy when I woke up and didn't think I should try to stand just yet.

Dizzy? Why? Did they hit you on the head? He growled the questions.

No. They used a strong herbal mixture to make me sleep. It's the same medicine we use to knock patients out for painful procedures. A headache and dizziness are common side effects. I'll be fine after a bit.

Ceros said a few unpleasant things about her captors. Danet wondered if he realized she could hear him.

What can you tell me about where you're being held? he asked.

She described the room she was in and a few of the crates nearby.

What about the window? What direction are the shadows falling?

There really aren't many shadows. What little bit of light is falling on the left side of the window though.

What about smells or sounds?

I'm afraid I still don't smell much more than the herbs they held over my face earlier. To distract him from his impulse to curse her kidnappers and their families she added, *But I can hear scraping. Like a tool scraping on rock.*

He paused, giving her the feeling he had relayed the information to someone. Probably Gehiji or one of his other friends.

Did you recognize anyone who took you? he asked.

I only saw one of the men in the garden. He looked somewhat familiar but not enough for me to place where I might have seen him before. One of the voices I heard outside my door a few minutes ago sounded familiar. But again, not enough for me to place it.

You didn't see them?

No. I pretended I was still out when they came in.

Danet felt Ceros' anger and frustration through their connection. She was flattered he cared enough to feel such strong emotion, but worried he might lose focus.

Was the voice outside the door the same man as the one in the garden? he asked.

No.

Do you think you can make it to the window?

I think so.

It was more of a struggle than she expected to sit up without the use of her hands. When she finally managed it, she had to let another wave of dizziness pass before she stood.

Ceros' concern rang through when he asked, *Are you sure you're okay?*

Yes. Truly, I am fine. The weakness shouldn't last much longer.

She scooted next to a stack of crates so she could lean against them as she stood. If the room spun unexpectedly, she didn't want to fall all the way down.

Because of a stack of boxes below the window, she couldn't get a clear view. *I can't see much. The roof of a small building or the end of this one. I'm not sure which.*

What kind of roof? What color? he asked.

I think the curved tiles are red, but I'm not sure. The way the sun is setting it might be a dark orange. The walls are an ordinary tan. Nothing remarkable about either that I can tell.

Anything else stand out about your surroundings?

No. Her shoulders slumped. *It's not very helpful, is it?*

Maybe. He paused. *Runihura is tracking their trail. We haven't heard anything from him so I'm taking that to mean that he's been able to follow but can't get away to send word just yet.*

How do you know he hasn't been found or hurt?

Because we know Runihura and the way he operates. Trust me. He'll find and disable your captors long before they know he's there.

But—

Trust me.

She searched her heart and found that she did trust him. More than seemed reasonable for having known him for so little time. *All right. I trust you.*

Good.

What else can I do?

He paused. His indecision rippled through their connection.

The most helpful thing you could do would be to find out who is behind all of this. But I don't want you putting yourself in danger to do it. If you see anyone you know or something unusual, tell me. Otherwise, I just want you to listen and watch.

I can do that.

I know you can.

His confidence in her eased some of her worry. She turned away from the window to sit on the floor again. *Oh, Ceros?*

Yes?

I may regret it later, but I'm glad I can talk with you this way. I would probably be a lot more scared right now if I couldn't.

I wish you weren't in this position at all. Especially since you've been taken because of me.

It's not your fault, you know, she assured him. *It's whoever is behind this. And I'm certain you'll figure it out and take the appropriate action.*

You really don't want to know what I consider appropriate with respect to your kidnappers.

She felt a deep, simmering anger and a need to maul something through their connection. Danet shuddered in reaction.

No sooner had she gotten situated on the floor than she heard someone at the door.

Someone is here. She pushed the thought to Ceros.

I'm still with you. Just be careful of what you say to them.

The door opened and a man stepped into the room. Danet had seen him somewhere before but couldn't place him. His manner of dress didn't give her any clues as to where she might have seen him before.

"Ah, good. You're awake," the man said. "Don't bother yelling. No one here will help you and you'll only force us to knock you out again so we don't have to listen to you."

"Why am I here?" she asked, not bothering to get up.

"Because we need the prince to do something and you are leverage to ensure that he complies."

A dozen questions sprang to mind, but she settled on one. "What do you need him to do?"

A strange look crossed the man's face. "That is between us and the prince."

"Why do you think he'll comply? I am nothing to him. I'm just his healer."

Danet felt a wave of irritation through her connection with Ceros.

The man at the door frowned. "We have been informed otherwise." Before she could ask another question, he continued, "Now, I must return and tell the others you are awake."

"Wait a minute! What if I—" The door closed despite her protest.

Harrumph. She was both irritated and relieved.

You don't know where you've seen him before? Ceros asked.

No. She tried to remember again, but it was pointless. She saw so many faces at the clinic and then again at the palace she couldn't keep them straight.

I was wondering about our connection.

What about it? Danet asked hesitantly.

Didn't you think it was hampered by physical distance at first?

She was relieved he didn't ask any of the hard questions she felt certain he eventually would get around to. *Yes.*

Do you think it still is?

It might be. She drew out "might" to emphasize her uncertainty.

So you could be close to the palace then.

It's a possibility. She took a fresh look around, trying to determine if the items in the room had any connection to the palace. Or if the red roof tiles were atop someplace she passed by.

Still, nothing came to mind.

I'm going to send a group to search the villas near the palace.

You can't just send guards into people's homes.

They don't need to enter anyone's homes. I just need them to find one with a red tile roof.

CHAPTER TWENTY-TWO

"A letter has arrived for you," Mdjai said without getting up from Ceros' lounge chair. To the casual observer, it would appear Mdjai was close to falling asleep.

Ceros knew better. He looked over his shoulder. A young servant boy stood in the doorway, nervously switching his weight from one foot to the other. Clearly the boy didn't want to be there. Ceros motioned him forward.

"I was told to give this to the prince and only the prince." The boy's eyes flicked from one face to the next then back to Ceros. "Is that you, sir?"

"Yes. I am he."

The boy put a folded note in Ceros' outstretched hand.

"Thank you." Ceros broke the seal and read the scribbled words inside. He nodded once to Gehiji to let him know it had been sent by the kidnapper then asked the boy, "Who gave you this note?"

"One of the girls from the market."

"Were you given any other instructions?" Ceros asked.

"No, my prince." The boy paused then added, "But I was told I was being watched and if I didn't deliver the note right away, they would find out where I lived."

"Were you paid anything for your troubles?"

"A copper pence, my prince."

Ceros reached into his desk and pulled out a money pouch. He handed the boy several coins. "Thank you. I'm sorry your day was disturbed."

The boy looked at the silver pieces in his hand. His eyes widened and a grin blossomed. "Oh, wow." He bowed as he backed toward the door. "Thank you, my prince."

As soon as the boy disappeared through the outer door, Ceros said to his waiting friends, "I'm to present myself on the west bank of the oasis before moonrise. Needless to say, I am to go alone. If I do not comply, they will deliver Danet's body in the morning."

"The oasis is east of the city?" Mdjai asked Ceros.

"Yes." He'd held on to his calm while the boy had been here, but he was sorely tempted to give in to his anger now that he didn't have an audience. At least an audience that was unfamiliar with his moods.

"I will gather what we'll need," Gehiji said. "I don't suppose I need to remind you that you need to calm yourself before you unintentionally shift."

"No, you don't," Ceros growled.

Ceros? What's happened? Danet asked through their connection. *You're very angry. Why?*

The note from the kidnappers came.

What did they want?

They want me to meet them at the oasis before moonrise.

Ceros held a hand up to Gehiji when he started to say something. He pointed to his head to let him know he was talking to Danet. Gehiji nodded his understanding.

You aren't going, are you? Danet asked.

Of course I'm going, he scoffed.

You can't!

Why can't I?

Because you're the prince! And we don't know whom or what you'll be facing. It's too risky.

Why do I feel as if I have just been insulted? Did the woman have no faith in him? *It's improbable that I'll be facing an entire army by myself. Not that I haven't done that before.*

I... You have?

It will be fine, he assured her. *I'll go and see what these people want, hopefully find out who is involved or behind it, we'll rescue you and return to the palace and all will be well. Nothing to it.*

Nothing to it? she asked incredulously. *Somehow I doubt it will be as easy as walking in, asking a few questions, making a few promises and leaving.*

No. Probably not. But we'll improvise. He forced himself to project confidence and more calm than he really felt.

Improvise?

Yes. Now, like I said earlier, you need to keep your eyes and ears open. Any information you can send me about your location and those with you will be helpful.

Please don't do this. I'm sure whoever is behind this will realize when you don't show that you couldn't put the throne at risk over a servant.

Ceros growled. *You are not a servant.*

I was. She sighed. *Even now, I'm really just a highly educated servant. My status simply allows me the luxury of choosing whom I serve.*

When we get back to the palace, we are having a serious discussion about how you see yourself.

Ceros, I can't stand the thought of you deliberately putting yourself in harm's way because of me.

Danet, he said mimicking her, *I can't stand the thought of you being harmed in any way because of your association with me. I will see that you are freed.*

Fine! Send one of your oversized friends to handle it. Why does it have to be you?

He growled again. *Because I need to do this.*

But—

Enough. We will also discuss your habit of arguing with me when we return.

She fell silent. Part of him wanted to continue arguing just to know she was well and unharmed but she would never convince him to stay in the palace while she was held captive.

It might have hurt her feelings that he cut her off but they didn't have much time and he needed to concentrate. He would make it up to her later.

Once she was safe in the palace.

And they were alone.

With a jar of honey.

What are you planning to do with the honey? she asked.

I didn't mean to transmit that. He rubbed his hand across his face. *You need to go lie down and not listen to anything else I might slip up and say.*

Uh huh. As if—

She stopped. *Wait. Someone is coming.*

I'm here, he reminded her.

To Gehiji and Mdjai, he said, "Someone is coming into her room."

Gehiji nodded that he'd heard.

Ceros' mind pictured all sorts of scenarios. He tried to keep them to himself and not transmit them to her. He also struggled to keep his rising anxiety for her to himself.

Not being able to see and hear what Danet did strained his patience.

I know him, she finally said. *He's one of the servants at the palace.*
Who is he?

I don't remember his name. Seems like it's Jabari or Jafari or something like that. Medium height, slender build and brown hair. He is obviously not a lower-caste servant. He carries himself as if he holds some rank.

Do you remember where he usually works or what he does? I could ask Mother.

He has something to do with arriving dignitaries. There was a pause. *They're taking me to the washing room. I'll be allowed a moment of privacy before we leave.*

Did they say where they are taking you? he asked.
No.

Ceros paced near his desk, waiting for her to say something else. A few minutes later she said, *The window in the washing room has been covered by something on the outside. I cannot see out. The only other window is the one in the roof overhead.*

That's okay. It's almost immaterial at this point. We'll have to leave soon to make the meeting.

I don't see anything I could use as a weapon. My hands are free but I don't want to do anything to the poor young girl who had to stand watch over me while I took advantage of the facilities.

Don't do anything foolish, Danet. I swear to you, we will be coming for you.

I know you will, but I don't want you getting hurt trying to rescue me. It's you they're after, not me.

Danet... he warned.

I'm willing to bet they haven't tangled with an angry mystic before.
Danet, don't.

He felt a swell of power through their connection, then it abruptly cut off.

Danet?

"Danet!"

"What's wrong?" Gehiji rushed to Ceros' side.

"I don't know." Ceros struggled to grasp their connection again but couldn't find the thread. "She was there. I was trying to talk her out of not doing something foolish. The last thing she said was they hadn't tangled with an angry mystic before." He shook his head to clear it. "It was weird. I felt a surge of energy then nothing. Like it was just cut off."

Gehiji pressed his lips into a grim line.

"Something happened," Ceros insisted. "We have to get to her now."

Gehiji put his hand on his shoulder. "Slow down. You must go to the oasis. You must meet whoever is behind this." He looked him in the eye. "But you can't go like this."

"Like what?" Ceros growled.

"Half furry with fangs and claws," Mdjai said, stepping up to Ceros' other side.

Ceros looked down at his own hands. His claws were growing longer. Hair had sprouted on his arms.

"You'd terrify your own people if you walked through the palace halls like this," Gehiji pointed out.

The outer door to his suites opened and closed, making them all freeze and look in that direction.

"Quick. Pull yourself together," Mdjai whispered.

"We'll stall whoever it is," Gehiji reassured him as they both walked to the doorway connecting the rooms.

Ceros scurried to the side of his study that was cast in shadow and watched his closest friends delay whoever showed up. He took several deep breaths and focused on being calm and focused. When he heard his mother's voice he knew he couldn't delay forever. He checked his hands to make sure they had returned to normal then stepped out to greet the queen.

"Mother. What brings you this way?"

She presented her cheek for him to kiss. He dutifully obliged.

"I heard a messenger had come." She gracefully slid over to the lounge and sank into the cushions. She raised a single eyebrow, indicating she was waiting for information and didn't intend to leave until she had it.

Ceros exchanged looks with Gehiji and Mdjai. Mdjai shook his head and walked out of the room. Gehiji dropped into a nearby chair.

Ceros sighed and ran a hand over his face.

"I don't suppose I can tell you later, could I?" Ceros asked.

"Why not tell me now?" she said with a wave of her hand.

"Because I only have a minute before I have to meet an unknown person to collect something that was taken from me."

"You were robbed?" She sat up suddenly, concern wreathing her face.

"Mother, can I please talk to you about this later? I really need to go."

She waved them away. "Certainly. Go, do whatever you need to do." As soon as she stood, she paused, a frown on her face. "What was taken?"

"Something far more precious than I realized."

CHAPTER TWENTY-THREE

Danet came to, lying in a patch of grass. She tried to roll over but, like earlier, her hands were tied behind her back. And once again, her head was pounding.

Only this time, the pounding didn't come from any herbs. It came from the lump she was sure was on the back of her head where she had been struck.

It was dark. She knew she had been brought someplace near the oasis because she could smell the water and the jamale flowers that only bloomed there.

Everything around her was quiet. Even the natural sounds of bugs and rustling grass were hushed as if all the creatures were holding their breaths, waiting for something.

Ceros.

She wiggled and rolled until she could sit up.

The movement sent a wave of dizziness through her pounding skull. She paused and took a few deep breaths.

Even though she knew she wouldn't be able to see much in the dark, she looked around her. Thanks to the moon's reflection, she knew the water was behind her. The thickness of the brush indicated it wasn't very far. She could make out a few trees to her left. To the right, she didn't see much at all.

Ceros? She called out through their connection.

A growl came from somewhere to her left.

Danet's breath caught in her throat. What kind of animal would be way out here after dark?

She gulped. Most likely not one that she wanted to come face-to-face with.

Well, at least the noise didn't come from a snake. A shiver ran down her spine.

Not wanting to be caught lying down by anyone or anything, she struggled to her feet. Are my odds better if I go to the left or right?

The sound of rustling grass drew her attention. Keeping an eye on that area, she backed away slowly.

Her retreat became blocked by a solid object behind her knees. Breath on her calf made her turn slowly and look down.

Even in the pale moonlight, she could see the golden fur of her beast standing behind her.

"Ceros?" she whispered.

The beast rubbed his nose against her leg.

"If that's you, Ceros, I hope you didn't come out here alone."

His odd yowling sound made Danet think he had said, "Of course not."

"I don't suppose you can untie knots while you're in that form, can you?" she asked, trying to keep her voice low.

The beast circled around and sniffed her bound hands. His growl made her hair stand on end.

"I'm going to take that as a no," she murmured.

A rustling behind her caught her attention. Ceros wrapped one arm around her waist and pulled her against him. He whispered in her ear, "I can't tell you how conflicted I am about finding you tied up. Part of me wants to hunt down the men who dared take you from me. Another part is tempted to back you up against that tree right there and lay claim to you in the most primitive way I know how. Yet another wants to haul you off to a cave in the middle of the desert and hold you until we both forget about this."

Danet shivered at the images his words created in her mind.

Ceros circled around to face her. "If those men had done more than tie you up— and believe me, I would know, I can smell them on you—I would not be standing here. The beast wants blood and I'm barely in control right now. I need for you to tell me that you are all right."

"Kiss me and let me prove to you how all right I am."

Thankfully she didn't have to ask twice.

He pulled her roughly against him and ravaged her lips. Danet sensed how much he struggled to keep the beast in check. Her knees threatened to buckle beneath the assault of intense emotions from him. Despite her instinct to respond in kind, she gentled her kiss and allowed her love for him to trickle through their connection. She hoped it would soothe both him and the beast.

Finally his grip eased and he returned her kisses in a gentler manner.

When he eased away from her lips, he dropped his forehead against hers and took a ragged breath.

"Thank you," he whispered.

"For what?"

"For understanding."

She smiled tenderly. "Anytime."

Somewhere in the haze his kisses created in her mind, it occurred to her that Ceros had just shifted from the beast into a man, and yet he wore a linen wrap. She didn't remember the beast having anything wrapped about its belly. Before she could ask about it, the leaves rustled nearby.

"What a touching scene," a familiar voice said from the nearby cluster of trees.

Ceros stiffened and pushed Danet behind him.

"Who is it?" Danet tried to look around Ceros.

"Aleric," Ceros said flatly.

"You're the one who has been trying to kill Ceros?" she asked incredulously as she peered around Ceros.

"Of course. The throne could have just as easily been my father's and therefore, mine."

Danet struggled to figure out what he was talking about.

Ceros kept himself between her and Aleric. "Our fathers were twins, but yours wasn't the oldest, Aleric."

"They were separated by mere minutes," Aleric sneered.

"And according to the high council, that was all they needed to determine who would rule after Grandfather."

Aleric waved a hand as if to dismiss what Ceros had said. "The high council," he practically spat the words. "A bigger bunch of ineffective old men I have yet to see." He walked to a sandy patch where the desert bled into the greenery of the oasis.

Danet tensed when two large, well-armed men stepped from the shadows and spread out on either side of Aleric.

Ceros continued as if the men posed no threat. "While I won't argue with your assessment, you realize you are considered a part of that group, don't you?"

"What better way to know what was going on in Licosia and the palace?" Aleric asked.

"It's important to stay informed." Ceros seemed to agree, but his tone belied his words.

"Especially about who holds any kind of power," Aleric pointed out.

Ceros shrugged. "The best way to know who to side with and who to eliminate if the tables are ever turned."

Aleric bowed his head in acknowledgement.

"Like Father," Ceros said quietly.

"His time was past. Licosia is ready for change."

"And you know this how?" Ceros asked.

"I make myself available to the people. They come to me and I listen."

With a lift of his chin, Ceros gestured to one of Aleric's guards. "People like the ones who helped you take Danet?"

"Them too."

"Were these the same people who helped you find an Aspenadder plant?"

Aleric put his hands behind his back. "Figured that out, did you?" He looked at Danet. "With a little help no doubt." He shrugged. "I wondered how you recovered so fast. I guess if you know what toxin was used, an antidote is easy to find."

"Easy, he says," Danet scoffed.

"No matter," Aleric sneered. "From what my friends have told me, even if you made it back to the palace, your lifesaver would soon be forced from the city."

Danet's eyes widened. Oh Gods, she hadn't thought of the long-term consequences when she tried to escape. How many people saw her use her gifts?

"And why would she need to flee?" Ceros asked.

"Her kind are forbidden in Licosia," Aleric said with contempt.

"What kind is that, exactly?" To most people, Ceros' tone would have been enough warning. Aleric, however, did not heed it.

"Is it possible you don't know?" The glee in Aleric's voice set Danet's teeth on edge.

"Do you mean her kind as in, she's a woman? Or her kind as in, she's an educated and intelligent woman?" Ceros stepped to the side and looked at her as if inspecting her for some flaw. "Perhaps you mean to classify her by her brown hair and laughing green eyes?"

"No, you fool, she is a mystic. How can you not see that?" Aleric demanded.

Ceros made a dismissive sound and shrugged one shoulder. "Oh, that."

"So you did know!" Aleric stepped closer. "Yet you did nothing. What kind of leader would you be if you so easily dismiss a royal decree?"

Danet felt the blood drain from her face. This was what she dreaded. She knew eventually Ceros would be forced to act on his knowledge of her heritage. She had hoped it would be later rather than now.

"What kind of man would I be if I condemned someone for something beyond his or her control, like lineage, particularly after having done so much for the royal family and the people of Licosia? And more recently, for me, personally?"

Aleric lifted his chin. "It doesn't matter. You have defied a decree. The high council will hear of this."

"Will you be telling them of it before or after you answer for the murder of their king? Or perhaps more recently, for the attempts on my life?" Ceros asked.

"You can't prove anything."

"You just confessed!" Danet blurted.

"To whom? To the two of you? Neither of you will make it back to the palace to tell anyone."

"They heard you," Danet nodded to one of Aleric's men.

"They are loyal to whomever pays them. And since they only speak broken Liconian, it is unlikely they will report anything they might or might not have heard while here."

Danet's heart sank.

"Mercs," Ceros said. "I thought they looked familiar." He said something to the man closest to him in another language. The guard looked surprised Ceros could speak to him.

"What are you saying to him?" Aleric sounded panicked.

As Ceros continued to speak to him the guard's expression changed. A frown creased his brow and he exchanged glances with his counterpart. The guard responded then looked again to the other guard.

"Stop that. What do you think you're doing?" Aleric said,

putting himself between the guard and Ceros.

The second guard seemed to think about whatever Ceros had said then nodded.

Almost as one, the two guards sheathed their weapons and turned and walked into the dark.

"Wait a minute! Come back here!" Aleric shouted at the guards' backs. "You'll not be paid a single coin if you walk away from here!"

With a growl he turned to face Ceros and Danet again.

"I don't know what you said to them, but it doesn't matter. I have a handful of men waiting for my command."

"Call them," Ceros challenged as he stepped closer to Danet.

"Ahmose! Haji!" Aleric shouted, still as cocky as when he set foot on the oasis. "Bring your swords!"

Danet tensed and searched the dark for signs of movement.

Ceros remained relaxed by her side. However his hand slid down her back to where her hands were bound. As they waited, his fingers worked the knot loose until she felt more blood flow in her hands.

He stilled her movements with a touch of his hand. *Don't let him know your hands are free.*

"Ahmose! Haji!" Aleric shouted again.

"I don't think they can hear you," Ceros pointed out. "Perhaps you'd like to go and look for them?"

"So you two can run away as soon as my back is turned?" Aleric sneered.

"No, no. We'll stay right here," Ceros assured him.

"Idogbe! Come here!" Aleric demanded.

Still no response.

Two shadows moved in the brush.

"Good thing you shouted," a familiar voice said. "We might not have found Ceros if you hadn't." Mdjai and Runihura stepped into the moonlit circle.

Danet slumped in relief.

Aleric's face fell.

"That's a pretty good trick you have there," Runihura said proudly. "Shifting forms over water makes it hard to follow. You're keeping me on my toes."

"I do what I can," Ceros said with a grin.

"If you're looking for your men, they're tied up next to their mounts. Don't expect them to come to your rescue," Mdjai informed Aleric. "Including the two we found on the other side of the oasis."

"And the one on the north side I took out when they first arrived," Runihura said.

"Oh, and the dark-headed one with the tiny knife near the water," Mdjai added.

Runihura shook his head sadly. "I wouldn't count him if we were keeping score."

"He really didn't put up a fight, did he?" Mdjai agreed.

Ceros snickered.

Aleric looked as if he grew angrier by the second.

"What do you want to do with this one?" Runihura indicated Aleric with a flick of his thumb.

"Tie him up and bring him with the others." Ceros quickly added, "But take care. He has a history of poisoning people."

Runihura scoffed then produced a length of rope and closed in on Aleric.

Ceros turned to Danet. "Are you all right?" He helped free her from the loosened bindings.

"Yes. I'm fine." She smiled up at him as she rubbed her wrists and hands to help the circulation.

He took her hands in his and took over the rubbing.

"I'm sorry. I didn't think about other people seeing me use my powers when I tried to escape," Danet said. "I only thought of getting away so you wouldn't have to come out here."

A frown creased his brow.

"I know I've put you in a delicate position," she continued.

"No, you haven't."

"We both know that is not true." She indicated Aleric with a lift of her chin. "He won't stay quiet about it."

"He has bigger problems to worry about right now," Ceros said.

"Maybe so but he clearly wants you off the throne and would probably do or say anything to make that happen."

"We'll see." He put one finger over her lips to stop any further argument. "We will discuss this later. Right now I need to help Mdjai and Runihura gather up the prisoners so we can return to the palace."

Danet nodded her agreement. "Very well." She looked to where Runihura stood next to Aleric. "What can I do to help?"

"If there are any injured men I'll have you—"

"Why couldn't you just die like your father?" Aleric yelled as he grabbed one of Runihura's knives.

Before she could call out a warning, Aleric threw the blade at Ceros' back.

Without thinking, she pushed Ceros aside then extended one hand and stopped the blade's momentum. With the other, she let a fireball loose.

Aleric yelled in pain when the orange sphere hit him in the center of his chest. He flew backward and hit the ground.

When she realized the blade still hung suspended in midair, Danet flicked her wrist and let it drop onto the sand.

"What the hell," Runihura exclaimed.

Ceros reached for Danet. "Why do I have to keep asking if you are okay?"

"I'm fine." She looked down at her hands. Surprisingly they looked the same. And weren't shaking. Yet. "I'm sorry for injuring your cousin."

"I'm not," Ceros mumbled.

"It seems I cannot control my abilities," she pointed out.

He lifted her face by the chin until she looked him in the eye. "Thank you for saving my life. Again."

Suddenly her emotions felt quite fragile. "You're welcome, my prince," she murmured with a tear in her eye.

"That had better be a term of endearment," he grumbled then grabbed her hand and tugged her behind him.

Mdjai picked up the knife Aleric had thrown. "That's quite the party trick you have there, princess."

"Yes, well, I didn't know I had it in me," she muttered as she stumbled along behind Ceros. At this point, she was too tired to even correct Mdjai on his improper use of a royal title.

Mdjai chuckled then went to help Runihura with Aleric.

CHAPTER TWENTY-FOUR

It didn't take long to return to the palace. Most of the men who had been captured went with them easily once they saw Aleric had been rendered unconscious then draped over a saddle.

Ceros escorted Danet to his rooms and left her in a servant's care with orders to soak in the tub as long as she wished then have some dinner. As soon as she felt refreshed, she should come to the king's receiving room.

He sent word to her father that she was safe. The note also requested Sebak join him and Danet at the palace in the morning.

Meanwhile he had to deal with the primary issue of Aleric and his treason.

Ceros watched as the queen paced back and forth in front of the desk.

"I cannot believe Aleric was behind all of this," she said for the fifth or sixth time.

"Believe it, Mother. He confessed to me and Danet. And I believe Mdjai and Runihura heard most of it as well." He looked to the two of them for confirmation.

Both nodded as they continued to stuff themselves with food from the many trays that had been brought in.

"They certainly witnessed his last attempt at killing me."

"Which you haven't fully explained yet," she reminded him.

"That's Danet's story to tell," he said.

"What do you mean? Why can't you simply tell me what happened?" she railed.

"Mother, can we please move on? I still need to decide what punishment Aleric should receive."

She stopped pacing. "The punishment for treason is beheading. The law is clear."

"I thought as much but I want to make sure that I won't be creating a political firestorm when I issue the orders."

"How so?" she asked.

Ceros began ticking reasons off on his fingers. "He is family. He is a high council member. He supposedly has been listening to what the people say and want. He seems to think he has a claim to the throne."

"He tried to kill you! More than once!"

"He was behind Father's death as well," he said quietly.

The queen went pale. Ceros moved to assist her as she slumped into a nearby chair.

"I can't prove anything, of course. But now that I know who was behind the attempts on my life, things add up based on the information we have gathered about Father's death."

"Oh Gods," she whispered with her hand at her throat.

"I'm sorry, Mother." He knelt beside her. "That is probably not what you wanted to hear."

She patted his hand where it rested on the arm of her chair. "No, it isn't. But I would rather know than not."

"I'm sorry I could not attend the lighting of Father's funeral pyre."

"I am too." She touched his cheek. "You still need to say your own farewell."

"I have." He indicated Gehiji and the others with a lift of his chin. "We paid our respects last night." His lips twitched. "As I stood there, I remembered what he used to say about city projects. That's when the idea of building a grand monument in his honor came to me."

A frown creased his mother's brow. "Your father would hate that."

Ceros smiled. "I know."

She chuckled. "You just have to get the last word, don't you?"

"Why break tradition now?"

The doors opened and Danet came in.

Ceros rose. Even Gehiji, Mdjai and Runihura came to their feet.

Danet slowed her advance and looked from one man to the

next. Her brow furrowed in confusion at their show of respect.

"I thought I left orders for you to rest," Ceros said.

She moved past the table of food and made her curtsey to the queen. "I did."

"Not very long," he mumbled as he reached for her hand. "We were just filling Mother in on the details of what happened."

"I understand I have you to thank once again for saving Ceros' life," the queen said to Danet.

Danet bowed her head. "I am just happy to have been able to help, my queen."

Ceros watched in silence as his mother waved to the chair next to hers.

"Now you'll have to tell me your version of events," she said to Danet. "Men don't always see things the same as us."

Danet looked to Ceros, a question in her eyes.

With her hand still in his, he led Danet to the chair his mother indicated and encouraged her to sit. He winked then returned to the desk, leaving her to his mother's mercies.

Throughout the question-and-answer session, Ceros kept one ear tuned in. He was surprised Danet answered without hesitation. Even when his mother got around to asking how Danet had managed to stop Aleric's knife.

He glanced up from the document he had been writing to see how the queen handled the news that Danet was a mystic. When he realized she didn't look the least bit surprised, he frowned.

"Mother, did you know about Danet's, er, talents?" he asked.

"Not specifically, no. But I knew her mother. And her grandmother. Both of whom were skilled mystics. So I knew it was possible Danet could have inherited their gifts. I just hadn't seen evidence of it yet." She patted Danet's leg and smiled. "Other than her uncanny ability to cure people even when they were beyond the capabilities of most healers."

Ceros and Danet exchanged glances.

He was relieved the queen had taken the news so well. Danet, however, looked as if tension held her together.

"How is it that you knew about her mother and grandmother and yet they were allowed to remain in Licosia? Mystics were banished long ago."

The queen waved her hand in the air as if to dismiss the idea. "Phish. That decree should have been overturned before your father ever sat on the throne. It was originally written during the Great Wars." The queen began telling the group. As she spoke, Mdjai, Gehiji and Runihura moved closer to listen.

"The king, your great-grandfather," she nodded to Ceros, "had been led to believe that one of his most trusted advisors, a very powerful mystic, was behind a series of treasonous acts that directly impacted the balance of power during the war." The queen turned thoughtful. "I don't remember exactly what he was accused of, but sleeping with the king's wife would have been a lesser crime."

Mdjai let out a low whistle.

"Thankfully they were able to prove the man was innocent before he was executed. However, to flush out the true culprit, the king and that advisor developed a plan. They knew a mystic was involved but they didn't know who it was." She looked to Danet apologetically. "It is far too easy for mystics to hide their gifts so they decided to banish all of them through this decree."

"They banished all mystics because of one bad one?" Danet protested.

"Yes. A rescinding order was supposed to be issued before the end of the week, once most of the families had left. They wanted to make it legal for the two who were chosen to return to Licosia to search for the traitor."

"But they didn't want to advertise that fact, otherwise the flood of mystics and their families would return, hampering their efforts," Ceros guessed.

"That's correct," the queen nodded.

Danet crossed her arms in front of her chest. Obviously she didn't care for his great- grandfather's plan.

As a soldier, he could see the value in their strategy. Especially during those harsher times. But he also knew it must have been difficult for those families who were forced out of their homes with very little notice.

War was never pretty.

"Would you get me a glass of wine, my dear? I'm getting rather parched telling this story," the queen asked Gehiji.

"I would be happy to." Gehiji made a slight bow and hopped up to get the requested drink.

If the frown on Danet's face was any indication, she was confused why she hadn't been asked to retrieve the wine for the queen. He saw her fighting the urge to get up out of the chair and do as the queen requested.

Gehiji delivered the cup with exaggerated flair, making the queen laugh. After she had a few sips, she continued.

"It took time to locate the traitor. Several cycles of the moon, I believe. By the time they did, the war had reached its height. Unfortunately, that rescinding order never got signed. Partly due to who the traitor ended up being."

She nodded as if she were telling one of the greatest secrets ever known. "The king's scribe. A seemingly simple and relatively unimportant position, but it put the traitor in a position to know all of the kingdom's business. And he had the power to alter documents, changing the meaning ever so slightly. More than one key document went missing in his care too."

Ceros shook his head. "No wonder Father handled his own correspondence."

"Exactly," the queen concurred.

The queen smiled at Danet. "I strongly suspect both families wanted to bring their loved ones and friends back, but since the last battles of the war were fought at Licosia's doorstep, no one wanted to return." She looked at Ceros. "It was some time before trade was reestablished with our neighbors. Communication would have been slow and irregular outside the city walls. Even if the decree had been rescinded, it is doubtful many would have returned."

He nodded his understanding. "So the bottom line is, I need to complete that rescinding order."

"That is correct," the queen agreed.

The stunned expression on Danet's face was priceless.

"That can't be one of your first orders as prince," Danet declared.

"Why not?" Ceros asked.

"Well… Because people might not approve," she blustered.

"Approve of what? Me dissolving some antiquated order that should have been rescinded two generations ago? Or me honoring you and your father's years of service to the royal family and the city of Licosia by dissolving that same order so you no longer have to worry about your heritage?"

When he saw a teardrop glisten on her lashes, he had to fight the urge to rush to her side like a lovesick fool. Before he could get out of his chair, his mother reached to comfort Danet.

"Why are you sad?" The queen put her arm around Danet's shoulders. "You should be proud. You come from a line of very brave, very loyal mystics. Why, your great-grandmother even saved his," she pointed at Ceros, "great-grandmother's life."

"I'm sorry." Danet wiped away her tears. "I'm just having a hard time coming to terms with the thought that I wouldn't have to hide what I am any longer. That I wouldn't have to worry that someone might take away our home or Father's clinic or even worse, harm Father, all because of me. It's just too much." She looked at Ceros. "But I don't want you to risk public displeasure by doing this."

Ceros moved to stand next to Danet. He put his hand on the back of her neck to offer what comfort he could in front of others. What he really wanted to do was scoop her up and drop her onto his lap and wrap his arms around her. But that wasn't going to happen anytime soon.

"I want to do this, Danet. I truly doubt there will be a public uprising. But I am willing to discuss it with the chancellor first. Will that make you feel better?"

"Yes, if you will promise to wait if he feels it will be an issue."

Ceros growled. "We need to discuss your tendency to argue with me."

That brought a smile to her face. She sniffed back her tears. "I'll put it on the list."

Satisfied they managed to avoid an emotional upheaval, he wiped a stray tear from Danet's cheek then turned to his mother. "There's one more thing to be dealt with."

"What's that? The date for your wedding?"

Gehiji snickered in the background.

Danet choked and turned pale. Ceros patted her on the back and shot his mother a look that spoke of retribution. "No, actually, I was thinking along the lines of Aleric and his allegations that he has a claim to the throne."

"That is just nonsense," the queen declared.

"I agree, but if he has spoken to a large part of the population, he's bound to have attracted some attention. Especially when those people don't know our family history," Ceros pointed out.

"Your father descended from a long line of kings. And the blood of the last known omegamorph runs in your veins," she said proudly. "He may share a similar heritage, but the throne rightfully falls to you."

Mdjai cleared his throat and gave Ceros a meaningful look. Gehiji looked at him in a similar fashion. Each of them believed he should have told his family years ago that he had become an omegamorph. There had been more than one heated debate on the subject.

Ceros took a deep breath. "There's something else you need to know, Mother." He toyed with a strand of Danet's hair, seeking comfort in the silky feel.

She reached for his free hand, silently offering her support.

"Just before I left for Shirghada, I was visited by one of our Gods. He came to me in a dream and said I was needed to maintain peace in our lands." He looked at his friends. "I was told I would journey to a faraway place. There I would meet others like me, brothers in arms, with similar destinies."

The queen looked at Gehiji, Mdjai and Runihura.

"Each of us would come from a different part of the world. And each of us would be gifted with a different talent."

"What is your talent?" the queen interjected.

Gehiji answered for him. "Strategy."

"I would have said justice," Mdjai added.

"They're both right," Runihura said.

Ceros bowed his head in thanks.

"What are your talents?" Danet asked, looking at each of them in turn.

"Gehiji has a silver tongue. He can obtain supplies when there are none to be had." Runihura's voice held only sincerity.

"He also has an uncanny ability to sense a lie. Even the most gifted trickster cannot fool him," Ceros said. The others nodded in agreement.

"Runihura can track anything. If it has breathed, much less moved, he can follow it," Gehiji said with a touch of pride.

Mdjai grinned. "And I like to blow things up."

"He is our explosives expert," Ceros admitted.

"Mdjai also has the ability to find water in the middle of the desert," Gehiji reminded them.

"Because he can control it and make it bubble to the surface," Runihura scoffed.

"And he can best anyone with a blade," Ceros added.

"Wow," Danet said. "You're just a mobile army, aren't you?"

"Pretty much." Ceros shrugged.

"So it's up to the four of you to keep the peace in the world?" the queen asked.

"No, we're one short," Ceros answered.

"Kneph," Gehiji said.

"Where is that whelp?" Runihura asked. "Couldn't be bothered with a puny issue like a throne being overturned?"

"I believe he mentioned a family issue that needed to be dealt with when we parted ways," Gehiji answered.

"What? Did his high-and-mighty father want to deliver another cart full of gold to him?"

Mdjai snickered. "Actually, I believe he said something about needing to get out of an arranged marriage."

Runihura sat stunned for a few seconds then doubled over in laughter.

While Runihura struggled to control himself, Gehiji diplomatically redirected the conversation. "I believe we interrupted your story, didn't we, Ceros?"

"Since I don't remember where I left off, I'll just jump right to it." He looked at his mother. "You may or may not be pleased to learn the Gods have blessed our family with another omegamorph." At her blank expression, he added, "Me."

She finally shook free of her shock. "When?"

"It was part of the dream I told you about. When I woke, I was in the middle of the desert on top of a rocky cliff and I was not my usual form."

"What form were you?" she asked quietly.

"That would probably be easier shown than explained," Danet suggested.

"You knew of this?" the queen asked.

Danet nodded slowly.

"You've seen his alternate form?"

"Yes," Danet said simply.

Looking back in his direction, his mother demanded, "Show me."

He exchanged a look with Danet. The support and what looked a lot like love in her eyes overrode any doubt he had. He stepped away from the furniture and transformed.

CHAPTER TWENTY-FIVE

Seeing the beast from her dreams in the same room with her, with no shadows to hide him, was surreal. To know without a doubt the beast and Ceros were one and the same made her a little dizzy.

His mother seemed to be handling the news well enough. Then again, the queen had always been a strong woman.

"Oh my," the queen murmured.

Does it hurt when you transform? Danet asked Ceros.

No.

Just checking.

He chuckled in her mind.

"If I hadn't seen him change, I wouldn't believe it," the queen said.

"Believe it," Gehiji said as he eased next to the queen.

Mdjai and Runihura moved closer to the entrance. It probably would create a scene if someone came in while Ceros was in this form.

Ceros padded over to his mother and nosed her knee.

She froze with her hand in midair as if she were torn between petting him and climbing over the back of her chair.

In his beast form, Ceros really was a large creature. The size of his head alone might make someone think he could chew an arm off.

Finally her hand settled on his head. Tentatively, but nonetheless, she touched his fur. Once she did, the texture seemed to fascinate her.

Tell her I won't bite. Ceros said. *Well, at least not her.*

Danet smiled. "He said he won't bite." She didn't think it was possible for the queen to appear any more surprised.

"He did?" the queen asked.

Danet nodded.

"But how…?" The queen's voice trailed off.

"He told me to tell you."

She doesn't look as if she's taking this well, Ceros said.

The queen looked at Gehiji, a question in her eyes.

He stood next to her with his arms folded across his chest and nodded in affirmation.

"We can talk to each other." Danet pointed to her own head. "We discovered it while he was immobilized with the plant poison."

"You were able to talk to him the whole time?" the queen asked.

"Yes. Most of it."

"Why didn't you tell me?" the queen demanded.

"First, it would have been hard to prove. And, second, we agreed it would be safer if you didn't know."

"Why? I'm his mother. I would have protected him," she insisted.

Nope. She's not taking this well at all, Ceros said. I'm changing back.

"We know you would have," Danet said gently. "But you needed to be able to face the high council and dozens of other people without any hint of what was really going on. Any of whom could have been the one trying to kill him."

Ceros backed away from his mother then transformed into his usual form. Like the time at the oasis, he wore a simple linen wrap. Only now that she wasn't disoriented and had light, she could see he also wore a royal-purple sash and gold armbands.

"I'm never going to get used to that," the queen mumbled.

"It is a bit unsettling to watch, isn't it?" Danet agreed.

"Not any more than watching your friend race into battle unarmed, then seeing an oversized animal come out the other side in his place, flinging bodies as he went." Gehiji shook his head. "For the longest time we thought he was crazy for not wearing any armor or taking any weapons with him."

"It was too hard to find where I dropped it," Ceros shrugged, "so I gave up carrying it."

Danet shook off the images of what he might or might not have done in the heat of battle. "Do you always transform back wearing the same thing?"

"You noticed that." Ceros smirked. "It's what I was wearing when the Gods made me an omegamorph." He shrugged. "At least I was wearing something that night."

Danet's cheeks heated as she imagined the places he might have been when he transformed back.

"I believe I've reached my limit for surprises for this evening." The queen stood and approached Ceros. She studied his face for a moment. "I am proud you were chosen and even prouder that you have accepted your destiny. The people of Licosia will rejoice the return of the omegamorph." She rose up on the tips of her toes and placed a kiss on his cheek. "We can finish talking tomorrow after I've had a chance to rest and absorb everything you've told me."

Ceros smiled down at his mother. "That may be the best idea I've heard all evening."

The queen turned and took Danet's hand. "Make sure this one," she pointed to Ceros over her shoulder, "gets some rest tonight."

"I will."

"Good night, my dear." The queen placed a quick kiss on Danet's cheek as well, leaving Danet baffled once again.

The queen opened her mouth to say something, caught Ceros' wary expression then seemed to change her mind. Mdjai, Gehiji and Runihura each wished her a good night's sleep as she regally swept out the door. One by one they turned to face Ceros.

"Is there anything else you need our help with this evening?" Gehiji asked with a quick glance at Danet. "Or will you be retiring soon also?"

"I believe we've all had enough for one day."

"Then we'll bid you a good night." With a tip of his head, Gehiji turned and gestured for Mdjai and Runihura to precede him.

Runihura grabbed his plate of food and made a gesture of farewell then lumbered out the door behind Mdjai.

When the door clicked shut, he looked to Danet.

"I suppose I should get my things." She stood. "Would it be asking too much to have an escort called for me?"

"No."

"Thank you."

"You mistake me. I meant, no, I won't call an escort for you."

He didn't need to prod her mind to know what she was thinking. The play of emotions across her face told him everything. It ranged from anxiousness to shock to irritation in only a few seconds.

Her back stiffened. "Very well. I can manage then." She turned to stomp off. "Have a pleasant rest of your evening, my prince."

He rolled his eyes then quickly reached out and grabbed her arm. "I meant you don't need an escort to find your way back to my room. I'll be happy to escort you personally."

She attempted to resist his grasp. "I can't go back to your room with you. That wouldn't be proper at all."

"Why not?"

"Because you're the prince and I'm not some tart that warms the bed of anyone who looks at them prettily."

"Damn right you're not." He pulled her fully into his arms even as she tried to wiggle free.

"Then you agree that it isn't proper for me to return to your room with you."

"No."

She stopped wiggling. "But, you just said…"

"I said you aren't some tart. And you most certainly won't be warming anyone's bed other than mine because I have every intention of you being there every single night and morning from now on."

"But…" Her mouth gaped open but no other words came out.

"Do you not understand yet?"

She shook her head.

"I want you as my bride. My queen. The mother of my children. I want you to be the one to stand beside me as I find better ways for my people to grow and prosper. I need you to remind me of my duty to be a better man and even better king."

Tears glistened on her lashes.

"Do you think you can do that? For me and for Licosia?" he asked quietly.

"I… But I'm a nobody."

"You are Danet. You are a respected healer. In your own way, you are a leader and a groundbreaker."

Her gaze sank to his chest. "Your family would never approve of you bonding with me."

"Mother already has."

She pulled back and looked him in the eye. "You talked to your mother about this already?"

"Yes."

"When?"

"Earlier today." He lowered his forehead until it rested against hers. "I think that is why Aleric kidnapped you. He overhead the two of us talking."

"Ah. Now it makes sense."

"What does?"

"The reason that I was kidnapped, and your mother's behavior this evening."

He chuckled. "I could tell that you were a bit confused by her actions."

"To say the least," she mumbled.

He raised his head. "Are you angry with me for talking with Mother first?"

She bit her lip. "No. It was the smart thing to do. And the politically correct thing also." She frowned. "Obviously, she doesn't think it will be an issue."

"So you'll stay then?"

She tried to pull back, but he tightened his hold on her.

"You're a prince. You should be courting princesses. Women who were raised to be graceful and elegant and diplomatic at all times." Her eyes implored him to understand. "Assets to their husbands." She shook her head. "That's not me, Ceros. I would probably embarrass you or do or say something out of line and create a public uprising or start a war."

He chuckled.

"Don't laugh. I'm serious," she said with a frown.

"I'm not laughing at you." He dropped a kiss on her nose. "I have the same fears, Danet. Why do you think I stayed so long out in the wilderness with Gehiji and the rest of them? I didn't want to come home and face this. But here I am. And just so you know, I think you are very graceful and elegant and far more diplomatic than I will ever be."

"But I—"

"You know almost everyone here in the palace, which means you know more about what goes on than I could hope to know. It wouldn't surprise me if you knew more than Mother."

"And that is why—"

"That is why you would be a huge asset to your husband. No pampered princess is ever going to take the time to get to know the people who work here. They won't care if the stableboy broke his leg last week or that the cook has a new grandson. You do. And you always will. You care about the people we are responsible for. I want that in a mate because that is important to me too. So, please, will you stay?"

Danet raised her chin defiantly and tried to blink away the tears on her lashes. "I haven't heard you formally ask me anything yet, my prince."

He smiled. "Danet." He kissed her lightly on the forehead. "Would you do me the great honor of becoming my bride?" He kissed her gently on one cheek. "My companion through the good and bad times?" Then he kissed her other cheek. "The mother of my children?" Her chin came next. "My mate in this life and any that may come after?" He dropped every defense, every wall he had and let all of his love and hope flow through their connection.

She let out a gasp then the tears began to flow freely. "How can I possibly say no?" Rising up on her toes, she pressed her lips to his.

He returned her kiss with ardor.

When the last of her defenses fell, he felt the full strength of her love. His beast purred in contentment. For the first time since being visited by the Gods, he didn't feel as if the beast was in more control than he.

Her arms slipped around his waist and she pressed her body closer.

Ceros ran one hand down her back then followed the curve of her ass. He pulled her up and ground his erection against her belly.

Heat sizzled between them. The urge to strip her bare and claim her as his own rode him hard. Only the last bit of his control prevented him from doing so.

He broke their kiss and rasped, "Come. If we don't go to my chambers now, you will find yourself splayed out on the table for anyone to walk in and see. And I really don't want to give the servants anything else to talk about, do you?"

It took a moment for his words to sink in but finally her dazed expression cleared and she shook her head.

"Good." He pulled her to the door. When she didn't move as quickly as he wanted, he asked, "Do I need to carry you?"

"No." She giggled. "But you'll still give people something to talk about if we're seen running through the hallways. Especially at this time of the night."

He slowed his pace to a somewhat fast walk. "Good point."

As they passed a darkened alcove, he pulled her in behind him and kissed her once more. The kiss not only scattered her wits but it ratcheted up his need to be joined with her.

"We really need to hurry," he muttered as he tugged on her hand and pulled her along behind him again.

He only slowed his pace as he neared the men standing guard at the entrance to his rooms.

"We are not to be disturbed," he said in his most authoritative voice. He stopped then backed up and added, "Not even by the queen."

Both men responded, "Yes, my prince."

Ceros motioned for Danet to pass through the door. He shut the doors behind him then leveled a serious look at her.

You have one chance to take off anything you don't want ripped off, he warned her though their connection.

CHAPTER TWENTY-SIX

Danet shivered in anticipation.

Their last coupling had been about bonding and healing. This time she wanted to know how much he truly desired her.

She stopped in the middle of the room and faced him. Beneath her dress, she slipped her feet from her sandals.

His struggle to maintain control was evident. His jaw was firm and his fists were clenched. Even his eyes had darkened to a muddier gold color. The tension practically vibrated off him in waves.

"I certainly don't want to have this lovely new robe that you left for me ruined." She hooked her thumbs under the front edge of the robe's opening and pushed the fabric over her shoulders, making the garment slip off and puddle on the floor behind her.

"And this gown is made of far too delicate fabric for you to handle right now." She held his gaze. "Perhaps it would be best if I took it off too."

Ceros watched, almost in thrall.

With a few tugs, she loosened the tie at her waist. Then she slowly pulled the fabric up, using one hand against her thigh.

His gaze followed the movement of the fabric as it traveled up her leg.

Danet rejoiced in her ability to captivate him. It bolstered her confidence and spurred her on.

With one swift movement, she pulled the dress over her head and let it drop onto the floor with the robe. She stood before him with nothing but a small scrap of fabric covering her most intimate place. His eyes roamed every inch of her, from head to toe.

The stark desire she saw on his face made her heart rejoice. Knowing she very likely played with fire, she beckoned to him with her finger as she backed toward the bed.

When he reached her, she stopped him by placing one hand on his chest before he could grab her.

"Will you allow me, my prince, to disrobe you?"

He seemed unsure of her question and she could tell his impatience almost won out. "Very well," he said reluctantly.

"Thank you, my prince," she said sweetly, silently rejoicing she had an opportunity to worship his body the way she had dreamed of doing.

She placed both hands on his chest and slid them under the edges of his robe. She eased the fabric up and over his shoulders then down both of his arms, pushing the garment off as she moved. Her movements were slow and deliberate. She knew if she didn't remain in control, he would seize the reins and she wouldn't be able to hold a clear thought for hours.

She circled around to his back, letting her fingers trail across the lines of muscle as she went.

His skin was heated but softened from the oils he had applied earlier in the day. She felt ripples in his muscles as if he fought to remain in place.

To get it out of the way, she loosened the latch that secured his necklace then reached around to his front and gently lifted the heavy gold piece. Knowing it was a valuable family heirloom, she placed it on the table next to the bed.

When she returned to his side, she found he had kicked his sandals off.

She lifted one eyebrow in question.

He shrugged. "One less thing for you to do."

"But it pleases me to touch you," she said, reaching for him once again. "And I had so dearly hoped to touch you…" She dropped her gaze to the lower half of his body. "Everywhere." When she raised her eyes to meet his, she allowed him to see how much she desired him.

The muscle in his jaw jumped. "Danet," he warned.

"I will continue," she said matter-of-factly then dropped to her knees in front of him. His cock jumped in response beneath the linen cloth he wore.

She untied the knot of his belt then worked the pleats loose that held the cloth in place. When both pieces fell to the floor, she looked her fill.

His fully engorged cock stood proudly before her, daring her to bring him under her spell.

She reached for him, placing both hands on his thighs. As she slid them up, she leaned in and nuzzled his member with her lips and cheek. Her fingers moved all the way up to his ribs then back down to his thighs again. When she slid her fingers once more up his thighs, she licked the entire length of his cock and swirled her tongue around the tip.

She heard him take a deep breath then release it.

Instead of sliding her fingers up his body, she caressed his sac with one hand and held his cock steady with the other. She slowly took the head of his cock into her mouth, making him suck in a ragged breath. Remembering what a married friend had told her, she flicked her tongue back and forth as she bobbed her head up and down.

Ceros gripped her hair, slowing her movement.

She peeked at his face to gauge his reaction.

His head was tipped back and his eyes were closed. But just as he started to piston his hips, he pulled back, out of her mouth.

With a growl, he reached for her and swept her up in his arms.

"But I wasn't finished," she protested.

"No, we most certainly aren't finished." He put a knee on the bed then crawled to the center, holding her. He laid her on her back but before her head hit the sheet, his lips had descended upon hers.

She wrapped her arms around his chest and held on as the world tilted.

All that she knew was him. The blood pounding in his veins. His scent filling her senses. All that mattered was him. That his lips were on hers, his flesh met hers and their bodies were entwined. All she needed was him. His touch. His breath mingled with hers. Their hearts beating as one.

His spirit called to hers. Or maybe hers called to his.

As their bodies joined, so too did their souls.

In the back of their minds, two golden lights twisted and turned and swirled around and into each other until neither could tell where one ended and the other began. With one last turn, time stopped and everything slowed. Finally the two became one in a great burst of light.

When Danet became aware of her body again, she was lying beneath Ceros. His face was buried in her neck. Their breaths were fast and shallow, as if they had run up the side of a mountain.

Even though she had little inclination to move, and even less energy to do so, she ran her fingers up and down his spine in a gentle caress.

Finally Ceros lifted his head. His brow furrowed in puzzlement. "Did you notice anything unusual when you found your fulfillment?"

She chuckled. "Define unusual."

Somewhat reluctantly, he asked, "Did you see a really bright burst of light and feel as if your world exploded?"

"Yes, actually, I did." She poked him in the ribs to try to make him roll off her so she could talk to him easier.

"Other than blindingly exceptional sex, what just happened?"

"Unless I am very much mistaken, that was a soul meld." She poked him again. He grabbed her hand and pinned it above her head.

"A what?" he asked.

"A soul meld." She sighed. "I need to read through Grandmother's diary to make sure of what I am telling you, but that's how I remember her describing it."

"But what is it?"

"It's just what it sounds like." She tried to twist and roll him off her, but he wouldn't budge. She sighed. "Two souls coming together."

When he didn't burst into laughter or begin cursing, some of the tension drained from her.

"So what does that mean exactly?" he asked, drawing the words out.

"If our souls really did meld, then we are forever joined. The mental connection we share will probably be stronger and it's most likely that we'll be able to sense where the other is. At an extreme, I've even read that couples who have melded their souls cannot live if one of them dies."

"Well then." He kissed her gently on the lips. "I guess we'll just have to take very good care of each other so that we live very long lives."

Danet felt tears gather in her eyes again. "Are you sure you're okay with this? I mean, it's not as if we tried to do the meld. It just happened. But neither of us knew what we were doing and you didn't ask to be tied to me for all eternity. And—"

He cut off her ramble with another kiss.

She sighed against his lips.

"Danet, I love you. I've already told you I want you as my mate and my queen. And if this bond means you're mine for all eternity, I couldn't ask for more." He dropped another kiss on her lips.

She wrapped her arms around him. "And I love you." She put all of her love into that kiss. Finally he rolled to the side and pulled her with him so she ended up sprawled across his chest. "I'll go home and dig out Grandmother's diary so we can find out more about this meld and what it'll mean for us."

"This is your home now. And while I'm somewhat curious to know more about this meld thing, I think we can find out what that means for us together. But I had an idea about your lack of knowledge of your heritage."

"Oh?"

"Once mystics are no longer forbidden in Licosia, I think we should track down one or two of your relatives and ask them to come. Either for a visit or an extended stay."

She didn't think it was possible, but her smile grew. "Do you really think we could find one of them? I've had no contact with Mother's family. I doubt Father has either."

"I know people who can track anyone to any place they might have gone."

"Why does that not surprise me about you, my prince?" she said as she pulled him closer for another kiss.

He gave in to her lips' demands before asking, "When are you going to stop addressing me as prince?"

"When you become king."

"I don't want anything that formal between us. I see you as my equal and I never want you to believe otherwise."

"What did your mother call your father?"

He paused, thoughtfully. "If I remember correctly it depended on who they were with. Formal occasions, she tended to address him as Dear or Highness. If it were just family, she used his name." He shrugged. "Sometimes Dear." He shook his head. "But I have no idea what she called him when it was just the two of them."

"I don't believe it would have been intended for anyone else's ears anyway."

He mock shuddered. "I'd rather not think about my parents being intimate while we're naked, so stop that thought right now."

She giggled. "I don't blame you." She pressed a quick kiss on his lips. "I will think on what I want to call you. But I suspect that as we spend more time together, it will naturally fall out."

"Does 'Keeper of My Heart and Master of My World' have any appeal for you?" His eyes twinkled in mirth.

She wrinkled her nose. "It's a bit long, don't you think?"

"Perhaps a bit. But I think with practice you could become fluent with it."

She poked him in the ribs. "You are terrible."

"You are delectable." He bent his head and licked her neck and collarbone, sending a shiver down her spine.

He nibbled, licked and kissed his way across her shoulder then down to her breast. When he sucked the nipple into his mouth she arched off the bed, silently begging for more. His hand grasped her other breast and pulled it toward the center of her chest so he could quickly switch his attentions between both nipples.

She gripped his arms and tried to pull him closer but he resisted. He continued to suckle her breasts, driving her mad with sensations. She squirmed and writhed beneath him and her breaths became pants.

Ceros grabbed her hands and pinned them against the mattress above her head. The intense look on his face ratcheted her desire even higher.

"Ceros. Please."

"Please what?"

"I want you inside me," she urged.

He shifted both her hands to one of his. The other slid down her arm to her ribs then over her hip. He nudged her thighs open with his knee and slipped his hand between them.

She squirmed even more when his finger found her clit. With just a few strokes she hovered near oblivion. He eased the pressure and slowed his movements and lured her away from the edge. Just as her breathing became easier, he renewed his efforts.

"Oh Gods," she pleaded.

He guided his cock to her opening and eased inside her, inch by agonizing inch. When he was all the way in, he held still. "Open your eyes and look at me."

The words barely registered through the haze of sensation he had created. She forced herself to lift her heavy lids and meet his gaze.

"I want you to see me as I ride you to the end." He slid his cock back and hovered near the edge of her opening. "Don't close your eyes or I'll stop," he warned through clenched teeth.

She struggled to lift her hips and increase the friction he had created, but he kept her pinned in place. She was at his mercy to prolong or grant her pleasure.

Every fiber of her being burned for him.

It was exquisite torture.

"Ceros." His name was a plea and a sigh on her lips.

She dropped her mental defenses and let him feel what he did to her. How she craved him. How much she needed him to fill her completely.

His eyes widened in surprise. With a growl, he released her hands then found a solid foundation on the mattress near her waist. He buried himself in her body like a man possessed.

Once, twice, three times he pistoned into her, making her pussy quiver and ripple around his cock. Again and again he rode her hard until she bowed up and cried out in pleasure. As she crested, he stiffened and fell into the same tidal wave of sensation.

Their hearts beat against their chests as they slowly floated back to reality.

Ceros shifted and took most of his weight off her, but kept her within the circle of his arms. "You know, I could do this every night," he mumbled.

"Oh really?" Her words slurred after being drained of all her energy.

"Absolutely." He pulled her closer to his chest. "I think I will have my schedule permanently blocked."

Her eyes popped open in surprise. "Every day?"

"Every day."

The thought that he could want her so much wrapped around her like a warm blanket. "So, I guess I had better block my schedule too, then, huh?" she teased.

"Definitely."

She smiled.

"Tomorrow. We'll do that tomorrow." He sighed. "Right after we do the bonding ceremony."

Her smile grew bigger. Tomorrow certainly looked promising. And somehow she didn't think living with Ceros would ever get dull.

I love you, she said through their connection.

I love you, too. He pressed a kiss against the side of her head.

On the other side of the dreaming, they met once more at the oasis. He as a golden beast and she as his fair maiden in white. Together, they walked side by side into the sunrise to face another day.

The End

ABOUT THE AUTHOR

Dena Garson loves to read romance—the hotter the better. When one of her BFFs said "one of us should be writing this stuff", she took up the challenge. If she isn't writing, she's designing jewelry but somehow she still manages to make it into the office on a regular basis.

Find Dena on the web at:

Website - www.denagarson.com
Blog - www.denagarson.net
Facebook - www.facebook.com/dena.garson.7
FB Author - www.facebook.com/AuthorDenaGarson
Twitter - @DenaGarson
YouTube - www.youtube.com/user/DenaGarson
Goodreads - www.goodreads.com/dgarson
Google+ - plus.google.com/+DenaGarson
Pintrest - http://www.pinterest.com/denagarson7
Email – dgarson@cox.net

OTHER BOOKS BY DENA GARSON

Risky Business
Down to Business
Cherie's Silk
Working It All Out
Ghostly Persuasion
Loss of Control
Your Wild Heart

Print Anthologies
Wedding Bliss
Modern Tastes

www.ingramcontent.com/pod-product-compliance
Lightning Source LLC
Chambersburg PA
CBHW020944180626
46814CB00003B/929